The Glamour

Books by Christopher Priest

THE GLAMOUR
THE AFFIRMATION
AN INFINITE SUMMER
ANTICIPATIONS *(editor)*
THE PERFECT LOVER
THE SPACE MACHINE
THE INVERTED WORLD
DARKENING ISLAND
INDOCTRINAIRE

Christopher Priest

The Glamour

Doubleday & Company, Inc., Garden City, New York
1985

For their invaluable help, the author wishes to thank:
Robert and Coral Jackson
Marianne Leconte
Stuart Andrews
Alan Jonas

All characters in this book are fictional and any resemblance
to actual persons, living or dead, is entirely coincidental.

DESIGNED BY LAURENCE ALEXANDER

Library of Congress Cataloging in Publication Data
Priest, Christopher.
The glamour.
I. Title.
PR6066.R55G6 1985   823'.914
ISBN *0-385-19761-6*
Library of Congress Catalog Card Number: 84-13679
Copyright © 1984 by Christopher Priest

To Lisa

The Glamour

Part I

I have been trying to remember where it began, thinking about my early childhood and wondering if anything might have happened that made me become what I am. I had never thought much about it before, because on the whole I was happy. I think the reason for this was that I was protected from knowing what was really going on. My mother died when I was only three, but even this was a blow that was softened; her illness was a long one, and by the time she actually died I was used to spending most of my time with the hired nurse.

What I remember best was something I enjoyed. When I was eight I was sent home from school with a letter from the medical office. A viral infection had been attacking many of the children at the school, and after we had all been screened it was discovered or decided that I was the carrier. I was placed in home quarantine, and was not allowed to mix with other children until I ceased to be a carrier. The outcome was that I was eventually admitted to a private hospital, and my two perfectly good tonsils were efficiently removed. I returned to school shortly after my ninth birthday.

The period of quarantine had lasted nearly six months, coinciding with the best part of a long hot summer. I was on my own for most of this time, and although at first I felt lonely and isolated I quickly adapted. I discovered the pleasures of solitude. I read a huge number of books, went for long walks in the countryside around the house, and noticed wildlife for the first time. My father bought me a simple camera, and I began to study birds and flowers and trees, preferring their company to that of my friends. I constructed a secret den in the garden, and sat in it for hours with my books or photographs, fantasizing and dreaming. I built a cart with the wheels of an old pram and skittered around the country paths and hills, happier than I had ever been before. It was a contented, uncomplicated time, one in which I built up personal reserves and internal confidence, and it changed me.

Returning to school was a wrench. I had become an outsider to the other children because I had been away so long. I was left out of activities and games, groups formed without me, and I was treated as someone who did not know the secret language or signs. I hardly cared; it allowed me to continue with a reduced form of my solitary life, and for the rest of my time at school I drifted on the periphery, barely noticed by the others. I have never regretted that long, lonely summer, and I only wish it could have lasted longer. I changed as I grew up, and I am not now what I was then, but I still think back to that happy time with a kind of infantile longing.

So perhaps it began there, and this story is the rest. At the moment I am only "I" although soon I shall have a name. This is my own story, told in different voices.

Part II

The house had been built so that it overlooked the sea. Since its conversion to a convalescent hospital, two large wings had been added in the original style, and the gardens had been relandscaped so that patients wishing to move around were never faced with steep inclines. The graveled paths zigzagged gently between the lawns and flower beds, opening out onto numerous leveled areas where wooden seats had been placed and wheelchairs could be parked. The gardens were mature, with thick but controlled shrubbery and attractive stands of deciduous trees.

At the lowest point of the garden, down a narrow pathway leading away from the main area, there was a secluded, hedged-in patch, overgrown and neglected, with an uninterrupted view of the bay. In this place it was possible to forget for a while that Middlecombe was a hospital. Even here, though, were precautions: a low concrete curb had been embedded in the grass to stop wheelchairs rolling too close to the rough ground and the cliff beyond, and fairly prominent among the bushes at the back there was an emergency signaling system connected directly to the duty nurse's office in the main block. Very few of the patients visited this place. It was a long way to walk down or back, and the staff were unwilling to push wheelchairs as far as this. The main reason, though, was probably that the steward service did not extend much beyond the terrace or the top lawns.

For all these reasons, Richard Grey came down here whenever he could. The extra distance exercised his arms as he worked the wheels of the chair, and anyway he liked the solitude. He could get privacy inside his room where there were books, television, telephone, radio, but when actually inside the main building there was subtle pressure to mix with the other patients.

He had always been an active man, and although he had been at Middlecombe for a long time, he had still not fully adjusted to the idea of being a patient.

Although there were no more operations to come, it seemed to him that his recovery was interminable. His days in the hospital were on the whole unpleasant. The physiotherapy was tiring, and left him aching afterward. On his own he was lonely, but mixing with the other patients, many of whom did not speak English well, made him impatient and irritable. Lacking friends, the gardens and the view were all he had to himself.

Every day Grey would come down to this quiet place to stare at the sea below. This was a part of the coast known as Start Bay, the western extremity of Lyme Bay, on the South Devon coast. To his right, the rocky headland of Start Point ran out into the dismal sea, sometimes obscured by mist or rain. To his left, just visible, were the houses of Beesands, the ugly neat rows of holiday caravans, the silent waters of Widdicombe Ley. Beyond these, the cliffs rose again, concealing the next village from him. The shore here was shingle, and on calm days he would listen to the hissing of the waves as they broke insipidly at the bottom of the cliff.

Above all, he wished for a stormy sea, something positive and dramatic, something to break his routine. But this was Devon, a place of soft weather and temperate seasons, the climate of convalescence.

It all reflected his state of mind, which had become unquestioning. His body had been severely injured, his mind less so, and he sensed that both would repair in the same way: plenty of rest, gentle exercise, increasing resolve. It was often all he was capable of—to stare at the sea, watch the tides, listen to the waves. The passage of birds excited him, and whenever he heard a car he felt the tremor of fear.

His sole aim was to return to normality. Using sticks he could stand on his own now, and he was sure the crutches were permanently in his past. After wheeling himself down the garden he would lever himself out of his chair and take a few steps leaning on the sticks. He was proud of being able to do this alone, of not having a therapist or nurse beside him, of having no rails, no encouraging words. When standing he could see more of the view, could go closer to the edge.

Today it had been raining when he woke, a persistent, drifting drizzle that had continued all morning. It meant he had had to put on a coat, but now it had stopped raining and he was still in the coat. It depressed him because it reminded him of his real disabilities—he could not take it off on his own.

He heard footsteps on the gravel, and the sound of someone pushing through the damp leaves and branches that grew across the path. He turned, doing it slowly, a step and a stick at a time, keeping his face immobile to conceal the pain.

It was Dave, one of the nurses. "Can you manage, Mr. Grey?"

"I can manage to stay upright."

"Do you want to get back in the chair?"

"No . . . I was just standing here."

The nurse had stopped a few paces away from him, one hand resting on the chair as if ready to wheel it forward quickly and slide it under Grey's body.

"I came to see if you needed anything."

"You can help me with my coat. I'm sweating under this."

The young man stepped forward and presented his forearm for Grey to lean on while he took the sticks away. With one hand he unbuttoned the front of the coat, then put his big hands under Grey's armpits, holding his weight, letting his patient remove the coat himself. Grey found it a slow, painful process, trying to twist his shoulder blades to get out of the sleeve without compressing his neck or back muscles. It was impossible to do, of course, even with Dave's help, and by the time the coat was off he was unable to conceal the pain.

"All right, Richard, let's get you into the chair." Dave twisted him around, almost carrying him in the air, and lowered him into the seat.

"I hate this, Dave. I can't stand being weak."

"You're getting better every day."

"Ever since I've been here you've been putting me in and out of this damned chair."

"There was a time you couldn't get out of bed."

"I don't remember that."

Dave glanced away, up the path. "You don't have to."

"How long have I been here?" Grey asked.

"Three or four months. Probably four now."

There was a silence of memory inside him, a period irretrievably lost. All his conscious memories were of this garden, these paths, this view, this pain, the endless rain and misted sea. It all blended in his mind, each day indistinguishable from the others by its sameness, but there was that lost period behind him too. He knew there had been the bedridden weeks, the sedatives and painkillers, the operations. Somehow he had lived through all that, and somehow he had been signed off, dispatched to convalescence, another bed from which he could not get out by himself. But whenever he tried to think back to beyond that, something in his memory turned away, slipped from his grasp. There was just the garden, the sessions of therapy, Dave and the other nurses.

He had accepted that those memories would not now return, that to try to dwell on them only hindered his recovery.

"Actually, I came down about something," Dave said. "You've got some visitors this morning."

"Send them away."

"You might want to meet one of them. She's a girl, and pretty too. . . ."

"I don't care," Grey said. "Are they from the newspaper?"

"I think so. I've seen the man before."

"Then tell them I'm with the physiotherapist."

"I think they'll probably wait for you."

"Can't you do something, Dave? You know how I feel about them."

"Nobody's going to force you to see them, but I think you should at least find out what they want."

"I've nothing to tell them, nothing to say."

"They might have some news for you. Have you thought of that?"

"You always say that."

While they had been speaking, Dave had leaned down on the handgrips and swung the chair around. Now he stood, pushing gently on the grips, rocking the chair up and down.

"Anyway," Grey said, "what news could they have? The only thing I don't know is what I don't know."

Dave let the chair tip down onto its two small wheels at the front, and moved around to Grey's side.

"Shall I wheel you up to the house?" he said.

"I don't seem to have any choice."

"Of course you have. But if they've come all the way from London, they aren't going to go back until they've seen you."

"All right, then."

Dave took the weight of the chair and wheeled it slowly forward. It was a long, slow climb up to the main house because of the uneven path. When propelling himself Grey had already developed an instinct about jolts and their effect on his back and hip, but when someone else pushed him he could never anticipate them.

They entered the building by a side door, which opened automatically at their approach, then rolled gently down the corridor toward the lift. The parquet flooring had a satin-smooth sheen, with no signs of wear. The whole place was always being cleaned; it smelled unlike a hospital, with polish and varnish, carpets, good food. The acoustics too were muted, as if it were really an expensive hotel where the patients were pampered guests. For Richard Grey it was the only place he knew as home. He sometimes felt he had been here all his life.

II

They ascended to the next floor and Dave propelled the chair to one of the lounges. Unusually, no other patients were there. At a desk in the alcove to one side James Woodbridge, the senior clinical psychologist, was using the telephone. He nodded to Grey as they came into the room, then spoke quickly and quietly and hung up.

Sitting by the other window was Tony Stuhr, one of the reporters from the newspaper. As soon as he saw him, Grey felt the familiar conflict on meeting this man: in person he was likable and frank, but the paper he worked for was a tabloid rag of dubious reputation and immense circulation. Stuhr's by-line had appeared in the past few weeks on several stories about a royal romance. The newspaper was delivered every day to Middlecombe, especially for Richard Grey. He rarely did more than glance at it.

Stuhr stood up as soon as Grey entered the room,

smiled briefly at him, then looked at Woodbridge. The psychologist had left the desk and was crossing the room. Dave stepped on the foot brake of the wheelchair and left the room.

Woodbridge said, "Richard, I've asked you to come back to the house because I'd like you to meet someone."

Stuhr was grinning at him, leaning over the table to stub out his cigarette. Grey noticed that his jacket was falling open and a rolled-up copy of the newspaper was stuffed into an inner pocket. Grey was puzzled by the remark, because Woodbridge must have known that he and Stuhr had met on several previous occasions. Then Grey noticed there was someone with Stuhr. It was a young woman standing beside him, looking at Grey, her eyes flicking nervously toward Woodbridge, waiting for the introduction. He had not seen her until this moment; she must have been sitting with the reporter, and when she stood up had been behind him.

She came forward.

"Richard, this is Miss Kewley, Miss Susan Kewley."

"Hello," she said to Grey, and smiled.

"How do you do?"

She was standing directly in front of him, seeming tall but not really so. Grey was still not used to being the only person sitting. He wondered whether he should shake hands with her.

"Miss Kewley has read about your case in the press, and has traveled down from London to meet you."

"Is that so?" Grey said.

"You could say we've set this up for you, Richard," Stuhr said. "You know we always take an interest in you."

"What do you want?" Grey said to her.

"Well . . . I'd like to talk to you."

"What about?"

She glanced at Woodbridge.

"Would you like me to stay?" the psychologist said to her over Grey's head.

"I don't know," she said. "It's up to you."

Grey realized he was unimportant to this meeting; the real dialogue was going on above him. It reminded him of the pain, lying in the intensive care unit in the London hospital between operations, dimly hearing himself discussed.

"I'll call back in half an hour," Woodbridge was saying. "If you need to see me before then, you can just pick up that phone."

"Thank you," said Susan Kewley.

When Woodbridge had left, Tony Stuhr released the foot brake on the chair and pushed Grey to the table where they had been sitting. The young woman took the chair closest to him, but Stuhr sat by the window.

"I've nothing to talk to you about," Grey said.

"I just wanted to see you," she said.

"Well, here I am. I can't run away from you."

"Richard, don't you remember me?"

"Should I?"

"Well, yes. I was hoping you would."

"Are we friends?"

"I suppose you could say that. Just for a time."

"I'm sorry. I can't remember much about the past. How long ago was it?"

"Not long," she said. She looked at him only infrequently when she spoke, glancing down into her lap, or at the table, or across to the reporter. Stuhr was staring through the window, obviously listening yet not participating. When he realized Grey was looking at him, he took the newspaper from his pocket and opened it to the football page.

"Would you like some coffee?" Grey said.

"You know I—" She checked herself. "No, I only drink tea."

"I'll get it." Grey propelled himself away from her

and went to the phone, asserting a sense of independence. When he had ordered the refreshments, he went back to the table. Stuhr picked up his newspaper again; obviously, words had been exchanged.

Looking at them both, Grey said, "I might as well say that you're wasting your time. I've nothing to tell you."

"Do you know what it's costing my paper to keep you in this place?" Stuhr said.

"I didn't ask for that."

"Our readers are concerned about you, Richard. You're a hero."

"I'm no such thing. I just happened to be there."

"You were almost killed."

"And that makes me a hero?"

"Look, I'm not here to argue with you," Stuhr said.

The tea arrived on a silver tray: pots and crockery, a tiny bowl of sugar, biscuits. While the steward arranged them on the table, Stuhr returned to his newspaper, and Grey took the opportunity to look properly at Susan Kewley. He remembered that Dave had described her as pretty, but that was hardly the right word. What Grey noticed most about her was that she lacked distinctive features. She was probably in her mid to late twenties. She was plain, but plain in a pleasant sense of the word; neutral was perhaps better. She had a regular face, hazel eyes, pale brown hair which grew straight, slender shoulders. She sat in a relaxed way, resting her narrow wrists and hands on the arms of the chair, her body erect and comfortable. She would not look at him, but stared at the crockery on the table as if avoiding not only his eyes but his opinion too. Yet he had no opinion, except that she was there, that she had arrived with Stuhr and therefore must be associated, directly or indirectly, with the newspaper.

How had he known her in the past? What *kind* of a friend? Someone he had worked with? A lover? But surely he would remember that, of all things?

For a moment it occurred to him that she might have been brought here by Stuhr as some kind of stunt, to provoke a response he could write about in the paper. MYSTERY WOMAN IN LOVE BID would be about par for the newspaper's course, and as true to the facts as most of the stories it ran.

When the steward had left, Grey said to her, "Well, what is it we have to talk about?"

She said nothing, but reached forward and pulled a cup and saucer toward her. Still she did not look at him, and her hair was tipping forward, concealing her face from him.

"As far as I can remember, I've never seen you before in my life. You'll have to give me more to go on than that."

She was holding the saucer, pale veins visible beneath her translucent skin. She seemed to be shaking her head slightly.

"Or are you here because *he* brought you?" Grey said angrily. He looked at Stuhr, who did not react. "Miss Kewley, I don't know what you want, but—"

Then she turned toward him, and for the first time he saw all of her face, slightly long, fine-boned, wintry in color. Her eyes were full of tears, and the corners of her mouth were twitching downward. She pushed back her chair quickly, toppling the saucer with its cup on the table, colliding with the wheelchair as she pushed past him. Pain jabbed down his back, and he heard a gulping inhalation of breath from her. She ran across the room and went into the corridor.

To stare after her would mean turning his head against the stiffness of his neck, so Grey did not try. It felt silent and cold in the room.

"What a bastard you can be." Stuhr threw aside his newspaper. "I'll call Woodbridge."

"Wait a minute . . . what do you mean?"

"Couldn't you see what you were doing to her?"

"No. Who is she?"

"She's your girlfriend, Grey. She's come all the way down here in the hope that if you saw her again it might trigger some memory."

"I don't have a girlfriend." But he felt again the helpless rage of his lost weeks. Just as he tried to avoid memories of the pain, so he shrank away from the weeks before the car bomb explosion. There was a profound blankness in his mind, one he never entered because he did not know how. "And if she is someone I know, what the hell is she doing here with you?"

"Look, it was an experiment."

"Did Woodbridge cook this up?"

"No . . . listen, Richard. Susan approached *us*. She saw the stories in the paper, and she came forward. She said that you and she had once had an affair, that it was all over, but that seeing her might help you regain your memory."

"Then it is a stunt."

"I won't deny that if you regained your memory I'd write about it. But really, this time I'm just here to drive the car."

Grey shook his head, and stared angrily through the window at the sea. Once he had discovered he was suffering from retroactive amnesia because of the concussion, he had been trying to come to terms with it. At first he had probed the feeling of blankness, thinking that if he could somehow find a way he would penetrate it, but to do so made him profoundly depressed and introspective. What he was doing now was trying not to think about it, to accept that the weeks he had lost would stay lost.

"Where does Woodbridge come into this?"

"He didn't set it up. He agreed to it. The idea was Susan's."

"It was a bad idea."

Stuhr said, "That's not her fault. Look at yourself—you're totally unmoved by this! The only reservation

Woodbridge had was that *you* might be traumatized. Yet you're sitting here as if nothing has happened, and the girl's in tears."

"I can't help that."

"Just don't blame her for it." Stuhr stood up. He thrust his newspaper back into his pocket.

"What are you going to do now?" Grey said.

"There's no point carrying on with this. I'll call and see you in a month or so. You might be more receptive then."

"What about the girl?"

"I'll come back this afternoon."

She was there, standing beside his wheelchair, a hand resting on the grip behind his left shoulder. At the sound of her voice, Grey started with surprise, jerking the stiffness in his neck, a completion of the movement he had failed to make when she left. How long had she been standing there, just beyond the periphery of his vision? Stuhr had given no indication she had returned.

Stuhr said to her, "I'll wait for you in the car."

He moved past them both, and again Grey felt that unpleasant sensation of everyone being taller than him. Susan sat down in the chair she had occupied before.

"I'm sorry about all that," she said.

"No—I'm the one who should apologize. I was very rude."

"I won't stay now. I need time to think, and I'll come back later."

Grey said, "After lunch I have to go for physiotherapy. Could you come again tomorrow?"

"It might be possible. Tony's driving back to London this afternoon, but I could stay."

"Where are you?"

"We were in a guest house in Kingsbridge last night. I could probably stay another night or two. I'll arrange something."

As before, she was not looking at him when they

spoke, except in short, darting glimpses through the strands of fine hair. Her eyes had dried but she looked paler than before. He wanted to feel something for her, remember her, but she was a stranger.

Trying to give her something warmer than this cold exchange of arrangements, he said, "Are you sure you still want to talk to me?"

"Yes, of course."

"Tony said that we—I mean you and I—were once . . ."

"We went out together for a while. It didn't last long, but it mattered at the time. I'd hoped you would remember."

"I'm sorry," Grey said. "I really don't."

"Let's not talk about it now. I'll come back tomorrow morning. I won't get upset again."

Wanting to explain, he said, "It was because you were with Tony Stuhr. I thought you worked for the newspaper."

"It was the only way I could find out where you were. I didn't understand the situation." She had picked up her bag, a canvas holdall with a long strap. "I'll come back tomorrow." She had laid one of her long hands lightly on his. "Are you sure you'd like me to?"

"Yes, of course. Come well before lunch."

"I should have asked you straight away: are you in much pain? I didn't realize you would be in a wheelchair."

"I'm better now. Everything happens very slowly."

"Richard . . . ?" She still had her fingers resting on the back of his hand. "Are you sure—I mean, you really can't remember?"

He wanted to turn his hand so that she would touch his palm, but that would be an intimacy he knew he hadn't deserved. Looking at her large eyes and her clear complexion he felt how easy he must once have found it to be with her. What was she like, this quiet-spoken woman who had once been his girlfriend? What did she know about him? What did he know of her? Why had they split up, when their relationship had mattered to them both? She was from beyond the coma, beyond the pain of ruptured organs and burnt-off skin, from the lost part of his life. But until today he had had no idea she even existed.

He wanted to answer her question truthfully, but something prevented it.

"I'm trying to remember," he said. "I feel as if I know you."

Her fingers briefly tightened. "All right. I'll see you tomorrow."

She stood up, went past his chair and out of his sight. He heard her footsteps soft on the carpet, then more distinctly in the corridor outside. Still he could not turn his head, without the pain.

III

Both of Richard Grey's parents were now dead. He had no brothers or sisters. His only relative was his father's sister, who was married and living in Australia. After leaving school, Grey went to Brent Technical College, where he took a diploma in photography. While at Brent he enrolled in a BBC training scheme, and when he had won his diploma he went to work at the BBC Television film studios in Ealing as a camera trainee. After a few months he became a camera assistant, working with various crews in the studios and on location. Eventually he graduated to full camera operator.

When he was twenty-four he left the BBC and went to work as a cameraman for an independent news agency based in North London. The agency syndicated its news film throughout the world, but principally to one of the American networks. Most of the news stories he was assigned to were in Britain and Europe, but he traveled several times to the States, to the Far East and Australia, and to Africa. During the 1970s he made several trips to Northern Ireland, covering the troubles there.

He established a reputation for courage. News crews are frequently in the thick of dangerous events, and it takes a particular kind of dedication to continue shooting footage in the middle of a riot or while under fire. Richard Grey had risked his life on several occasions.

He was twice nominated for a BAFTA Award for documentary or news filming, and in 1978 he and his sound recordist were given a special Prix Italia for film reportage of street fighting in Belfast. The commendation read, "For obtaining unique and shocking pictures under conditions of extreme personal danger." Among his colleagues, Grey was popular, and in spite of his reputation he never found people unwilling to work with him. As his stature grew it was recognized that he was not foolhardy, endangering himself as well as others, but used skill and experience and knew intuitively when a risk could be taken.

Grey lived alone in the apartment he had bought with the money his father had left him. Most of his friends were people he worked with, and because his work involved so much travel he had never settled down with a steady girlfriend. He found it easy to drift from one encounter to the next, never forming ties. When he was not working he often went to the cinema, sometimes to the theater. About once a week he would meet some of his friends for an evening in a pub. He generally took solitary holidays, camping or walking; once he had extended a working trip to the States by renting a car and driving to California.

Apart from the deaths of his parents, there had

been only one major disruption to his life, and that had happened about six months before the car bomb.

Richard Grey worked best with film. He liked the weight of an Arriflex, the balance of it, the quiet vibration of the motor. He saw through the reflex viewfinder as if with an extra eye; he sometimes said he could not see properly without it. And there was something about the texture of film itself, the quality of the picture, the subtlety of its effects. The knowledge that film slipped through the gate, halting and advancing, twenty-five times a second gave an intangible extra feel to his work. He was always irritated if people said they could not tell the difference, on television, between a film sequence and one recorded on an electronic camera. It seemed to him that the difference was manifest: video "footage" had an empty quality, a brightness and sharpness that was unnatural and false.

But for a news medium film was slow and unwieldy. Somehow the cans had to be taken to a lab, then to a cutting room. Sound had to be synched in or overdubbed. There were always technical problems during transmission, especially when a local news studio had to be used or if the film had to be sent by satellite to one of the syndicating stations. The difficulties were increased when working abroad or in a war zone; sometimes the only way to get the story out was by taking the unprocessed film to the nearest airport and putting it on a plane to London, New York or Amsterdam.

News networks around the world were changing over to electronic cameras. Using portable satellite dishes, a crew could transmit pictures direct to the studio as they were being shot. There they could be edited electronically and transmitted without delay.

One by one the news crews were going over to video, and it came, inevitably, to Grey. He went on a retraining course and thereafter had to use an electronic camera. For reasons he never really understood, he found it difficult to transfer his skill. He could not "see" without the intervention of film, the silent whirring of the motor. He became self-conscious about the problem, attempting to overcome it by fundamentally rethinking his approach. He tried to adjust his eye so he could see again, a concept to which his colleagues were sympathetic even though most of them were making the same transition successfully. He kept telling himself that technology was a mere instrument, that his ability was innate and not a product of the medium. Even so, he knew he had lost his flair.

There were other jobs open to him. The BBC and Independent Television News were also changing over to electronic news gathering, and even though he was offered a film job with ITN he realized that in the end the same problem would arise. Another job offered to him was with an industrial documentary unit, but he had cut his teeth on news filming and it was never a real alternative.

The solution came when the agency unexpectedly lost its contract with the American network. Staff had to be made redundant, and Richard Grey volunteered himself. He had no particular idea in mind—simply took the redundancy money, intending to use it to buy time to reconsider his career. In the first month he went on a holiday to the States, then returned to his flat in London to plan what to do next.

He was not short of money. He had bought his apartment outright with his father's money, and the redundancy lump sum would last at least a year. Nor was he idle, because he was given occasional free-lance work.

But then there was a gap.

His next memories were fitful: he was in intensive care at Charing Cross Hospital in London, surviving on a ventilator, undergoing a series of major operations, in pain and under sedation. After this there was an agonizing journey in an ambulance, and ever since he had been at Middlecombe Hospital, convalescing on the South Devon coast.

Somewhere in the gap in his life he had been in a London street, where a car bomb had been planted outside a police station. It exploded while he was passing. He suffered multiple burns and lacerations, back injuries, fractures of pelvis, leg and arm, and ruptured internal organs. He had nearly died.

This was the extent of his memories on the day Susan Kewley came to see him, and she nowhere fitted into them.

IV

There was a conflict of medical opinion about Grey's amnesia, and for Grey himself this was complicated by a conflict of personal opinion.

He was being treated by two men at the hospital: the psychologist James Woodbridge, and a consultant psychiatrist called Dr. Hurdis.

Grey disliked Woodbridge, because he found him high-handed and often remote, but he took a line that Grey found acceptable. Woodbridge, while acknowledging the traumatic nature of the injuries, and the effects of concussion, believed that retrograde amnesia could also be psychologically based. In other words, that there were additional events in his life, unconnected with the explosion, which Grey was now repressing. Woodbridge believed that the memories of these should be coaxed out gently by psychotherapy, and that the benefits of using other techniques to open up the memories would not be worth the risks. He thought that Grey should be rehabilitated gradually, and with a return to normal life he would be able to come to terms with his past, his memory returning in stages.

On the other hand, Dr. Hurdis, whom Grey actually liked, had been pressing him in a direction he tried to resist. Hurdis believed that progress with orthodox analytical psychotherapy would be too slow, especially where organic loss of memory was involved.

Against his personal feelings, Grey had so far responded better to Woodbridge than to Hurdis.

Until Susan Kewley's arrival, Grey had not been too concerned about what might actually have happened in the weeks he had lost. What worried him more was the sense of *absence*, a hole in his life, a dark and quiet period that seemed forever remote from him. His mind instinctively shied away from it, and like the sore places in his body he had been trying not to use it.

But Susan Kewley had come to him from out of the absence, unrecognized and unremembered. She had known him then, and he had known her, and now she was awakening in him the need to remember.

V

In the morning, when Richard Grey had been bathed and dressed, and was waiting in his room for news of Susan's arrival, Woodbridge came to see him.

"I wanted to have a quiet word with you before Miss Kewley gets here," Woodbridge said. "She seems to be a very pleasant young woman, don't you agree?"

"Yes," Grey said, suddenly irritated.

"I wondered if you had any memory of her."

"None whatsoever."

"Not even a vague feeling that you might have seen her somewhere?"

"No."

"Did she tell you anything about what happened when you knew her?"

"No."

"Richard, what I'm getting at is that you might have had some kind of row with her, and afterwards perhaps dealt with it by trying to bury the memory. It would be perfectly normal to do so."

"All right," Grey said. "But I don't see why that matters now."

"Because retroactive amnesia can be caused by an unconscious wish to banish unhappy memories. I think you should recognize this."

"Is it going to make a difference?"

"Seeing her now could deepen your unconscious wish to block her."

"It didn't yesterday. It deepened my wish to know her better. It just seems to me that she might be able to remind me of things I can't remember by myself."

"Yes, but it's important that you accept she is not going to provide you with the solution on her own."

"But surely it can't hurt?"

"We'll have to see. If you want to talk to me afterwards, I'll be here for the rest of the day."

Grey remained stubbornly irritated after Woodbridge had left. It seemed to him that there was a subtle but definite distinction between his private life and his presence in the hospital as a patient. He sometimes thought that his amnesia was seen as a professional challenge by the people who were treating him, something unrelated to his real life. If Susan really had been his girlfriend, their knowledge of each other was presumably intimate and deeply personal. Woodbridge's questions intruded on this.

A few minutes after Woodbridge left, Grey took the

book he was currently reading and went out of his room and along to the elevator. He propelled himself out to the terrace and moved to the far end. This was not only some distance away from the other patients, but gave him a vantage point over most of the gardens and the drive leading to the visitors' car park.

The weather was cool and gray, with low clouds moving in darkly from the northwest. The sea was normally visible from the terrace, glimpsed through trees, but today there was a dulling haze over everything.

He settled down to read, but the wind was blustery and after a few minutes he called a steward and asked for a blanket. After an hour, the other patients went inside.

Vehicles arrived at intervals, nosing their way up the turning incline into the steep tarmacadamed drive. Two of them were ambulances, bringing new patients; there were several tradesmen's vans, and a number of cars. With the arrival of each of these, Grey's hopes rose and he waited excitedly for her to appear.

It was impossible to concentrate on his book, and the morning passed slowly. He felt cold and uncomfortable and, as midday approached, more and more resentful. She had promised, after all, and must have known what the visit would mean to him. He started to invent excuses for her: she had had to hire a car and there had been a delay; the car had broken down; there had been an accident. But surely he would have heard?

With all the helpless egocentricity of the invalid, Grey could think of nothing but this.

The time drew near to one o'clock, when luncheon was served and he would be taken into the dining room. He knew that even if she arrived in the next few minutes they could only have a short time together; at two he had to go for physiotherapy.

At five minutes before the hour a car turned into the drive. Grey regarded the sight of its silver roof and sky-reflecting windows with fatalistic certainty that it was Susan. He waited.

She appeared on the terrace with one of the nurses, Sister Alicia, and the two women walked across to him.

"They're serving lunch now, Mr. Grey. Shall I wheel you in?"

Looking at Susan, he said, "I'll be there in a few minutes."

"I can't stay long," she said, looking not at Grey but at the nurse.

"Shall I tell them you're staying for lunch too?"

"No, thank you."

"Now you mustn't miss a meal, Mr. Grey," the nurse said, looking from one to the other of them. She walked away.

"Richard, I'm sorry I couldn't get here before."

"Where have you been?"

"I was delayed."

"Was it the car?"

"What? Oh no—I hired that last night."

"I've been waiting for you all morning," he said.

"I know. I'm really sorry."

She sat down on the low concrete parapet of the terrace. Her fawn raincoat fell away on each side, revealing her lower legs. They were thin, and clad in ankle socks over her stockings. He noticed that she was wearing a flowered skirt.

She said, "I had to telephone the studio this morning, and all sorts of problems have come up."

"Studio?"

"Where I work. You must remember—no, I'm sorry. I'm a free-lance artist, and I work three days a week for a design studio. It's my only regular job."

She leaned forward to take one of his hands. Grey stared at the ground, realizing dismally that for the second time he was feeling hostile toward her.

"I'm sorry," he said.

"And, Richard, I have to go back to London today."
He looked up at her, quickly. She added, "I know . . .
but I'll come back next week sometime."

"Can't you come before then?"

"I really can't. It's very difficult. I need the money,
and if I let the studio down they'll find someone else. It's
very hard getting the work."

"All right, all right." Struggling against his disappointment, Grey tried to get his thoughts straight. "Let
me tell you what I've been thinking since yesterday. I
want to look at you."

He had already noticed that she rarely turned her
face fully toward him, always presenting a quarter profile
or keeping her head lowered. Her hair fell about her face,
obscuring her features. It had seemed an attractive man-
nerism at first, a shyness, a reticence, but he wanted to see
her properly.

She said, "I don't like being looked at."

"I want to remember you."

She tossed her hair back with a light shaking motion of her head and looked straight at him. He regarded
her, trying to remember or see her as he might have done
before. She held his gaze for a few moments, then cast her
eyes downward once more.

"Don't stare at me," she said.

"All right." They were still holding hands. "But
you see, I believe that if I can remember you then I'll
remember everything else."

"That's why I'm here."

"I know . . . but it's so difficult for me. I'm always
being told what to do by the staff, the newspaper keeps
trying to make me tell my story, I'm stuck in this chair,
and all I want to do is to get back to normal. The truth is,
Susan, that I don't remember you at all."

She said, "But—"

"Let me finish. I *don't* remember you, but I feel as if
I know you. I honestly can't tell if that's because I really

do know you, or because I'd like to . . . but whatever it is, it's the first real feeling I've had since I've been here."

She nodded mutely, her face hidden from him again.

"I need to see you as often as you can manage it."

"I can't afford it," she said. "I've already spent most of what I have, just renting the car. And I've got to pay the train fare back to London."

"I'll pay for it all—I've got money. Or the newspaper can pay. Something could be arranged."

"It's just not very easy."

"Are you going out with someone else now?"

She was staring down the length of the empty terrace, and he wished she would face him.

"No," she said. "There's no one else." Her hand was fidgeting, the fingers stroking the material of her skirt as if trying to tease up a fragment of the cloth. "There was someone else . . . but not anymore."

"Is this why you haven't been here before?"

"Partly. He knew how much I was missing you, but now it's all over."

Grey felt excitement in him, a tightening of muscles, a feeling he had not known since before he could remember.

"Susan, tell me what happened between us. At the end. Why did we part?"

"You really don't know, do you?"

"No."

She shook her head. "It seems impossible you could forget."

"Can't you tell me?"

"Well, it no longer matters. Now I've seen you again it's as if it didn't happen."

"But I want to try to remember!"

"It wasn't any one thing. I suppose it had never really worked from the beginning."

"Was it a row? What was said?"

"No, not a row. It had been going wrong for some time, and we both knew we couldn't carry on as we were. It was complicated. This—other person was around, and you were unhappy about that. You wanted to stop seeing me, but nothing was resolved. Then the next thing I heard was that you'd been hurt by the bomb."

"Can't you tell me more than that?" Grey said.

"Do you remember the cloud?"

"Cloud? What sort of cloud? What do you mean?"

"Just . . . the cloud."

One of the stewards had appeared on the terrace, a napkin folded over his arm. "We're about to serve the main course, Mr. Grey. Will you and your friend be requiring lunch?"

"I'm missing lunch today," Grey said, and turned back to Susan. She had stood up. "What are you doing? You can't leave now!"

"I've got to. I have to take the car back to Kingsbridge, then there's a long bus ride to Totnes to catch the train. I'm already late."

"What were you talking about just now? What did you mean about the cloud?"

"It was something I thought you'd remember."

"I've no memory of anything. Tell me something else."

"Do you remember Niall?"

"No."

"What about those people sunbathing? Do you remember that?"

He shook his head. "Should this mean something?"

"I just don't know what you want to hear! Look, we can talk properly next time. I've really got to go, and you should be having lunch."

She was leaving; already she had turned away from him.

"When will you come again? Next week?"

"I'll come as soon as I can," she said. She crouched

down by his chair and squeezed his hand very gently. "I *want* to see you, Richard. I'd stay with you now if I could. Do you believe that?"

She brought her face to his and kissed him lightly on the cheek. He raised his hand to touch her hair, and turned his head, finding her lips. Her skin was cold, from the weather. She held the kiss for a few seconds, then drew back from him.

"Don't go," he said quietly. "Please don't leave now."

"I really must." She stood up and moved away from him. Then she stopped. "I nearly forgot! I brought you a present."

She came back to him, reaching down into her deep canvas bag. She drew out a white paper bag, folded over and sealed with a strip of clear tape.

"Shall I open it now?" he said.

"Yes. It isn't much, I'm afraid."

He broke the seal with his thumb and pulled out what was inside. There were about two dozen postcards of assorted sizes and kinds. They were all very old, and most of them were black and white or sepia-tinted. Some of them were views of English seaside resorts, some were expanses of countryside, some were from the European continent: German spas, French cathedrals, Alpine scenery.

"I saw them in an antique shop in Kingsbridge this morning."

"Thanks . . . they're very nice."

"I suppose you might have some of them already. In your collection."

"My *collection?*"

She laughed then, a short sound, oddly loud. "You don't even remember that, do you?"

"You mean I collect old postcards?" He grinned at her. "How much more am I going to learn from you?"

"Actually, there is something. You never used to call me Susan. It was always Sue."

She kissed him again, then left, walking quickly across the terrace and vanishing into the building. He waited, and a short time later he heard a car door slam, then the sound of an engine starting. Soon he saw the windows and roof of her car as it drove slowly down toward the lane.

VI

Dr. Hurdis visited Middlecombe that weekend, and spent a large part of Saturday afternoon with Grey. Hurdis adopted a sympathetic approach, listening more than speaking, never leading his patient with sudden or surprising questions. He treated Grey as a participant in a problem rather than as a recipient of treatment, and often their sessions together were more like conversations than analysis, although Grey realized this was probably not the case.

He was in a communicative mood that day, because at last he felt he had something to talk about, and had an interest in himself that was lacking before.

Not that the two short meetings with Sue had solved anything; his amnesia remained as profound as ever, a fact which Hurdis quickly elicited from him. The principal knowledge she had brought him was the reassurance that he had actually existed in the lost period. Until now, he had not truly believed in himself; the sense of absence behind him seemed to exclude him. But Sue was a witness to the fact of himself. She remembered him, when he did not.

He had of course thought of almost nothing but her since she left. His mind and life were filled with her. He wanted her company, the touch of her hand, her kisses. Most of all he wanted to see her, to look properly at her, but in a strange miniature of his larger problem he found it difficult to remember what she was like. He could visualize peripheral details about her: the canvas bag, the stockinged ankles, the flowered skirt, her coat, her masking hair. He knew she had looked him straight in the face, as if allowing him a secret sight of her, but afterward he found he could not see her face in his mind's eye. He remembered her plainness, the regularity of her features, but these too acted like a mask to her appearance.

"I think Sue is my best chance of recovering my memory," he said. "She obviously knows me well, and she was there during the weeks I've lost. I keep thinking that if she only tells me one thing that jogs my memory, it could be enough."

"You might well be right," Hurdis said. They were in the office he used on weekends, a comfortable place with big leather chairs and a bookcase. "But a word of caution. You mustn't be too anxious to remember. There's a condition known as paramnesia, hysterical paramnesia."

"I don't think I'm hysterical, Dr. Hurdis."

"Clearly not, in the usual sense. But occasionally someone who has lost his memory will grasp at any straw, any hint of a memory, and without knowing how accurate it might be let it lead to a whole sequence of invented memories."

"I'm sure that couldn't happen with Sue. She would put me right."

"As you say. But if you started confabulating, you might not be able to tell the difference. What does Mr. Woodbridge think about this?"

"I think he's against my talking to her."

"Yes, I see."

Grey's preoccupation, since Sue had left, had been

in trying to pry loose any memories she might have touched on. Fired by his new interest in her, the few things she had said became enormously important, and he examined them in his mind from every angle. He talked them out with Dr. Hurdis, glad to have an uncritical listener, someone who contributed by encouraging him to talk on and on.

In actual fact she had said remarkably little about their past together. It was symptomatic, according to Hurdis, that he should seize on such fragments and try to find relevance in them.

He had solved one minor mystery on his own: the matter of the postcards. At first he thought he had stumbled on something from his lost weeks, something hitherto forgotten, but then, surfacing from the old past, the memory came to him.

He had been working in Bradford, in the north of England. During an afternoon off he went wandering by himself through the back streets, and came across a junk shop. He had a small collection of antique film equipment, and was always on the lookout for more. This particular shop had nothing of this sort, but on the counter he came across a battered shoe box crammed with postcards. He looked through them for a while, mildly interested. The woman who ran the shop told him the price of each card was marked on the back, and on an impulse he asked her how much she would want for the lot. A few seconds later the deal was closed for ten pounds.

When he got home a few days later, Grey went through the several hundred old postcards he now owned. Some of them had obviously been bought and collected by someone in the past, because they were unused; many of them, though, had messages on the back. He read all the ones he could decipher, scrawled in fountain pen or indelible pencil. Almost all of them were prosaic dispatches from holidays: a lovely time being had, the weather improving, visited Aunt Sissy yesterday, the scenery is beautiful, raining all week but we're bearing up, Teddy doesn't like the food, weather glorious, the gardens are so peaceful, the sun brings out the mosquitoes, we've all been swimming, weather, weather, weather.

Many of the cards went back to the Great War and before, their halfpenny stamps mute tokens of how prices had changed. At least a third of the cards had been sent from abroad: grand tours through Europe, rides on cable cars, visits to casinos, insufferable heat. They were messages from a leisured class now irretrievably vanished: travelers in an age before tourism.

The actual photographs were even more interesting to him. He saw them as stills from some long-lost travelogue of the past, glimpses of towns and scenes that in one sense no longer existed. Several pictures were of places he knew or had visited: Edwardian gentlemen and ladies strolling on sea-front esplanades which now were littered with high-rise hotels, amusement arcades and parking meters; country vales where now broad motorways had been driven; French and Italian shrines now cluttered with souvenir stalls; peaceful market towns now jammed with traffic and chain stores. These too were memories of a vanished past, alien but recognizable, unattainable in every real sense.

He sorted the cards into groups by country, then returned them to the box. Whenever friends sent him cards after that he added them to the stack, thinking that they too would one day come to represent a certain past.

Sue's reminder of this had surprised him, but the cards did not come from his amnesiac period. He had been in Bradford while still working for the agency, pre-dating by at least a year any possible first meeting with her.

However, the fact that she knew about the postcards meant she must have seen them, or they had talked about them.

The rest of what she had told him was more vague. They had obviously been lovers, although for a short time.

They had split up. There was someone else in her life, and the name Niall had been mentioned. She was Sue, not Susan. Then two odd details: the sunbathers, the cloud.

What had gone wrong with the relationship? The two times he had seen her at the hospital he had been initially hostile to her; was this an awakening from the unconscious? If there was someone else, had everything been wrecked by jealousy?

And what was the significance of the people sun-bathing, the cloud? The two brought a mental image of a hot beach, people spread out in the sun, the interruption of a clouded sky. They were commonplaces; why had she selected these?

But taken as a whole, nothing she said stirred the slightest memory in him. From the traceable reference to the postcards to the enigmatic cloud, nothing helped.

Dr. Hurdis listened attentively, wrote down a few notes as Grey was speaking, but at the end sat with his notebook closed on his lap.

"There's something I'd like to try," he said. "Have you ever been hypnotized?"

"No. Would that work?"

"Well, it might. It's sometimes helpful in recovering lost memory, but it's imperfect and by no means a sure method. It could make a difference in your case, though."

"Why haven't you suggested this before?"

Hurdis said, smiling: "You're motivated now, Richard. I'm due to make another call here on Wednesday. We'll give it a try then."

In the evening, Grey spent an hour in the pool in the basement of the hospital, swimming to and fro very slowly, floating on his back, thinking about Sue.

VII

She telephoned on the Tuesday evening. Grey took the call on the pay phone in the corridor; he had his own telephone in his room, but she must have been given the other number. As soon as he spoke to her he knew she was going to let him down.

"How are you, Richard?" she said.

"I'm a lot better, thanks."

There was a short silence. Then, "I'm on a pay phone, so I can't talk too long."

"Hang up, and I'll call you back from my room."

"No—no, there's someone waiting. Look, I've got to tell you something. I won't be able to get down there this week. Will next week be all right?"

"No it won't," he said, against a thudding and inevitable feeling of disappointment. "You promised you'd come."

"Well, it's not possible."

"What's the problem?"

"I can't afford the train fare, and—"

"I've told you, I'll pay."

"Yes, but I can't get the time off. There's a deadline, and I've got to go in every day."

Two of the other patients walked slowly down the corridor, not speaking. Grey held the receiver closer to his ear, trying for privacy. The patients went through the door into the lounge, and he briefly heard music from the television set.

When the door had closed, he said, "Don't you understand how important this is to me?", but halfway

through his sentence the pips interrupted him. He heard a
coin fall, and the line opened again.

"I didn't hear that," Sue said.

"I said it's very important that I see you."

"I know. I'm sorry."

"Will you definitely come next week?"

"I'll try."

"You'll *try?* You said you wanted to come."

"I do, I really do."

Another silence.

Then Grey said, "Where are you speaking from? Is
anybody with you?"

"I'm at home—the phone in the hall."

"*Is* somebody with you?"

"No, Richard. I'm just working in my room, trying
to finish a piece of artwork."

Grey realized that he had no idea where she even
lived. A bead of sweat ran down his face beside his eye.
"Look, the phone's going to cut off in a minute. Have you
got another coin?"

"No, I'm going to have to finish."

"Please don't. Get some more money, and call me
so we can talk. Or give me the number, and I'll call you."
Time was slipping away.

"I'll try to come at the weekend, to make up for it."

"Do you mean that? It'd be—"

But the pips started, and Grey groaned in frustra-
tion. This time no coin fell. The line opened again, the
few seconds extra the machine always allowed.

"Please . . . call me now. I'll wait by the phone."

"All—" The line went dead.

He put the receiver back, churning with disappointment and fury. The whole building felt deeply silent,
as if his words had sounded about the place for all to hear.
It was an illusion, though: he could still hear the television
set faintly through the door, and somewhere below him
the central heating boiler was making its customary dis-

tant noise. He could hear voices at the far end of the corridor.

He sat in his wheelchair, the telephone just above head height, trying to calm his feelings. He knew he was being unreasonable; he was treating her as if she were answerable to him for all her actions and thoughts, as if vows were being broken.

Ten minutes passed, and then the phone rang. He snatched it down, hearing the damned pips again.

Sue said, "I was only able to borrow one coin. We can talk for about two minutes."

"All right, about the weekend—"

"Please, Richard. Let me speak. I know you think I'm letting you down, but when I found where you were I came down to see you without thinking of the consequences here. I have to sort out my work, but I'll come at the weekend—that's a promise. You'll have to send some money, though."

"I don't know your address!"

"Do you have some paper? Or can you remember it?" Speaking quickly, she dictated an address in north London. "Have you got that?"

"I'll send a check tomorrow."

"Now, there's something else. Don't interrupt, because there isn't time. I'm all mixed up because you can't remember me . . . but since I saw you, I've been thinking and thinking about you. I still love you."

"Still?"

"I always did, Richard, right from the start. You'll remember soon, I know you will."

He was smiling; he could hardly believe what he was hearing.

"I'm not going to be here much longer," he said. "Maybe a week or two. I'm feeling a lot better."

"It's terrible seeing you in that chair. You were always so active."

"I walked a long way today—five times across the

room. I'm doing more every day. You'll see at the weekend. You will come, won't you?"

"Of course! I can hardly wait to see you again."

The mood of depression she had cast him into had
evaporated. "I'm sorry about everything . . . I'm so cut
off down here. It'll be different next time."

"I know." The pips started, but now they didn't
matter. When the line cleared, Sue said, "I'll come Friday
evening."

"All right. Goodbye."

"Goodbye, love." The line died.

He hung up, then propelled himself down the corridor, thrusting down on the push wheels with all his
strength. At the end of the corridor he swung around and
speeded back to the elevator.

Once inside his room, he went through the cardboard box of personal documents that had been sent down
by the police and looked for his checkbook. Just to see
these pieces of card and paper was like glimpsing his old
identity again: a driver's license, two credit cards, a check-
guarantee card (now expired), membership of the British
Film Institute, an A.C.T.T. union card, a BBC Club card,
an insurance certificate for his car, a bank statement,
membership of the National Trust . . .

He found the checkbook and wrote a check for one
hundred pounds. He scribbled a note on the hospital's paper and slipped it into an envelope with the check. He
wrote the address Sue had dictated to him, then propped
up the envelope, ready for mailing in the morning.

He sat back in his chair for a while, dwelling pleasurably on her intimate and affectionate words at the end
of the conversation. He closed his eyes, trying to remember her face.

A little later he returned to the documents he had
scattered across the table. These had been in his possession
since arriving in Devon, but he had scarcely looked at
them. Nothing could have seemed more irrelevant. His

affairs, such as they were, were being looked after by a solicitor retained by the newspaper, and in fact the check to Sue was the first he had written since the car bomb.

Suddenly interested in himself, he opened the checkbook and looked through the counterfoils. About half of the twenty-five checks had been used, and the dates scrawled on the counterfoils were all in the period immediately prior to the bomb. Hoping for a clue, he looked at each one but soon realized he could learn nothing from them. Most of them were made out to cash; there was one to British Telecom, one to the London Electricity Board, one to a bookshop, and one to G.F.&T. Ltd for the sum of £12.53. This last item was the only one he failed to understand, but he couldn't see that it was significant.

His address book was also in the box—a small, plastic-bound notebook. He knew most of it was blank, because he had never been very good at writing down addresses, but nevertheless he turned to the page for K. There was no entry for Sue—unsurprising, but vaguely disappointing. It would have been a sort of proof, a link with his forgotten past.

He went through the entire book, examining everything. Most of the addresses were of people he could remember: colleagues, old girlfriends, the aunt in Australia. Several of the names had just telephone numbers against them. Everything in the book had that familiar feeling from his known past, providing him with nothing new.

Just as he was about to put it aside, he thought to look at the back of the last page, a memory stirring that he sometimes used it for scribbled notes. There he found what he was looking for: amid a number of obscure pieces of arithmetic, a reminder of a dental appointment and a couple of doodles was the word "Sue." Next to it was a London telephone number.

For a moment he was tempted to pick up his phone and call her immediately, celebrate the fact that he had found her in his own past, but he held back. He was con-

tent with what had passed between them. He would see
her on the weekend, and did not want to risk her changing
her mind yet again.

He put the address book in his pocket, thinking he
could easily check with her that this was still her present
number. That would be enough to give him the sort of
proof he needed, verify the link with himself.

VIII

The following morning Grey visited Dr. Hurdis's office.
He was still in the optimistic mood of the evening before,
had slept well, and had done so for the first time without
painkilling medication. The psychiatrist was waiting for
him, and introduced him to a young woman who was also
in the room.

"Richard, this is one of my postgraduate research-
ers, Miss Alexandra Gowers. Richard Grey."

"How do you do?"

They shook hands formally, Grey registering that
she looked very young. She was wearing a red skirt with a
black woollen pullover, and had spectacles and long dark
hair.

"With your permission, Richard, I'd like Miss
Gowers to be present while you are hypnotized. Would
you have any objections to that?"

"Not at all."

"This is just a preliminary session. What I'd like to
do is put you into a light trance and see how you react to
that. If it goes well, I might try to deepen the trance a
little."

"Whatever you think is right," Grey said. That

morning he had been feeling curious about what hypnosis might be like, but not nervous at the prospect.

Dr. Hurdis and the young woman helped him out of his wheelchair, and then Hurdis took his weight as he lowered himself into one of the leather chairs and made himself comfortable.

"Now, do you have any questions, Richard?"

"I'd like to know about the trance—does it mean I will lose consciousness?"

"No, you'll be awake the whole time. You'll remember everything afterwards. Hypnosis is simply a form of relaxation."

"That's all right, then."

"What I want you to do is try to cooperate as far as possible. You can speak, move your hands, open your eyes, and none of this will break the trance. The main thing I want you to realize is that we might not get results straight away, and you mustn't feel disappointed."

"I understand that."

"All right." Hurdis was standing to his side, and he reached over and stretched out an angle-poise lamp so that it was somewhere above Grey's head. "Can you see this?"

"Yes."

Hurdis moved it back a little. "What about here?"

"Just about."

"Keep looking up so the lamp is on the edge of your vision. Relax your body as much as you can, and let your breathing get very steady and easy. Listen to what I'm saying, and if your eyes feel tired, let them close." In the room, Grey was aware that Alexandra Gowers had moved away and was sitting on one of the straight-backed chairs against the walls. "Keep the lamp in sight and listen to me, and while you do so I would like you to start counting backwards to yourself, count to yourself, count from three hundred downwards, start now, keep counting, and listen to what I'm saying, but keep counting slowly *299* to yourself, and breathing *298* very gently and slowly, and think

297 of nothing but looking up at the lamp and *296* counting slowly backwards listening *295* to what I'm saying, and feeling your body very relaxed *294* and comfortable, very comfortable, your legs *293* feel very heavy, your arms feel very heavy *292* and now your eyes are beginning to feel *291* very tired, so if you wish you can close them, let them close, but keep *290* counting slowly and listening, your body is very relaxed *289* and now your eyes have closed but you are *289 288* still counting slowly, while you feel you are drifting backwards, very relaxed as you drift slowly backwards, and now *287* you are feeling very drowsy, very comfortable as you drift backwards, feeling drowsy, listening to what I'm saying but getting drowsy, drifting deeper and deeper into sleep, but still listening to what I'm saying . . ."

Grey felt comfortable and relaxed and drowsy, but was still aware of all that was around him. He had his eyes closed and was listening to Dr. Hurdis, but he could also sense further. Outside in the hall two people walked past, talking to each other, and somewhere in the room Alexandra Gowers had made a clicking noise with a ballpoint pen, and rustled some paper. In the next room a telephone rang, and someone answered it. Obedient to Hurdis's suggestions his body felt completely relaxed, but his mind was alert.

". . . drifting backwards, feeling drowsy, listening to me, your body is relaxed and you are sleepy. Good, Richard, that's excellent. Now stay breathing very steadily, but what I want you to do is concentrate on your right hand. Think about your right hand, and how it feels, and concentrate on it, and perhaps you find it is resting on something very soft, something very light, very light, something that is supporting your hand, something that is pressing up very gently from below, lifting your hand, lifting your hand . . ."

As Hurdis said these words, Grey felt to his amazement that his hand was lifting away from his lap. It went gently upward until his arm was upright, or almost so.

"Good, that's fine. Now feel it in the air, feel the air around it, supporting it gently. The air is holding it up, the air is holding it, holding it, and now you cannot pull the hand down again, the air is holding it . . ."

Thinking he should try, Grey tightened his arm muscles and attempted to bring his hand down . . . but the sensation of something soft and supporting was definite, and his hand stayed where it was.

". . . holding it up, but now I want you to lower your hand as soon as I have counted to five, as soon as I count from one to five, your hand will fall back, but not until I reach five, Richard, one . . . two . . . your hand is still held up by the air . . . three . . . four . . . now you feel the air is releasing your hand . . . five . . . your hand is free. . . ."

Seemingly of its own will, the hand fell slowly back into his lap.

". . . that's fine, Richard, that's fine. Now I want you to stay breathing slowly, your whole body relaxed, but when I tell you I want you to open your eyes, not until I tell you, you can open your eyes and look around the room, and when you open your eyes and look around the room, I want you to look, but not until I tell you, I want you to look for Miss Gowers, look for Miss Gowers, but you will not be able to see her, she is here but you will not be able to see her, but don't open your eyes until I have counted to five, when I count from one to five I want you to open your eyes . . ."

Hurdis droned on and on, and Grey, listening closely, found the quiet speaking voice irresistible, compelling.

". . . open your eyes when I reach five . . . one . . . two . . . three . . . four . . . I want you to open your eyes . . . five. . . ."

Grey opened his eyes and saw Dr. Hurdis standing

slightly to one side looking at him, half smiling in a friendly way.

"You can't see Miss Gowers, Richard, but I want you to look for her, look around the room but you cannot see her, look now. . . ."

Grey turned toward the row of chairs against the wall, knowing she was there. He had heard her sitting down, and just now he had heard her with her pen and notebook, but when he looked she was not there. Thinking she must have moved, Grey looked quickly around the room, but there was nowhere she could be. He looked back at the chairs, *knowing* she was there but unable to see her. Weak sunlight came through the window and struck the wall, but there was not even a shadow of her. He tried to imagine her red skirt and black top, but that was no help.

"You can speak if you wish, Richard."

"Where is she? Has she left the room?"

"No, she is still here. Now, please sit back again and make yourself comfortable. Close your eyes again, steady your breathing and let your limbs relax, you're feeling drowsy. Fine, that's fine. You can feel yourself starting to drift again, starting to move slowly backwards, and now you feel very sleepy indeed, very sleepy, and you are drifting deeper and deeper, that's fine, deeper and deeper, and now I'm going to count to ten, from one to ten, you will drift deeper and deeper, and with every number you will drift deeper, and feel sleepier and sleepier, one . . . very deep . . . two . . . you are drifting further and further . . . three. . . ."

But then there was a gap.

Grey next heard: ". . . seven . . . you will feel very refreshed, very happy, very calm . . . eight . . . you are beginning to awaken, you will be fully awake, fully alert, very calm . . . nine . . . your sleep is now very light, much lighter, you can see the daylight against your eyelids, and in a moment you will open your eyes

and be fully awake, and you will be calm and happy . . .
ten . . . you can open your eyes now, Richard."

Grey waited a few more seconds, comfortable in
the chair, his arms folded in his lap, sorry that it was over.
He was reluctant to break the spell; he had been free of the
stiffness in his body all through the hypnosis, with no
threat of pain. But his eyelids fluttered, and a moment
later he opened his eyes fully.

Something had happened. This was his first
thought as he looked at the other two; both stood beside
the chair, looking down at him.

"How are you feeling, Richard?"

"Fine," he said, but already the pains of his body
were returning, the familiar stiffness creeping over his
hip, his back, his shoulders. "Is something wrong?"

"No, of course not. Would you like a cup of coffee?"
Grey said he would, and Alexandra Gowers put down her
notebook and left the room. Hurdis's manner was abrupt
and awkward. He moved to the other chair and sat down.

"Now, I want to ask you: do you remember everything that just happened?"

"I think so."

"Would you mind describing it to me? What is the
first thing you remember?"

"You told me to start counting backwards from
three hundred, and I did. It was difficult to concentrate,
and I gave up after a while. The next thing I remember
was that my hand rose up in the air, and I couldn't get it
down until you released it. Then you made Miss Gowers
disappear."

Hurdis nodded slowly. "The only thing I'd say is
that you were doing these things, not me."

"If you say so."

"What do you remember next?"

"I . . . think you wanted to go further, but then
you seemed to change your mind. I'm not sure what happened. I started waking up."

"And that's all you remember?"

"Yes."

Alexandra Gowers returned to the room, carrying a small tray with three cups of coffee. As she passed them across, Hurdis repeated what Grey had just said. Returning to her seat, she said, "Then it's spontaneous."

"I think so too," Hurdis said.

Grey, whose feeling of mild euphoria had been quickly dispersed by the chilly atmosphere, said, "Would you mind telling me what you're talking about?"

"You turn out to be an excellent hypnotic subject," Hurdis said. "I was able to take you into a deep trance without any difficulty at all. Normally the subject is able to remember this afterwards, but in some cases he is not. I think you are one. You were in deep trance for about forty-five minutes. I was hoping you would be able to remember this."

"It's known as spontaneous amnesia," Alexandra Gowers said, and Hurdis glanced sharply at her.

"It's just a technical term, Richard."

"Of course," he said quietly. Most of what he had been forced to listen to in recent months consisted of technical terms, sometimes explained, sometimes not. He no longer cared; he was looking forward to hearing ordinary people saying ordinary things.

"The point is that I regressed you to the period obscured by the amnesia. It would obviously be better if you could remember by yourself, but if not it might help if we gently jog your memory."

"Then you did take me back?" Grey said, interested now.

"When you were in deep trance I asked you to try to recall the events of last year. We can roughly date it to the end of last summer, the car bomb incident being at the beginning of September. Is that right?"

"Yes."

"As I had expected, you sounded traumatized. Your

voice became emotional and it was difficult to make out a lot of what you said. I asked you to describe where you were, but you didn't. I asked if there was anyone with you, and you said there was a woman."

"Susan Kewley!"

"You called her Sue. I must tell you, Richard, that none of this is conclusive. It will take more sessions than just this one. We were unable to make sense of most of what we heard. For instance, some of what you said was in French."

"*French!* But I don't speak French! Well, hardly any. Why should I speak French under hypnosis?"

"It can happen."

"Well, what did I say?"

Alexandra Gowers had her notebook open. She said, "At one point we heard you say *encore du vin, s'il vous plaît,* as if you were in a restaurant."

Grey smiled; it was more than three years since he had been in France. Then he had traveled to Paris with a crew to cover the French presidential elections. They had taken a research assistant to interpret for them, and during the whole trip he had hardly uttered a word of French. What he most remembered of the trip was that one night he had slept with the assistant.

"I can't explain that," he said.

"Maybe," Hurdis said. "But you must not discount it either."

"But what am I supposed to assume? That I was in France last summer?"

"It's not safe to make assumptions. But there's one more thing I think you should see." He passed Grey a sheet of paper, apparently torn from a notebook. "Do you recognize this handwriting?"

Grey glanced at it, then in surprise looked more closely. "It's mine!"

"Do you know what it means?"

"Where did you get it? I don't remember writing

this." He read the words quickly: they were a description of what appeared to be a passenger lounge in an airport, with crowds of people, P.A. announcements, airline desks. "It looks like part of a letter. . . . When did I write this?"

"About twenty minutes ago."

"Oh no, that can't be true!"

"You asked for some paper, and Miss Gowers gave you her notebook. You said nothing while you were writing, and you only stopped when I took the pen away."

Grey read the page again, but nothing about it struck any chord of memory. The passage had a familiar ring to it, but only in the sense that it conveyed the sense of bustle, boredom and nervous anticipation of airports. Grey had flown many times in the course of his job, but somehow that last hour before actually boarding was always a minor ordeal. To say he was scared of flying would be an overstatement, but he was nervous and unrelaxed, wanting to get the journey over and done with. This might then be something he would conceivably write or describe, but nothing could have been farther from his mind that morning.

"What could this be?" he said to Hurdis.

"You've no idea yourself?"

"No."

"It could be part of a letter, as you suggest. It could be an unconscious memory, released by the hypnosis. It could even be an extract from a book, or something else you might have read in the past."

"What if it's an unconscious memory? Couldn't this be the answer?"

"Of all the possibilities, that's the one I believe you should be most cautious about." Hurdis had glanced at the clock on the wall.

"But surely that's what I'm trying to find!"

"Yes, but you must be very careful. We have a long way to go. Perhaps we should meet again next week?"

Grey felt a stirring of discontent. "I'm hoping to be out of here soon."

"But not by next week?"

"Well, no . . . but soon I hope."

"Very good." Hurdis was clearly on the point of leaving. Alexandra Gowers had also stood up.

Still in the armchair, Grey said, "But where does this leave me? Have I made any progress?"

"At our next meeting I'll implant the suggestion that you retain what happens in deep trance. Then we might have a better chance of interpretation."

"What about this?" Grey said, meaning the page of handwriting. "Should I keep it?"

"If you wish. No, on second thought I think I'll keep it with my case notes. I'd like to study it properly, and next week we might use it as the basis for regression."

Hurdis took the paper from his unresisting fingers. Grey was curious about it, but in itself it did not seem important.

Before she left, Alexandra came over to him.

"I'm grateful to you for letting me stay," she said. She extended her hand, and they shook as formally as they had at the beginning.

"When I was trying to see you," Grey said, "were you here, in this room?"

"I never moved from the chair."

"Then how could I not see you?"

"At one point you looked straight into my eyes. It's a common test of suggestibility, called induced negative hallucination. You knew I was there, you knew how to see me, but your mind would not register me. Stage hypnotists work a similar effect, but they usually make their subjects see people without their clothes on." She said this seriously, clasping her notebook to her side. She pushed her glasses up to the bridge of her nose.

"Yes," said Grey. "Well, it was a pleasure to look for you, anyway."

"I do hope you regain your memory," she said. "I shall be fascinated to know what happens."

"So will I," Grey said, and they both smiled.

IX

That evening, alone in his room, Richard Grey levered himself out of his wheelchair and walked to and fro across the room, using his sticks. Later, feeling like a non-swimmer casting off from the side, he walked the length of the corridor and returned. It was a major effort. After a short rest he did it a second time, taking much longer, pausing for rests whenever he could. At the end of it his hip felt as if it had been hammered and bruised, and when he went to bed he could not sleep for the pain. He lay awake determined that his long convalescence must end as soon as possible, sensing that his mind and body would heal in unison, that he would remember only as soon as he could walk, and vice versa. Before, he had been passively content for time to take its course, but now his life was different.

The following day he had a session with James Woodbridge, but said nothing about what had happened under hypnosis. He wanted no more interpretations, no more technical terms. He was convinced that his forgotten past now had to be remembered, that it was in some way symbolic of overall recovery, that it opened the way to his personal future. Somehow those weeks leading up to the car bomb had been significant and relevant. Perhaps it was nothing more than a love affair with Sue, but it was important to remember even that. There too, the silent gap in his life gave promise of the future.

Thursday passed slowly, or seemed to, but then it

was Friday. He tidied his room, obtained clean clothes from the hospital laundry, exercised his body, and concentrated all over again on trying to remember. The staff knew he was expecting Sue, and he took their teasing with good grace. Nothing could deflate his mood now. Everything was heightened by her, given form and meaning. The day went slowly, the evening came, and hope was modified by apprehension. Late, far later than he had expected, she called him from a pay phone. She had arrived at Totnes station, and was about to hire a taxi. She was with him half an hour later.

Part III

Part III

I

The departures board showed that my flight was delayed, but I had already gone through passport control and there was no escape from the passenger lounge. Although it was a huge area, lined all along one side with plate-glass windows looking out across the apron, it was noisy, hot and oppressive. The lounge was crowded with people, many of whom were in package-tour groups headed for Benidorm, Faro, Athens and Palma. Babies cried, children ran in energetic games, and flight announcements came through the loudspeakers at regular intervals.

Already I was regretting that I had not taken the train and boat to France, but it was high season and once before I had traveled on a cross-Channel ferry at this time of year. Air travel always had the temptation of speed, even for a short journey like mine, yet since leaving home that morning I had been subjected to one delay after another: crossing London on the Underground, with two changes of train, the slow journey to Gatwick Airport with the railway carriage crowded to the doors, and now the wait for the plane.

Restlessly, because in spite of having flown more times than I could remember I always felt apprehensive before a flight, I walked around the lounge, trying to distract myself. I looked through the books and magazines, and bought a paperback; I examined the toys and gifts that were on sale; I went slowly past the airline information desks: British Caledonian, British Airtours, Dan-Air, Iberia. There was nowhere to sit down, nothing much to do except stand or walk about and look at the other passengers. I diverted myself with a game I had often played before in similar circumstances, trying to guess which of the people were on my own flight, why they were flying, where they were going to go to afterward, who they were. By some knack I was often able to guess correctly which people were on my flight. I remembered the time I had flown to Australia, when in the crowded Heathrow departure lounge I had spotted a particular woman in a noticeable, brightly colored dress. Four days later, in Swanston Street, Melbourne, I saw the same woman in the same dress.

Today, playing the same idle game, I picked out a middle-aged man with two immense pieces of cabin luggage, a young woman dressed demurely in a light jacket and jeans, a businessman with a financial newspaper.

The delay was finally overcome, and three flights were called in quick succession. The crowd thinned out, and the people I had picked remained in the lounge with me. The next flight called was mine, and I followed the crowd through the boarding gate and into the extensible ramp. In the turmoil of finding seats I lost sight of the other three, and thought no more about them.

The flight was extremely short, the plane having barely gained its operating altitude before starting the approach into Le Touquet. Half an hour after leaving Gatwick we had reached the terminal. We were all waved smoothly through customs and immigration, and I went to find my train; most of the other passengers headed for the Paris connection. Mine was to be a long journey, so before boarding the train I bought a supply of food: fresh bread, cheese, a little cooked meat, some fruit, and a large bottle of Coca-Cola.

My first train was a local, stopping at every tiny station and halt on the line. It was well into the afternoon when I arrived in Lille, where I was to change. This was to the express train to Basel, but if anything it drove more slowly, and stopped more often, than the first. At the fourth stop a great silence descended on the train and station. Ten or fifteen minutes passed.

I was reading the paperback I had bought, and was only marginally aware that someone walking down the corridor had stopped outside my compartment. I heard the door slide open, and I looked up. It was a young woman of medium height and build, standing in the doorway.

She said, "You're English, aren't you?"

"Yes." I raised my paperback for her to see.

"I thought so. I saw you on the other train, to Lille."

"Are you looking for a seat?" I said, because I was already bored with my own company.

"No, I booked one in London. My luggage is in the other compartment. The trouble is I don't speak French very well, and there's a family in there who keep talking to me. I don't want to be rude, but . . ."

"It gets to be a strain after a while, doesn't it?"

The train lurched, then halted again. Somewhere underneath the carriage a generator started churning. Outside on the platform two men in SNCF uniforms walked slowly past the window.

"Would you mind if I joined you for a while?" she said.

"Of course not. I'd like some company."

She slid the door to, then sat in the window seat opposite mine. She was carrying a large canvas bag bulging with possessions, and she placed this on the seat beside her.

"I've seen you before!" I said. "Weren't you on the plane—I mean, did you fly from Gatwick?"

"Yes—I saw you too."

"This morning!" I was laughing in surprise, because I had suddenly recognized her as one of the passengers I had picked out in the departure lounge.

"Where are you going now?" she said.

"I'm hoping to get to Nancy tonight."

"That's a coincidence—so am I."

"I probably won't stay more than a day or two. What about you? Are you visiting friends?"

"No, I'm on my own. I thought I might go and see some people in the south, but they don't even know I'm in France yet."

She had straight brown hair, a pale face, thin hands. I guessed her to be somewhere in her late twenties. I found her company very attractive, partly for the relief from my own boredom but mostly because she was so likable, so ready to talk. She seemed interested in me, making me talk a lot.

"You don't happen to know if there's a restaurant car?" she said. "I haven't had anything since breakfast."

"I've brought plenty of food," I said. "You're welcome to it." I had already eaten some, and had been intending to save the rest for later, but I opened the bag and passed it to her. I took an apple, but she ate the rest.

While we had been talking the train had started, and already we were moving through the flat and uninteresting countryside. The sun was shining straight in through our window, and because it could not be opened it was warm in the carriage. When she arrived she had been wearing the jacket I had noticed earlier, but now she removed it and placed it on the rack overhead. While she turned away from me I could not help appraising her body. She was slim, slightly bony around the shoulders, but she had an attractive body. I noticed the white lines of her bra visible beneath her blouse. I was thinking vaguely erotic thoughts, wondering where she was planning to stay that night, whether she would like a traveling companion for more than this train journey. It was almost too good to be true, to meet someone like this on my first day. I had planned and expected to spend the holiday on my own, but not out of a principle.

We continued to talk while she finished off the food, and exchanged names at last: hers was Sue. She lived in London, not particularly close to me but in the same general area. There was a pub in Highgate we both knew, and must have visited at different times. She said she was a free-lance illustrator, had been to art school in London but had been born in Cheshire. Of course I talked about myself, some of the stories I had covered and the places I had been to, why I had given up work and what I was planning to do next. We were very interested in each other; certainly I could not remember the last time I had met someone to whom I could talk so freely in such a short time. She listened to me intently, leaning forward across the space between our seats, her head slightly to one side so that she appeared to look at the seat beside me. I consciously tried to change the subject several times and draw her out of herself. She answered direct questions but otherwise did not appear to want to talk about herself.

I kept wondering: why is she alone? Because I found her attractive, it was difficult to believe she did not have a boyfriend somewhere, perhaps one of these friends she said she was visiting in the south.

The subject did not come up. I had a friend called Annette at the back of my mind. Part of the reason for my own trip was that Annette was in Canada visiting her brother, leaving me at a loose end in London. But there was no firm commitment with her, and our friendship was casual; sometimes we slept together, sometimes we did not. I had lived moderately promiscuously, often away from home for weeks on end, sleeping with women I hardly knew, never forming ties.

Sue and I both stayed away from the subject of others. We were after all virtual strangers to each other, passing time on a train, so there was no reason why anything should be said. Even so, we were already at ease with each other; minor confidences were exchanged; opinions, jokes. I kept wanting to touch her, wishing she would move over and sit beside me, or that I had the nerve to sit next to her. I was shy of her but excited by her, and the longer we talked on the more obvious it was that we were avoiding the subject of other people.

As the train approached Longuyon at last, I said, "I think we change trains here."

"My God, I've forgotten my luggage! It's in the other compartment." She stood up abruptly. "Will you meet me on the platform?" she said. "I'm not sure which train to catch for Nancy."

"Neither am I." She was opening the door to the corridor. "Don't forget your jacket." I passed it to her. "I'll meet you outside."

The train started braking almost as soon as she had left. I took my own suitcase from the rack and moved out to the corridor. Several other passengers were making the same change and the doors were blocked. When the train stopped there was a press of bodies, but when I was on the platform I put down my bag and went in search of Sue. Train doors slammed and most of the people walked away. Silence fell.

Then, abruptly, a door flew open and a dumpy, middle-aged woman with a head scarf climbed down to the platform. She was carrying a suitcase which she deposited on the ground. She reached into the train and brought out a second bag. Sue followed, looking harassed. There was a brief, one-sided conversation completed by the pecking of both cheeks. The woman returned to the train, closing the door behind her. I went over to help Sue with her luggage, and she was smiling.

An hour later we were on the local train to Nancy. We sat next to each other, the fatigue and tedium of travel giving us a kind of tired familiarity. I could feel the light pressure of her arm against mine, but the break had interrupted the first headiness.

It was evening when the train arrived. We asked at the tourist office for a recommendation to an inexpensive hotel reasonably close to the station, then set off down the road with our bags. When we found the place, Sue came to a rather abrupt halt outside and put down her luggage.

"Richard, there's something we haven't discussed," she said.

"What's that?" I said, although I knew what she meant.

"I don't want there to be any misunderstandings about tonight."

"I wasn't assuming anything," I said.

"I know, but here we are, we've only just met, and although it's been very pleasant . . ."

She looked away from me, across the street. There was a lot of traffic in the town, with many people walking about in the warm evening.

"Would you like to find another hotel for yourself?" I said.

"No, of course not. But we should have separate rooms. We haven't said anything about this, but I'm meeting somebody when I get to Saint-Raphaël. A friend."

"That's all right," I said, regretting that I had left it to her to bring up the subject. The longer it had gone unaired, the more it was inevitable we would make assumptions.

The hotel was able to let us have a room each, and outside the elevator we prepared to separate.

Sue said, "I'm going to take a shower, then lie down for a bit. What about you? Are you going out for a meal?"

"Not just yet. I'm tired too."

"Shall we have dinner together?"

"If you'd like to."

"You know I would. I'll knock on your door in an hour."

I I

In the center of Nancy was a magnificent broad square, surrounded by eighteenth-century palaces, known as the Place Stanislas. We entered it from the south side, coming into great emptiness and peace. It was as if the bustle of the main town was unable to penetrate to this place. No more than a few people strolled or stood in its vastness. The sun beat down, striking sharp shadows on the sandstone pavings. An autobus was parked outside L'Hôtel de Ville, formerly the Duke of Lorraine's palace, and some distance behind this four black-painted saloon cars were parked in a neat row. No other traffic entered the square. A man wearing a cloth cap wheeled his bicycle slowly across the plaza, passing the statue of the Duke which stood at the center.

In one corner of the square was the Fountain of Neptune, a glorious rococo construction with nymphs and naiads and cherubs, water trickling across scalloped levels into the pools below. The wrought-iron archways of Jean Lamour surrounded the fountain. We walked over the cobbled road, gazed up at L'Arc de Triomphe, then passed through into the Place de la Carrière. This was lined on both sides with terraces of beautiful old houses; two rows of mature trees ran down the center of the Place with a narrow park between them. We walked through this, utterly alone. Over the roofs to our left we could see the spire of the cathedral.

A car drove through, trailing smoke and a clattering noise. At the far end there was a colonnade in front of the former Palais du Gouvernement, and here another

couple walked slowly past. We looked back the way we
had come, to the vista of Place Stanislas glimpsed through
the Arc: the bright sunlight made the clean lines of the
buildings, the stately sculpted view, seem static and monochrome. The car with the smoke had passed through into
the square, and now nothing moved anywhere we could
see.

We left Carrière and walked through a narrow
shaded lane to one of the main shopping streets. Sounds
grew around us, and we saw the press of people. In Le
Cours Léopold there were a number of sidewalk cafés, and
we went to one of these and ordered *demis-pressions*. The
evening before we had visited one of the restaurants on
the opposite side, and after the meal had stayed drinking
wine together until after midnight. We had spoken, in
mostly general terms, about the other people in our lives,
people from the past, although I had described my relationship with Annette as an unspecific counter to Sue's
boyfriend waiting for her in Saint-Raphaël.

Now, after our sightseeing walk, she was more
ready to talk about the present.

"I don't like living in London," she said. "It costs so
much money just to stay alive. I've never really had any
money, not since leaving home. I'm always broke, always
scraping along. I wanted to be a real artist, but I've never
been able to get started. It's all commercial work."

"Do you live alone?" I said.

"Yes—well, I've got a room in a house. It's one of
those large Victorian houses in Hornsey. It was broken up
into flats and bed-sitters years ago. My room is on the
ground floor. It's quite large, but I can't work in natural
light—there's a wall outside the window."

"Is your friend an artist?"

"My friend?"

"The one you told me about yesterday. In Saint-
Raphaël."

"No, he's a sort-of writer."

"What sort of writer is a sort-of writer?"

She smiled. "It's what he says he does. He spends most of his spare time writing, but he never shows it to me and I don't think he's had anything published. I'm not allowed to ask about it."

She shook her head, staring at the little plate of salted *bretzels* the waiter had brought with the drinks. "He wanted to move in with me, but I wouldn't let him. I'd never get any work done."

"Then where does he live?"

"He moves around from one place to another. I'm never sure where he is until he turns up. He doesn't pay rent, and just sponges off other people."

"Then why . . . ? Look, what's his name?"

"Niall." She spelled it for me. "Niall's a hanger-on, a parasite. This is the only reason he's in France. The people he was staying with were going on holiday, and the choice was to leave him alone in their house or take him with them. So Niall gets a free holiday on the Riviera, and that's why I'm going down there to see him. He says he needs me."

"You don't sound very keen on the idea."

"I'm not." She looked frankly at me. "If you want the truth, I can't afford it, and I was beginning to enjoy not having Niall around me all the time, when he started calling me from France." She swallowed the rest of her drink. "I shouldn't say this, but I'm sick of Niall. I've known him too long, and I wish he'd leave me alone."

"Well, ditch him."

"It's never as easy as that. Niall's a clinger. I've known him too long, and he knows how to get his own way. I've kicked him out more times than I can remember, and yet every time he manages to worm his way back into my life. I've given up trying."

"But what sort of relationship is that?"

"Let's have another drink. I'll get these." She signaled to the waiter as he was passing.

"You didn't answer my question."

"I didn't want to. What about your girlfriend, the one who's in Canada? How long have you known her?"

"You're changing the subject," I said.

"No, I'm not. How long have you known her? Six years? That's how long I've known Niall. When you've been with someone as long as that, he *knows* you. He knows how to manipulate you, how to hurt you, how to use things against you. Niall's especially good at that. I can't get away from him because every time I try he finds something new to blackmail me with."

"But why don't you—?" I paused, trying to imagine such a relationship, trying to think of myself in a similar situation. It was completely outside my experience.

"Why don't I what?"

"I can't understand why you let it go on."

The waiter arrived with two more glasses, and removed the old ones. Sue paid him, and he laid out the change on the table, putting the note away in the small leather pouch he carried around his waist.

"I can't understand it either," she said. "I've never found anyone else, and so I suppose it's easier just to keep going. It's my own fault, really."

I said nothing for a while, leaning back in the seat and pretending to watch the passers-by. She was so unlike the passive self she was depicting. It seemed to be a destructive relationship, the way she described it. I wanted to say to her: I am different, I do not cling, you've found someone else now. Leave this man Niall, stay with me. You don't have to put up with him.

Eventually I said, "Do you know why he wants to see you?"

"Nothing special. He's probably browned off, wants someone to talk to who will listen."

"I don't see why you put up with this. You say you're broke, and yet you're traveling across France just so he can talk to you."

"It'll be more than talking," she said. "Anyway, you don't know him."

"It seems very irrational to me."

"Yes. I know it does."

III

We stayed one more night in Nancy, then took another train to the town of Dijon. The weather had changed for the worse, and as the train moved slowly through the extensive suburbs of the city a heavy rain began to fall. We discussed whether or not to stay, but I was no longer in any hurry to reach the south, and we agreed to stick to the plans we had worked out the previous evening.

Dijon was a crowded, busy city, with some kind of business convention going on, and the first two hotels we called at were full. The third, Hôtel Central, had only double rooms available.

"We can share," Sue said as we retreated from the reception desk to consult. "Ask for a twin-bedded room."

"Are you sure you don't mind?"

"It'll be cheaper than two rooms, anyway."

"We could try somewhere else."

She said quietly, "I don't mind sharing."

Our room was on the top floor, at the end of a long corridor. It was small, but it had a large window with a balcony and a pleasant view across the trees of the square below. The two beds were placed close together, separated by a small table with a telephone. As soon as the porter had left, Sue put down her canvas bag and came across to me. She embraced me tightly, and I put my arms around her. The back of her jacket, and her hair, were wet from the rain.

"We don't have long together," she said. "Don't let's wait any more."

We started kissing, she with great passion. It was the first time we had held each other, the first time we had kissed. I had not known what she would feel like, how her skin and lips would taste. I knew her only to talk to, only to look at; now I could feel and hold her, press her against me, and she was different. Soon we were eagerly undressing each other, and then we lay on the nearest bed.

We did not leave the hotel until after dark, driven out by hunger and thirst. We had become physically obsessed with each other, and could hardly stop touching. I held her close to me as we walked along the rain-swept street, thinking only of her and what she now meant to me. So often in the past sex had merely satisfied physical curiosity, but with Sue it had released deeper feelings, greater intimacy, a new appetite for each other.

We found a restaurant, Le Grand Zinc, and nearly passed it by, thinking it must be closed. When we went in we discovered we were the only customers: five waiters, dressed in black waistcoats and trousers, with stiff white aprons that reached to their ankles, stood in a patient row beside the serving door. When we were shown to a window table they moved into action, attentive but discreet. Each had short dark hair plastered to his scalp with shiny dressing, and each had a pencil-thin mustache. Sue and I exchanged glances, suppressing giggles. We had found it did not take much to make us laugh.

Outside, a storm had started: brilliant, pink-hued flashes of lightning, far away, thunderless. The rain continued to sheet down, but traffic was sparse in the street. An old Citroën was parked by the curb, glistening in the rain, the double inverted V on its radiator grille reflecting back the red lamp lights from the restaurant.

Remembering a lesson learned during an earlier

visit to Paris, I suggested we have the *plat du jour*, and in due course the comic-opera waiters served us *saucisson en croûte*, followed by *côtes de porc*. It was a memorable meal, garnished with private thoughts and secret signs.

At the end of the meal, sipping brandy, we held hands across the tabletop. The waiters stared away.

"We could go to Saint-Tropez," I said. "Have you ever been there?"

"Isn't it crowded at this time of year?"

"I suppose so. But that's no reason not to go."

"It would be expensive. I'm running out of cash."

"We can live cheaply."

"I can't afford to go on eating in places like this," she said.

"This is a celebration."

"All right, but did you notice the prices?"

Because of the rain we had not checked the prices before entering, but they were clearly printed on the *carte*. The prices were in old francs, or seemed to be. I had made a halfhearted attempt to convert them, but had come to the conclusion they were either ridiculously low or outrageously high; the quality of the cooking and service indicated the latter.

"We're not going to run out of cash," I said.

"I know what you mean, and it's not going to work. I can't sponge off you."

"Then what's going to happen? If we're going to travel together and it will bankrupt you, how much longer can we go on?"

She said, "We've got to discuss that, Richard. I'm still going to visit Niall. I can't let him down."

"What about me? Don't you think that will let me down?" She shook her head, looking away. "If it's just money, let's go home to England tomorrow."

"It isn't only the money. I promised I would see him. He's waiting for me."

I took my hand away from hers and stared at her in exasperation. "I don't want you to go."

"And neither do I," she said in a low voice. "Niall's a bloody nuisance, of course I realize that. But I can't just not turn up."

"I'll come with you," I said. "We'll see him together."

"No, no—that would be impossible. I couldn't stand that."

"All right. I'll go with you to Saint-Raphaël and wait for you while you tell him. Then we'll go straight back to England."

"He's expecting me to stay with him. A week, maybe two."

"Can't you do *something?*"

"I don't think so."

"Well, I'll at least pay the damned bill here." I snapped my fingers at the waiters, and in seconds a folded bill on a plate was put in front of me. The total, *service compris*, came to 3600 francs, written the old way. Tentatively, I put 36 francs on the plate, and it was accepted without demur. "*Merci, monsieur.*" As we left the restaurant the waiters stood in an impeccable row, smiling and nodding to us, *bonne nuit, à bientôt.*

We hurried along the street, the storm effectively postponing any more wrangling over the problem. I was angry as much with myself as anything: only the day before I had been congratulating myself on being unpossessive toward women, and now I was feeling just the opposite. The way out was obvious—to give in, let Sue go on to see her boyfriend, and hope to run into her again in London one day. But she had already become acutely special to me. I liked her and she made me happy, and our physical lovemaking had confirmed all this and promised more.

Upstairs in the room we toweled our hair and stripped off our damp outer clothes. It was warm in the room, and we threw open the window. Thunder rumbled in the distance and traffic swished by below. I stood for a while on the balcony, getting wet again, wondering what to do. I wanted to put off the decision until the morning.

From the room, Sue said, "Will you help me?"

I went in. She had pulled back the covers from one of the beds.

"What are you doing?" I said.

"Let's put the beds together. We'll have to move the table."

She was standing in her bra and pants, her hair tousled and still damp. Her body was slim, slightly curved, the thin underwear barely concealing her. I helped her move the beds and table, and we began remaking the beds, interleaving the sheets to form a large double, but before the job was half finished we started kissing and touching again. We never completely made the beds that night, although they stayed pressed together.

In the morning I made no decision, realizing I would only lose her. Talking about the problem worsened it. After breakfast at a table outside the hotel we set off to explore the town. We said nothing about continuing our journey southward.

At the center of Dijon was the Place de la Libération, the ducal palace faced across a cobblestone plaza by a semicircle of seventeenth-century houses. It was on a smaller, more human scale than Nancy, but we noticed that here too the crowds and traffic stayed away. The weather had improved again and the sun was hot and brilliant. Several wide puddles lay in parts of the plaza. An area of the palace had been made over into a museum, and we wandered around admiring the grand halls and rooms as much as the exhibits. We lingered for a time before the eerie tombs of the Dukes of Burgundy, stone manikins set among gothic arches, each mounted in a grotesquely lifelike pose.

"Where is everybody else?" Sue said to me, and although she spoke softly her voice set up sibilant echoes.

"I thought France would be crowded at this time of year," I said.

She took my arm and pressed herself against me. "I don't like this place. Let's go somewhere else."

We wandered for most of the morning through the busy shopping streets, rested once or twice in cafés, then came to the river and sat down on the bank under the trees. It was good to escape temporarily from the crowds, the endless noise of traffic.

Pointing up through the trees, Sue said, "The sun's going to go in."

A single cloud, black and dense, was drifting across the sky in the direction of the sun. It did not look like a rain cloud, but it was large enough to blot out the sun for half an hour. I squinted up at it, thinking about Niall.

"Let's go back to the hotel," Sue said.

"Suits me."

We returned to the city center. In the room we discovered that the chambermaid had made the beds for us. They were where we had left them, standing together, and when we pulled back the covers we found the sheets neatly interleaved, to make a double.

IV

We traveled farther south, changing trains at Lyons to reach Grenoble, a large and modern city in the mountains. We found a hotel, this time booking a room with a double bed, then, because it was still midafternoon, went out to look at the town.

We were becoming dedicated travelers, dutifully seeing the sights in each of the towns we visited. It gave us an external purpose, an excuse to be together, something that gave us a rest from our obsession with each other.

"Shall we go up the mountain?" I said. We had come to Quai Stephane-Jay, and here was the terminal of a funicular system. From the broad concourse at the front it was possible to see the cables stretching up out of the town toward a high rocky promontory.

"Those things aren't safe," Sue said, gripping my arm.

"Of course they are." I wanted to see the view from the top. "Would you rather just walk the streets for the rest of the day?"

We had yet to discover the old part of the town, and much of Grenoble was concrete high-rise with litter and wind-tunnel effect at street level. The city guide recommended that visitors tour the university, but it was out on the eastern edge.

I talked her into it, but she feigned nervousness and held on to my arm. Soon we were lifting away from the city, gaining height quickly. For a while I stared back at the city, seeing its huge spread through the valley, but then we moved to the other side of the car to watch the slopes of the mountain rising beneath us. It was an ultramodern cable system, four glassy globes moving together in convoy, steady in the sky.

As the cars slowed down at the top we had to scramble to get out, and then we walked through the noisy engine house into the cold wind of the ridge. Sue slipped her arm around me under my jacket, holding close. To be with a girl I really liked, whom I wanted to go on liking, was a unique feeling for me. To myself I was renouncing my past, never again wanting superficial sexual conquests; after many years I had found the person I wanted to be with all the time.

"We can get a drink here," I said. A restaurant and café had been built on the farthest extremity of the promontory, with a viewing platform that overlooked the val-

ley. We went inside, glad to be out of the wind. A waiter
brought us two cognacs and we sipped them, feeling deca-
dent because it was still daytime. Later, Sue visited the
Ladies' and I went over to the souvenir stand and bought a
few postcards. I was thinking I should send some to
friends, but the truth was that since meeting Sue I had lost
interest in almost everything except her.

She found me at the stand.

"I'm feeling warmer now," she said. "Let's look at
the view."

We went out into the wind, hugging each other
again, and moved to the edge of the platform. Three coin-
operated telescopes tipped down toward the valley from
the raised parapet. We stood between two of them, leaning
against the concrete wall and staring down. On the hori-
zon were the mountains surrounding the town to the
south; to our left, the snow-capped peaks of the French
Alps were sharp against the blue.

Sue said, "Look, I suppose that's the university."
She was pointing toward a group of beautiful old buildings, turreted and spired, along by the river. "It's closer to
the town than we thought."

There was a plan built into the top of the parapet,
indicating what could be seen. We traced the various
landmarks.

"It's smaller than I thought," I said. "When we
came in on the train, the city seemed to spread right up
the valley."

"Where are all those office blocks? I can't see them
anymore."

"They were by the hotel." I looked on the plan, but
it was not marked. "There was a whole area of them, near
where the cable cars started." I followed the cables with
my eyes down the mountainside, but the terminal was hidden from us. "It must be a trick of the light."

"Perhaps they were designed that way, to blend in
with the old buildings."

It said on the plan that Mont Blanc could be seen to the northeast, so we turned in that direction. There were clouds behind us though, and the view of the mountains was indistinct. Beyond the restaurant were the ruins of an old fort, and we walked over to them. We found there was a charge for entering, so we changed our minds.

"Another brandy?" I said. "Or back to the hotel?"

"Let's do both."

Half an hour later we returned to the platform for another look at the city. Lights were coming on down there, and tiny points of warm orange and yellow glinted from the buildings. We watched the evening for a while, then took the cable car down the mountain. After we had breasted one of the rises, the city again came into full view. A mist was forming, but now we could see the newer section very clearly: blue-white fluorescent strip lights shone from the glass towers. It seemed to us impossible that we could not have seen them from the top. I took out the postcards I had bought: one of them was a photograph of the view, and in this the modern buildings clearly stood high above the others.

"I'm getting hungry," Sue said.

"For food?"

"That as well."

V

We arrived in Nice. It was the height of the tourist season, and the only hotel we could find that we could afford was in the north of the town, lost in a maze of narrow streets, a long walk from the sea. With our arrival my feeling of dread became dominant. We had at best another day or two together; Saint-Raphaël was only a few kilometers along the coast.

Niall had become a forbidden subject, ever-present but never discussed. Even the silence about him became obvious. We knew exactly what the other would say, and neither of us wished to hear it. If I had a way of dealing with the problem it was to give my best to Sue, to hope to convey to her what we were about to lose. She seemed to be doing the same. We both had the power of concentration, and turned it full upon each other.

I was in love with her. The feeling had started in Dijon, and every waking minute with her confirmed and enlarged it. She delighted me in every way, and I was obsessed with her. Yet I drew back from saying the words, not through doubts but because she might think them coercive.

I still did not know what to do. On our first night in Nice Sue fell asleep beside me while I sat up with the light on, ostensibly reading but in fact brooding about her and Niall.

Nothing would work. An ultimatum, a choice between me or him, would fail. There was a stubbornness in Sue about Niall, and I knew I could not shift her. Discarded too was the idea of portraying myself as the wounded loser; that was actually how I felt, but nothing would make me use it as a ploy. Reason, too, was out. She freely acknowledged that her relationship with him was irrational.

She had rejected my other ideas—my hanging around in the background while she saw him; a premature return to England.

Hours of introspection produced nothing but the lame hope that she might change her mind by herself.

We stayed in our hotel room for most of the next day, leaving it every two or three hours for a walk or a drink or a meal. We saw very little of Nice, but because of my preoccupation I hated what I saw. I identified the town with my sense of loss, and blamed it for it. I disliked the ostentatious wealth on display: the yachts in the harbor, the Alfas and Mercedes and Ferraris, the women with their face-lifts and the men with their business paunches. I equally disliked the showy inverse: the English debs in rusty Minis, the worn-out Nike running shoes, the chopped-off jeans, the faded clothes. I resented the topless sunbathers, the palm trees and aloe vera plants, the shingly beaches and the exquisite blue sea, the casino and the hotels, the villas on the hills, the skyscraper apartment blocks, the suntanned youths on motorbikes, the wind surfers and paraskiers, the speedboats, pedalos and beach huts. I begrudged them all their pleasure.

My only pleasure was the source of my misery: Sue herself. Provided I pushed Niall to the back of my mind, provided I did not think beyond the next few hours, provided I held on to my lame hope, all was temporarily well.

Of course she knew.

She too had her introspections; once I found her crying on the bed. Our lovemaking became urgent, and whenever we were out we constantly touched or held each other. Often we sat in a bar or a restaurant holding hands, staring away at other people, other places.

We decided to stay a second night in Nice, even though it would only prolong the wretchedness. We agreed tacitly that we would leave for Saint-Raphaël in the morning, and there we would part. This was our last night together.

We made love as if nothing were to change; then, restlessly, we sat together on the bed, the window and shutters wide open to the night. Insects hummed around the light. At last she broke the silence.

"Where are you going to go tomorrow, Richard?"

"I haven't decided yet. I might just go home."

"But what were you going to do before we met? You must have made plans."

"I was just traveling around. Now there's no point, without you."

"Why don't you go to Saint-Tropez?"

"On my own? I want to be with you."

"Don't say that."

"It's the only thing I'm sure of."

She was silent, staring down at the rumpled sheets on which we sprawled. Her body was so white, and suddenly I had a jealous image of seeing her again in London in a few weeks' time and finding that she had acquired a suntan.

"Sue, are you really going to go through with this?"

"I've got to. We've been over all that."

"Then this is the end, isn't it?"

"I think that's up to you."

"How can you say that? I don't want this to finish! You must know that by now."

"But Richard, you're making an issue out of this. You're acting as if we can't see each other again. Why does it have to be final?"

"All right, I'll see you back in London. You've got my address."

She shifted position, pulling at the creased sheet below us, freeing it from her weight and laying it over her bare knees as she kneeled beside me. Her hands fretted it as she spoke.

"I've got to see Niall. I'm not going to break a promise. But I don't want to hurt you. . . . I'd never see Niall again, if I had my way."

"Then what are you saying?"

"I'll see him tomorrow. You go on with your holiday, tell me where you'll be and I'll join up with you as soon as I can."

"Do you mean that?" I said.

"Of course I do!"

"What will you say to him? Are you going to tell him about me?"

"If I can."

"Then why don't I wait for you here?"

"Because . . . I can't just *tell* him. I'll have to stay with him for a while."

"How long will that be?"

"I don't know. Three or four days . . . maybe a week."

"A week!" I turned away from her angrily. "For God's sake, how long does it take to tell someone you're finished with him?"

She bent her head. "Let me do it my way. You don't understand the problem with Niall. I'll have to break it to him in stages. First of all he's got to be told I've met someone else, someone who matters more than him. Don't you think that's enough to be going on with? I can say the rest when he gets used to that idea."

I left the bed and poured us both some wine from the bottle we had bought earlier. There was no other way but her way, I knew that. I passed her a glass of wine but she put it aside untouched.

"When you see Niall, will you be sleeping with him?"

"I've been sleeping with him for six years."

"That's not what I asked."

"It's none of your business."

It hurt to hear it, but it was true. I looked at her naked body, trying to imagine some other man with her, deeply abhoring the idea. She had become so precious to me. Her head was bent, her hair concealing her face. I went to touch her, laying my hand on her arm. She responded at once, clasping my hand.

"All right, Sue. I'll do what you suggest. I'll leave you in Saint-Raphaël tomorrow and go on down the coast. If you haven't caught up with me within a week, I'll either go on without you or head back to England."

"It won't take a week," she said. "Three days, maybe less."

"Just make it as soon as you can." I found I had drained my glass of wine without even noticing I had started it. I put it aside. "Now, what about money?"

"What about it?"

"You said you were almost out. How are you going to travel after you leave Niall?"

"I'll borrow some from somewhere."

"You mean you'll get it from Niall."

"Probably. He's always got plenty."

"You'll borrow his money, but you won't borrow mine. Don't you see that gives him just one more hold over you?" She shook her head. "Anyway, I thought you said he didn't have any money."

"I said he didn't have a job. He's never short of cash."

"Where does he get it? Does he steal?"

"I don't know. Please don't go on with this. Money means nothing to Niall. I can get what I need."

It was a small insight into what must have been their relationship. She could intend to tell him she was throwing him over in favor of someone else, and still expect him to lend her money. Everything I knew about Niall, all of it from her, was unpleasant: a bully, a parasite, a manipulator, perhaps a thief. At that moment I even hated his damned name.

I got up from the bed again, and while she watched silently I pulled on a pair of trousers and a T-shirt. I left the room, closing the door noisily. I walked along the corridor, then went down the four flights of stairs to the ground floor.

Outside, in the warm night, I walked down the street toward the café on the corner. It was closed. I turned the corner and started down the next street. This was a neglected, ill-lit part of Nice, the houses crowding one on the next, the plaster peeling and broken in many places. Lights showed from a few windows, and ahead of me at the next intersection I could see traffic moving to and fro. I went as far as this road, then came to a halt. I knew I was being unfair, that I had no hold over her, that in my own way I was being as manipulative as Niall. Just then I did not care, seeing Sue as someone who provoked such behavior in men, who probably always would. A week ago I had not known she even existed; now she pre-occupied me entirely. I wanted her more than I had ever wanted any other woman.

Minutes passed, and my quick anger subsided. I blamed myself: I had walked into her life and now ex-pected her to change everything. By my demands on her I was forcing a choice on her, making her see us as alterna-tives to each other. She knew Niall better than she knew me, and I knew nothing of him.

I turned and hurried back to the hotel, convinced that I was going to lose her. I took the stairs two at a time and went quickly into the room, half expecting to find her already gone. But she was there, lying in the bed with her back to the door, a single sheet covering her thin body. She made no move as I entered.

"Are you asleep?" I said softly.

She turned to look at me; her face was damp and her eyes were red.

"Where have you been?" she said.

I pulled off my clothes and climbed onto the bed beside her. We put our arms around each other, kissing and holding tenderly. She cried again, sobbing against me. I stroked her hair, touched her eyelids, and then at last, far too late but wholly meant, I said the words I had been holding back.

All she said, indistinctly, was, "Yes. And me. I thought you knew."

VI

The morning brought another silence between us, but now I was content. We had made a sort of accommodation. She knew my itinerary, and where and when we could meet.

We boarded a bus in the center of Nice, and soon set off westward. Sue held my hand and pressed herself close against me. The bus drove first to Antibes and Juan-les-Pins, then to Cannes. Passengers changed over at every stop. After Cannes we passed through some of the most beautiful scenery I had seen in France: wooded hills, steep valleys, and of course one vista of the Mediterranean after another. Cypresses and olive trees grew beside the road, and wild flowers flourished in every untended patch of ground. The roof panels of the bus were open, and rich scents blustered in; sometimes, because of the road, the smell was of gasoline or diesel oil. The whole coastline was scattered with houses and apartment blocks, high on the hills or standing among the trees; occasionally they ruined the view, but so too, in a different way, did the road.

We saw a sign saying that Saint-Raphaël was another four kilometers, and immediately we drew closer, holding each other tightly and kissing. I wanted both to prolong the farewells and be done with them, but there was nothing more to say.

Except one thing. As the bus halted in the center of Saint-Raphaël, a square opening out onto the tiny harbor, Sue put her mouth to the side of my face and said quietly, "I've got good news for you."

"What's that?"

"I started my period this morning."

She squeezed my hand, kissed me lightly, then went down the center aisle with the other passengers. I stayed in my seat, looking at her as she waited for her luggage to be unloaded from the hold. Once or twice she glanced up at me, smiling nervously. The little square was crowded with holidaymakers, and I looked at them, wondering if Niall was somewhere among them. Everyone was young, tanned, attractive. Sue stood by my window, looking up at me, and I wished the bus would leave.

At last we were off. Sue stayed still, smiling up at me and waving. The bus turned into a side street, heading back to the main road, and I lost sight of her.

Alone, I fell almost at once into a depressed mood. I thought only of the worst: that I would never see her again, that in Niall's hands she would be manipulated against me, that her feelings would diminish, that torn between two men she would settle on the one she knew better.

Apart from anything else, I simply missed her. I had never before felt so isolated.

VII

As soon as I had found somewhere to stay in Saint-Tropez, I took a walk around the village and discovered I liked it. Perversely, what I liked were exactly the same things I had disliked in Nice. There were the same kinds of people there, the same overt displays of wealth, the same glamour and hedonism. Unlike Nice, though, Saint-Tropez was small and the architecture was attractive, and it was possible to believe that at the end of the season the place would have its own identity. It was also far more cosmopolitan, with great numbers of people apparently camping or sleeping rough outside the village, and coming in every day.

I called in at the local Hertz office to book a rental car in three days' time, when I was planning to leave. I was lucky: because of demand, only one car was available then. I paid the deposit, signed the form. The Hertz girl had a name tag pinned to her blouse: Danièle.

My arrangement with Sue was to wait for her every evening at six at Sénéquier, the large open-air café directly overlooking the inner harbor. I did walk past this on my first evening, but of course there was no sign of her.

My thoughts about Sue were infrequent during the next day. I felt worn out by her, and so I devoted myself to the less strenuous activity of lying on the beach and from time to time walking down for a swim. In the evening I went to Sénéquier, but she did not appear.

I was on the beach again the next day, rather more cautious about the sun. Well smeared with shielding ointment, and sitting under a rented beach umbrella, I passed the day regarding the people around me and thinking inevitably of Sue. She had aroused an immediate physical need, and now she was not there.

I was surrounded by female nudity: bare breasts stared sunward on every side. The day before I had hardly given this a second thought, but now I was missing Sue again, thinking of her with Niall. I could not imagine away these nubile French, Germans, British, Swiss, with their *cache-sexe* bikini briefs, their suntanned breasts. Not one of them could replace Sue for me, but each one reminded me of what I was missing. Yet the irony was that seminudity, supposedly a form of vulnerability, actually created a new kind of social barrier. It was impossible to strike up a conversation with someone I knew only by body appearance.

That evening I waited again in Sénéquier for Sue, wishing she would appear. I wanted her more than ever, but in the end had to walk away without her.

I had one more day and one more night in Saint-Tropez, and in the morning I decided to kill time a different way. The beach was too distracting. I spent the morning in the village itself, wandering slowly around the boutiques and souvenir shops, the leathergoods stores, the crafts workshops. I strolled around the harbor looking enviously at the yachts, their crews, their affluent owners. After lunch I walked along the shore in a different direction, away from the center of the village, clambering over rocks and walking along a concrete sea wall.

At the end of the wall I leaped down to the sand and continued on. The crowds were thinner here, but the beach did not present a favorable aspect to the sun: trees shaded part of the sand. I passed a sign: *Plage Privée*. Beyond, everything changed.

It was the least crowded beach I had seen in Saint-Tropez, and by far the most decorous. Here there was no display of seminude bodies. Many people were enjoying the sun, and some were swimming, but as far as I could see there were no topless women, no men in G-string briefs. Children played, a sight I had not seen elsewhere, and on this beach there was no open-air restaurant or bar, no beach umbrellas or mats, no magazine vendors or photographers.

I walked slowly across the beach, feeling outrageous in my cut-off denim shorts, my Southern Comfort T-shirt, my sandals, but no one took any notice of me. I passed several groups of mostly middle-aged people. They had brought picnic meals to the beach, vacuum flasks, and little paraffin-fired Primus stoves for heating their kettles. Many of the men were wearing shirts with rolled-up sleeves, and gray flannel trousers or baggy khaki shorts. They sat in striped deck chairs, clenching pipes between their teeth, and some of them were reading English newspapers. Most of the women were wearing light summer dresses, and those who were sunbathing sat rather than lay, and were clad in modest one-piece suits.

I went down to the water's edge and stood near a group of children who were splashing and chasing one another in the shallows. Beyond, heads protected by rubber bathing caps bobbed in the waves. A man stood up and waded out of the sea. He was wearing shorts and a singlet, and goggles over his eyes. As he passed me he took off the goggles and shook out the water, making a spray across the white sand. He grinned at me and moved on up the beach. Offshore, a cruise liner was at anchor.

Ahead, a paraskier rose up on his cable, soaring behind the outboard motor speedboat that towed him. I walked on, out of the private section and to another beach where rows of straw-roofed shelters had been erected in straight lines across the sand. In their shelter, or spread out in the full glare of the sun, crowds of topless sunbathers lay in their familiar abandonment. This time I walked up the beach to an open-air bar and bought myself a glass of extortionately expensive iced orange juice. I was now some distance from the village itself, so I left the beach and walked back along the road.

It was still early afternoon, so I returned to the beach I had used before. I settled back to look pleasurably, if innocently, at the girls. An hour or so passed.

Then I noticed someone walking along the beach who looked different from all the others; she was wearing clothes, and I was not the only man on the beach to look at her. She had on skin-tight designer jeans and a transparent white blouse, and looked cool and self-possessed under a wide sun hat. As she approached I recognized her: it was Danièle, from the Hertz office. She came to within a few meters of me, then took off her sun hat and shook out her hair. While I watched, she stripped off her jeans and blouse and walked calmly into the sea. When she came out she put on the blouse over her wet body, but not the jeans, and lay back on the sand to dry out.

I went over to speak to her, and in a while we agreed to meet for supper that evening.

I was at Sénéquier at six, looking for Sue. If she had turned up I would have abandoned my date with Danièle without qualms, but Danièle had given me an inner reassurance. That evening would not be another lonely one, and if Sue did not appear my pride had a salve. I was feeling guilty about having picked up Danièle, and my reasons for doing so, and as a result blamed Sue. I thought of her with Niall, the sort-of writer, the rival, the bullying manipulator, and how if Sue were suddenly to appear everything could be put right.

I waited long past the hour, then finally conceded that she was not going to turn up.

I went from Sénéquier to a boutique I had been in earlier, where I had noticed they sold a wide range of postcards. Still feeling unreasonably vindictive about Sue, I chose a card. The picture was a reproduction of a prewar view of Saint-Tropez, before the commercialization. Fishermen mended nets on the harbor wall and the only boats in sight were fishing smacks. Behind them, where now the holidaymakers milled past in an endless flow and where the fashionable Sénéquier was situated, was a narrow yard with a wooden warehouse.

I took the postcard back to my room, and before changing my clothes I sat on the bed and addressed the card to Sue's flat in London. "Wish you were here," I wrote sardonically, and instead of signing it I printed an X.

A few minutes later, on my way to meet Danièle, I mailed it.

Danièle took me to a restaurant called La Grotto Fraîche, the only one, she said, that stayed open all year round, the restaurant the locals used. Afterward, we went to the apartment she shared with three other girls. Her bedroom was next to the main room, where two of them were watching television. As we made love I could hear the television through the wall, and occasionally the voices of the girls. When we were finished I thought only of Sue, and regretted everything. Danièle sensed that I was triste, but did not inquire. She put on a housecoat and made some coffee brandy. Soon I was walking back to the hotel.

I saw Danièle again in the morning, when I collected the Renault. She was wearing the Hertz uniform, was friendly, bright, unremorseful. Before I drove away we exchanged the double-cheek kiss.

VIII

I drove inland from Saint-Tropez, wanting to avoid the heavy traffic along the coast roads. The Renault was difficult to drive at first, the gearshift stiff to move and placed on the right, breaking my coordination. To drive on the right demanded constant attention, especially as the road wound sharply through mountain country. At Le Luc I joined the main autoroute and headed west on the broad divided highway, and driving became less of a strain.

I knew I was moving farther and farther away from Sue, but we had agreed on our rendezvous, and my main concern now was to see her again.

I drove along the autoroute as far as Aix-en-Provence, then turned south toward Marseilles. By lunchtime I had checked into a small *pension* in the dock area, and spent the afternoon wandering around the city. Well before six o'clock I went to our agreed rendezvous, the Gare Saint-Charles, and waited for her in as prominent a place as I could find. At eight, I went to find dinner.

I had another day to kill in Marseilles. I visited the Quai du Port, with its streetcars and wharves, the three- and four-masted barks lined up against the docks, the whole place deafeningly loud with the noise of the steam cranes. In the afternoon I went on a tourist boat for a tour of the great waterfront, passing the grim edifice of Fort Saint-Jean, then out into the calm bay to circle Château d'If. I spent the early part of the evening wandering on the concourse of the station, staring anxiously at the crowds whenever a train arrived from the Riviera. I was worried I would not recognize her.

IX

I came to Martigues, a short drive from Marseilles. Martigues was on a narrow but hilly isthmus between the Mediterranean and Étang de Berre, a vast freshwater lake. The center of the town was the original village, but nearby oil refineries had swelled the size and the population all through the twentieth century. It was impossible to drive into the center, Île Brescon, because a number of small but picturesque canals took the place of streets. I left the Renault in a town parking lot, then walked with my suitcase to find somewhere to stay.

This was the last agreed meeting place with Sue; if she did not appear here, I knew I was on my own.

The village was no place to be lonely. Many other visitors were there, walking along the narrow alleys or cruising through in boats, and it looked to me as if every- one else was in couples or groups. I began to dread the evening, knowing Sue would inevitably let me down. The

worst of it was the persistent hope, weakening my determination to put her behind me.

The Quai Brescon was the place we had agreed, the
opening of the main canal to Étang de Berre. I went there
as soon as I arrived, to familiarize myself with it, and returned several times during the day. It was a placid back-
water of the town, the houses built directly against the
water, with numerous small rowing boats and skiffs tied
up along the narrow towpaths. Few of the visitors found
the quai, and there were no restaurants, shops or even a
bar. Here the old people of the village gathered, and when
I arrived for my evening vigil they had already assembled,
sitting outside their peeling houses on an assortment of
old wicker chairs and boxes. The women all wore black,
the men wore weathered *serge de Nîmes*. They stared at me
as I sauntered along the quai, their conversation dying
around me as I passed. At the mouth of the canal, looking
out at the smooth black water of the lake, I could smell
sewage.

The warm evening darkened, night fell, lights came
on in the tiny houses. I was alone.

X

I drove around the Camargue to the village of Saintes-
Maries-de-la-Mer, the site of a shrine. I wanted to go to a
place I had not mentioned to Sue, somewhere she could
not find me if she tried. I also wanted to be by the sea
again, to throw stones at waves and wander moodily along
a beach.

But it was a mistake. The tiny village was crowded,
and buses blocked the streets and parking lots. I found a

place to leave the car and walked around for a while. The shrine, a miraculous well, was contained in a stone-built chapel, handwritten testimonies to its healing power attached to every wall. I read a few of these pathetic, joyful messages of gratitude, then returned to the bright and sunlit streets. Almost every building in the center was a commercialization of the shrine: effigies, candles, crosses, replicas were sold in every place. The only restaurant open was a vast modern cafeteria—plastic-topped tables and metal trays. I went inside seeking lunch, but was driven out by the crowds and the flies.

As I walked down to the beach I was attacked by the largest flying insect I had ever seen; it was yellow and black like a grotesquely swollen wasp. I assumed it was a hornet, and managed to elude it. From then on I kept a watchful eye open for more, but I did not stay long. The beach was open and flat, not used by the visitors, and when I reached the water the tiny waves broke feebly on the white sand. Just then I hungered for an ocean beach, with rocks and waves and sea wind, a sense of natural drama.

XI

The next day I went to a town called Aigues-Mortes. When looking at the map with Sue I had noticed the name and wondered what it meant. We had looked it up and found it was a corruption of the Roman name: Aquae Mortuae, "the dead waters." The town turned out to be a walled city, massively fortified in the Middle Ages and surrounded by a number of shallow lagoons. I parked the car outside the wall, then in the humid heat followed the course of the former moat. I soon tired of this and climbed a low hill close by, staring back. The town had a monochrome quality, like an old sepia-tinted photograph: light fell uniformly, blurring colors. I could see the roofs within the walls, and in the near distance beyond the town there was an industrial site with a number of high but unsmoking chimneys. The lagoons reflected the sky.

It struck me then that this was what France had become for me: without Sue to enliven me, it was a flat, silent and unreal place, drifting past as I traveled, locking into immobility when I stared. If I thought back over the last few days, Sue dominated everything. I remembered her company, her laughter, her love, her body. But behind her, almost unnoticed, were my images of France. Sue had distracted me from them, first by her presence, then by her absence. The empty plazas of Nancy, the old-fashioned restaurant in Dijon, that mountain sight of Grenoble, the modest bathers of Saint-Tropez, the docks of Marseilles—they were static in my mind, moments I had passed through with my thoughts elsewhere. Now Aigues-Mortes: frozen in the shimmering sun, like some vestige of memory, it had an arbitrary, random quality, its stillness reflecting some forgotten thought or image, something distinct from Sue. France was haunting me, semi-glimpsed beyond my preoccupations. How much more of France had I not noticed, how much more lay ahead?

My presence on the hill was attracting mosquitoes, which were whining unpleasantly around me, so I hurried back to where I had left the car, walking briskly through the town itself to get to the other side. The stillness had been an illusion, and bright colors cut the air.

At the entrance to the parking lot I noticed two suitcases standing together, and I thought how odd it was of someone to have left them there. I found the Renault, opened the door.

"Richard! *Richard!*"

She was running between the cars, dodging around

them, her hair flying about her face. I felt the sense of
unreality lifting from me, and all I thought was how much
she looked the same, how like herself she was. Holding her
again, feeling her willowy body against mine, I loved the
familiarity of her, and how natural it was to have her in
my arms.

XII

Driving southwest, the windows open against the heat,
leaving the Riviera behind:

"How did you find me?"

"Just luck . . . I was about to give up."

"But why that place?"

"You'd mentioned it, I knew you would go there. I
arrived last night, and I've been hanging around all day."

We were looking for somewhere to stay, somewhere
to be alone together. She had been on buses for three days,
traveling from one place to another, running low on cash,
trying to save enough for the journey home. Niall had
given her some money, she said, but he was broke too. It
hadn't been how she expected.

We stopped in Narbonne and checked into the first
hotel we found. Sue plunged into the bath, and I sat on the
side of it looking down at her. I noticed she had a bruise
on her leg, one that had not been there before.

"Don't stare at me." She slumped low in the water,
raising a knee to conceal her crotch from me but bringing
the bruise fully into view.

"I thought you wanted me to."

"I don't like being looked at."

Something had changed; I had always looked at her

before. I left the tiny bathroom, pulled off my clothes and lay on the bed. I listened to Sue splashing around, then draining the water. A long silence, followed by the rustle of a paper tissue as she blew her nose. When she appeared, she had put on panties and a T-shirt.

Glancing down at me she prowled around the room, stared out through the window at the yard below, fidgeted with her clothes on the top of her suitcase. Finally she came to sit on the end of the bed, where I could not reach her without sitting up and stretching toward her.

"Where did you get that bruise?" I said.

She turned her leg to look at it. "A sort of accident. I fell against something. There's another." She twisted around and pulled up her T-shirt to reveal a second dark bruise on her back. "They don't hurt," she said.

"Niall did that, didn't he?"

"Not really—it was an accident. He didn't mean it."

Because of the distance between us, I knew that she had resolved nothing, but I was glad just to have her back and said nothing. After a few minutes we dressed and walked into the town for a meal. I hardly registered the surroundings; I was travel-fatigued, had been in too many different places. And Sue preoccupied me. Narbonne felt real and alive, was not a tableau, but she distracted me away from it.

Over dinner, she at last gave me a full account of what had happened.

Niall's friends were staying outside Saint-Raphaël itself, in a converted farmhouse. Niall was not there when she arrived; she was told he was away on a trip. She waited for a day and a half, torn between having to wait and abandoning him altogether. When Niall turned up he was in a group of five people—another man and three young girls. No one said where they had been or what they had been doing. There were now nine people, including Sue, crammed into the house, and regardless of any other considerations she had been forced to share a bed with him. He was in a jumpy, violent mood at first, making Sue assume that something had been going on with one of the girls. There was an argument. The next day Niall vanished again, taking one of the cars. Sue decided to leave to join up with me, and got as far as packing her bags but Niall returned in time to stop her. She told him about me, and he started to beat her up. The others pulled him off her, and Niall's mood immediately changed: first he became melancholy and clinging—in a way Sue said she knew how to deal with—but then changed again, saying that if she had made a decision then he would not stand in her way.

"This is what made it difficult," she said to me. "If he had gone on acting badly I could have walked out on him. Instead, he pretended he didn't care any more."

"But at least you're here," I said. "Surely that's all that matters?"

"Yes, but I don't trust him. He's never acted like this before."

"What are you saying? That he might be following you?"

She was looking tense, fidgeting with the cutlery on the table. "I think it's more likely he was sleeping with one of those girls and couldn't be bothered."

"Can we forget him now?" I said.

"All right."

We went for a walk around the town after the meal, but our real interest was in each other and we soon returned to the hotel. We went up to the room, opened the windows wide to the warm night and closed the curtains. I took a bath and lay in the water staring blankly at the ceiling, wondering what to do. Nothing seemed to appeal, not even getting into bed with her. The bathroom door was open and I could hear her moving about, hanging up clothes, opening and closing the wardrobe door. At one point I heard her bolt the main door to the room. She did not come in to see me, and it meant nothing that she did or did not. We appeared to have reached a sort of sexless familiarity, one in which we shared a room, undressed in front of each other, slept in the same bed, yet were still separated by Niall.

When I had finished I went into the bedroom. Sue was sitting up in bed, looking through a magazine. She was naked. She put the magazine aside as I climbed in beside her.

"Shall I put out the light?" I said.

"Last week, when we were in Nice, you said something to me. Did you mean it?"

"That depends what it was."

"You said you loved me. Was that true?"

"It was at the time," I said. "I loved you then more than anyone I have ever known. In fact, there never has been anyone else."

"That's what I thought. What about now?"

"It's not a good time to ask. I'm feeling alienated."

"Then it's the best time to ask. Do you love me?"

"Of course I do. Why do you think all this matters so much?"

She shifted down in the bed so her head was on the pillow. "That's what I wanted to hear. Don't put out the light. I hate making love in the dark."

XIII

Collioure was a fishing village on the extreme southwesterly coast of the Mediterranean. It was built on a small bay, with a fort and a cluster of stone cottages, and was surrounded by rocky hills, brown-green under the blaze of the sun. As soon as we arrived I was struck again by a quality of frozen timelessness, that there was an unchanging life here that we could pass into and through, yet never really penetrate. It reminded me of the stasis of Aigues-Mortes, and my realization that the distractions of Sue made me unable to see properly.

But because I was with Sue, at last truly *with* her, I felt able to deal with this, realizing that both she and the village were different aspects of my perceptions. If I allowed them to, each one could interfere with the other, but now for the first time I was relaxed and very happy. We had no more discussions of ourselves.

During the days Collioure was almost deserted, the shutters of the houses closed against the heat. We would wander in the narrow cobblestone streets and climb the hills and watch the boats; in the evenings the locals would bring out their chairs and wine to sit in the long shadows and watch the day's catch being loaded into ice for the trucks. There were no hotels or apartments in Collioure, in spite of what the tourist guidebook said, and so we stayed in a small room over a bar. We were *les anglais* to the people in the village, smiled at maternally by the women when we walked about after dark, stared at by the men, but in general left alone by everyone. There were no other visitors in the village while we were there.

Except one. We noticed him on our second day while climbing up to the hills on the eastern side of the village. As the narrow road rose above the houses it turned across the rise, making a loop from which it was possible to see down across the cottages around the harbor. From this position the walls and angles of the roofs seemed foreshortened, piling against each other to make an irregular geometric pattern lit by the morning sun. There was an artist sitting here, a small canvas propped on an easel in front of him.

He was a small man with a round head and a hunched figure. It was difficult to guess his age: not old,

perhaps forty to fifty. As we passed we nodded to him, but
he made no answer. I felt Sue's hand slip from mine and
she looked sharply at him, then at me, then again at the
artist. She was obviously trying to tell me something, but I
had no idea what it was. As we walked on she was looking
back, as if trying to get a glimpse of the canvas.

When we were out of earshot she said, "That
looked like Picasso!"

"He's dead, isn't he?"

"Of course he's dead! It couldn't have been him—
but that man looked exactly like him."

"Did you see what he was painting?"

"It wasn't possible. I've never seen anything like it!
He looked just like the photographs."

"Perhaps it's a relative . . . or someone who wants
to look like Picasso."

"That must be it."

We walked on, talking about the way some people
try to imitate the appearance of those they admired, but
Sue would not accept that. To her it was a deeper mystery,
and she kept returning to it.

In the end I said, "Do you want to go back for
another look?"

"Yes, let's."

I half expected that he would have disappeared by
the time we returned, but he was still there at the turn of
the road, crouching on his stool and painting slowly.

"It's incredible," Sue whispered. "It *must* be a relative. . . . Did Picasso have sons?"

"I've no idea."

We were walking back on his side of the road, so
that this time we would see his canvas. As we approached,
Sue called out, *"Bonjour, monsieur!"*

He raised his free hand, but did not turn. *"¡Hola!"*

We passed behind him. The canvas was only half
completed, but the angles of the roofs had been blocked in,

the pattern was forming. We walked on down the hill into the village, Sue practically dancing with curiosity.

"There's a print of that in one of my books!" she said.

We were in Collioure for a total of four days, and on each of them, at some time, we walked up the hill to see if the artist was still there. Every day he was at his easel, painting slowly and patiently. He was in his own stasis, and progress was slow; on our last look he had added very little to what we had first seen.

Before we left Collioure we asked the woman who ran the bar if she knew who he was.

"*Non. Il est espagnol.*"

"We thought he might be famous."

"*Pah! Il est très pauvre. Un espagnol célèbre!*" And she laughed and laughed.

XIV

We should have finished in Collioure, but we planned to fly back to England, and after a two-day drive through the Pyrenees we came to Biarritz. The staff in the reception of the hotel booked us a flight, but it was not for two days. After the first night I took the car and turned it in at the local Hertz office.

Sue was waiting for me at the hotel, and I knew immediately that something was wrong. She had the evasive, indirect look I had grown to recognize from the bad times, and I felt a sudden dread. I knew at once it was something to do with Niall.

But how? Niall was hundreds of miles away, and could have no idea where we were.

I suggested a walk to the beach and she agreed, but we walked apart, not holding hands. When we reached the path that led down to La Grande Plage, Sue came to a halt.

"I don't really feel like the beach today," she said. "You go if you want."

"Not without you. I don't care what we do."

"I think I'd like to do some shopping on my own."

"What's the matter, Sue? Something's happened."

She shook her head. "I just want to be on my own for a while. An hour or two. I can't explain."

"If that's what you want." I gestured irritably at the beach. "I'll go and lie around until you feel like being with me again."

"I won't be long."

"But I don't understand what you want to do."

She had already moved away from me. "I want some space to think for a while, that's all." She came back, pecked me on the cheek. "It's nothing you've done. Really."

"Well, I'll go back to the hotel in an hour or two." She was moving away as I said this, missing most of it. I walked off in a huff, going quickly down the cliff path.

The beach was uncrowded. I found a place for myself, and there I spread out my towel, took off my jeans and shirt and sat back to brood.

She had distracted me again, but now I was alone I took in my surroundings at last. The beach was . . . still. I sat up straight, looking around, aware that something had ceased around me.

This was different from the Mediterranean beaches I had seen. There was no topless sunbathing, and unlike the Riviera coast the heat of the sun was pleasantly tempered by a sea breeze. The sea itself had muscle: long steady breakers came rolling in, making the satisfactory roaring noise familiar to me from British beaches. So there was movement and sound, denying the stillness, but still I felt locked in something that had settled, become stable.

Looking around at the other people on the beach I noticed that many of them were using changing huts, like tiny Arab yurts, erected in three parallel rows one behind the other. The people who emerged from these hastened down the beach and ran into the surf with a peculiar crouching motion, reaching forward with their arms. As the first breaker hit them they would jump up against it, turning their backs and yelling in the cold. Most of the swimmers were men, but there were a few women and these all wore shapeless one-piece bathing suits and rubber caps.

I lay back in the sunshine, still feeling uneasy, listening to the cries of the holidaymakers and thinking about Sue's behavior. How had Niall contacted her? How did he know where she was?

Or had she contacted him?

I felt irritated and hurt. I wished Sue would take me more into her confidence about Niall. If only she would tell the truth, then we had a chance of working together to solve the problem.

I sat up again, restless. Overhead the sky was a deep, pure blue, the sun striking down from above the casino. I glanced up at it, narrowing my eyes.

There was a cloud, the only one in sight. It was a white, woolly-looking cloud, the sort you see on a summer's day when the sun raises thermals from the fields and woodlands. This one, though, was by itself. It stood close to the sun, apparently unaffected by the breeze from the ocean. If the sun went in, what effect would it have on the beach scene around me? I imagined a sudden breaking of the gentle stasis, the people scurrying back to their changing tents, pulling on their flannelette dresses and their baggy slacks.

The cloud made me think of Niall, just as once before, from the riverbank in Dijon. Then and now I was preoccupied with him.

Niall was invisible to me; he existed only through Sue, her descriptions, her reactions.

I wondered what he was really like, whether he was as unpleasant as Sue made out. The odd thing was that we had much in common, because we were attracted to the same woman. Niall would see and know Sue much as I did, her sweet nature when happy, her evasiveness when she felt threatened, her irrational loyalties; above all he would know her body.

And Niall, of course, would know me only through her. How would she portray me to him? Impulsive, jealous, petulant, unreasonable, gullible? I would prefer to think that Sue described me in the way I saw myself, but I had a feeling that this would not survive translation. She had a way of conveying only the unpleasant qualities in someone's character, and in this way kept alive the sense of rivalry between us.

The beach was beginning to repel me; I felt like an intruder, entering a living diorama and interfering with its natural balance. There was still no sign of Sue, so I dressed and walked up the cliff path, heading for the hotel. At the top I glanced back: the beach now looked more crowded, the rows of changing tents had vanished, and out in the breakers a number of people in wet suits were riding the surf.

I left a note in the hotel room telling Sue that I had gone for a meal, then walked down into the busy streets to find a café. I deliberately passed a few, hoping I would see her somewhere around, but there were so many people I knew I could easily miss her.

I was tired of traveling; I had been in too many different places, slept in too many different beds. I began to wonder what was in the mail for me at home, if any jobs were being offered. I had almost forgotten what it was like to feel the weight of a camera on my shoulder.

I found a sidewalk café and ordered Coquilles Saint-Jacques with a carafe of white wine. I was irritated

with Sue for leaving me like that, for not being at the
hotel, for not telling me what was going on. But it was
pleasant there in the sun, and after the meal I ordered
more wine. I decided to sit out the rest of the afternoon in
the café. The drink was making me drowsy. I was looking
forward to going home and being with Sue in London. In
spite of everything we still hardly knew each other.

Unexpectedly, I saw her walking down the street
on the other side. I had been staring lazily in that direction, and my first impression was that she was walking
with another man. I sat up at once, craning to see better. I
must have been mistaken: she was on her own, but she was
walking in that way people do when they are with someone else. She walked slowly, kept turning her head to the
side and was not looking where she was going. By every
appearance she was deep in conversation with someone,
but I could see nobody with her.

She reached the street intersection and paused, but
not for a gap in the traffic. She was frowning, then she
shook her head angrily. After a few moments she walked
on, turning the corner and heading away from me.

I had not finished my wine, but I left the table and
followed her, intrigued by her behavior. I briefly lost sight
of her, but by the time I had turned the corner I could see
her again, for all the world in the middle of an argument
with her unseen companion. I found it touching to catch
her in this unguarded moment. She appeared to be about
to halt again, so I turned and walked away from her. I
returned to the street crossing, then walked quickly along
the main road until I found another side street. I hurried
along this, and at the next street I doubled back in her
direction. When I came around the corner she was standing still, facing toward me. I walked up to her, hoping for
a sign that her mood had changed, but she merely gazed
blankly at me.

"There you are," I said. "I've been looking for
you."

"Hello."

"Have you finished shopping? Or do you want to do some more?"

"No, I'm through."

She was not carrying any purchases. We walked on in the direction she had been going before; it was clear that it did not matter whether or not I was with her.

"What shall we do?" I said. "It's the last night of our holiday."

"I don't care. Anything you like."

Irritation rose in me again. "All right, I'll leave you alone."

"What do you mean?"

"That's obviously what you want."

We had stopped walking and were facing each other. "I didn't say that," she said.

"You didn't have to."

I turned away from her, angry with her passivity. I heard her say, "Richard, don't be difficult," but I walked on. When I reached the corner I looked back. She was still where I had left her, making no effort at conciliation. I felt that had to come from her; I made an exasperated gesture in her direction and walked away.

I returned to the hotel and went to the room. There I had a shower and put on fresh clothes, then lay on the bed and tried to read.

She returned late in the evening, after ten o'clock. As she entered the room I pretended to ignore her, but was acutely aware of her as she moved around, putting down her bag, slipping off her sandals, brushing out her hair. I watched as she took off her clothes and went into the shower cubicle. She stood in the shower a long time, and I lay on the bed waiting for her. It felt then as if everything was over, that even if she made one of her about-faces and became loving and affectionate and sexy again, I would reject her. There was something insurmountable between us, whether it was Niall himself or simply something he embodied. I could not stand these sudden withdrawals, her obstinacy, her irrationality.

At last she emerged from the shower, and stood at the end of the bed toweling her hair. I stared frankly at her naked body, finding it for the first time unappealing. She was too thin, too angular, and with her hair wet and swept back from her face she had a plain, vague expression. She caught me watching her and bent forward, toweling her hair from the back of her head; I could see the bony ridges of her spine.

With her hair still damp she pulled on a T-shirt, then turned back the sheet and got into the bed. I had to shift position slightly to let her in. Sitting up, the pillow propped behind her, she regarded me with wide eyes.

"Get undressed, come to bed," she said.

"I don't want to just yet."

"You're angry with me."

"Of course I am."

She drew a breath. "If I tell you the truth, will you forgive me?"

"Why wouldn't you tell me the truth this morning?"

"Because I had to do something, and you would have tried to stop me. And you could have, if you'd tried. It's Niall—he's here, in Biarritz. I've spent the day with him. But you knew that, didn't you?" I nodded, shocked by the news confirming the inevitable. "I saw him this morning while you were taking the car back. He said he wanted to speak with me alone. I'll never see him again after this. That's the truth."

"What did he want?" I said.

"He's unhappy, and wanted me to change my mind."

"What did you say?"

"I told him I'd made up my mind, and that I was with you now."

"And it took all day to say that?"

"Yes."

I still felt cold toward her, unforgiving of the truth. Why wouldn't she act on her decision? I said, "What I want to know is how the hell he followed us here."

"I don't know."

"Was he following us when we were in Collioure? Was he there?"

"I don't think so."

"Can't you see the damage this does? You just let Niall barge in on us whenever he feels like it, you don't tell me, and it drives me away from you. I'm sorry if he's unhappy . . . but why do *you* act like this? What's going to happen the next time he feels unhappy?"

"It won't happen again."

"I don't believe you. I'd like to, but I don't."

"I've told you the truth!"

"All right." I subsided, realizing how futile all this was. Sue's face was drained of color: her skin, her lips, even her eyes looked paler than normal. As her hair dried she looked less gaunt, but now she was as angry as I was. I kept thinking that what we should do is hold each other, kiss, make love, put the clock back, the other formulas for making up, but this time it was not possible.

We sat up late into the night, both of us entrenched in our needs, angry with each other because it all mattered so much. In the end I undressed and got into bed with her, but we lay awake without making love. Neither of us would make the first move.

At one point in the night, knowing she was awake, I said, "When I met you in the street, what were you doing?"

"Trying to work things out. Why?"

"Where was Niall?"

"Waiting for me somewhere. I had gone for a walk, then you appeared."

"You looked as if you were talking to someone."

"So what?"

We lay on in the warm darkness, the sheet thrown down from our bodies. When I opened my eyes I could just make out her shape next to me. She always lay still in bed, without tossing, and in the dark I was never sure whether she was asleep or not.

I said, "Where is Niall now?"

"Somewhere around."

"I still don't understand how he found you."

"Never underestimate him, Richard. He's clever, and when he wants something he's persistent."

"He seems to have power over you, whatever you say. I wish I understood what it was."

There was a long silence from her, and I thought she must have fallen asleep at last. But then she said, very quietly, "Niall's glamorous."

X V

We spent most of the next day traveling: a taxi to the airport, then two flights, with a long wait for the connection in Bordeaux. From Gatwick we caught the train to Victoria, and took a taxi to Sue's house. I asked the driver to wait while we went inside.

There was a small pile of mail waiting for her on a table in the hall, and she picked this up before unlocking her own door. I carried her suitcases inside, and put them down. Her room came as a surprise: I think I had expected the usual cramped chaos of bed-sitter existence, but the room was large, very tidy, and what furniture there was had been chosen with taste. In one corner was a single bed, and next to this was a bookcase filled with expensive art books. Under the only window was a desk, with a drawing board, several glasses filled with brushes, pens and knives, a container for paper, and a large angle-poise lamp. There was stereo equipment but no television set. Against one wall was a hand basin, a small cooker and a massive, antiquated wardrobe. As she closed the door to the room I noticed she had fitted two heavy bolts, one at the top, one at the bottom.

"I'd better not keep the taxi waiting," I said.

"I know."

We were facing each other, but not looking. I felt very tired from the journey. She came up to me and suddenly we embraced, more warmly than I would have expected.

"Are we going to see each other again?" I said.

"Do you want to?"

"You know I do. The only thing wrong with us is Niall."

"Then there's nothing to worry about. I promise you Niall won't bother me again."

"All right, let's not discuss it now."

"I'll give you a ring later this evening," she said.

We had exchanged addresses and numbers soon after meeting, but we went through the routine of making sure we still had them. Sue's address was easy to remember, so I had never written it down, but I had scribbled her telephone number in the back of my address book.

"Shall we meet for a meal tomorrow evening?" I said.

"Let's decide that later. Now I just want to unpack and look at my mail."

We kissed again, and this time it was decidedly warm. It reminded me of how she tasted, how she felt against me. I started to regret my behavior of the day before, but she pulled back from me smiling.

"I'll call you later," she said.

The London rush hour had started, and it was much later when the taxi dropped me outside my flat. I let myself in and put down my bag, looking at the pile of mail on the mat. I left it there and went upstairs.

After so long away, so many different places seen, the rooms had that disorienting air of familiarity and strangeness. The flat smelled slightly of damp, so I opened some windows, then switched on the water heater and the fridge. My apartment had four main rooms, apart from kitchen and bathroom: there was a lounge, bedroom, a spare room, and the fourth room which I thought of as my study. It was here that I kept the various pieces of elderly film equipment I had picked up over the years, as well as copy prints of some of the stories I had worked on. I had a 16-mm projector and screen, and an editing bench. All these were tokens of a halfhearted intention of starting up as an independent film maker one day, even though I knew that most of this stuff would have to be replaced with modern equipment of professional standard. I should also have to rent a proper studio.

The flat felt cool after the summer weather in France, and outside it was raining. I wandered around, feeling anticlimactic and already lonely for Sue. It had been a bad note on which to end the holiday; I didn't know her well enough to judge the changes in her mood, and I had left her just as we were on another upswing. I thought for a moment I should telephone her, but she had said she would call me, and anyway there was much to do around the flat. I had a suitcaseful of dirty clothes that had to be washed soon, and there was no fresh food. But I felt unmotivated and lazy, missing France.

I made a cup of black instant coffee and sat down with it to go through the mail. A pile of accumulated letters always looks more interesting before they are opened. What had built up for me was a number of bills and circulars, subscription copies of magazines, halfhearted replies to halfhearted letters I had written before I went away. A postcard had arrived from Annette in Canada. The best pieces of mail were two checks I had been expecting, for film work a couple of months before, and a note from a producer asking me to call him urgently. His letter was a week old.

My humdrum life was reintegrating around me. How Sue had the capacity to distract me! She had become so important to me, so immediate. When I was with her she put everything else out of my mind. Maybe in London she would seem different, the relationship would continue at a lower pressure in the context of everyday existence. What I knew for sure was that we could not possibly conduct a long-term affair in the way we had started.

I telephoned the producer who had written to me; he had left, but there was a message on his answering machine to contact him at home. I called there, but there was no answer. I walked down to the lock-up garage where I kept my car, and much to my surprise the engine started on the first attempt. I drove back to the house and parked outside. Then I collected my dirty clothes and a shopping bag, dumped the clothes in a machine at the local laundromat, and went to buy some groceries. When all this was finished I went home.

While I ate my rudimentary version of home cooking, I read a copy of the morning's newspaper, wondering what might have happened in the world while I was away. My job had given me a peculiar attitude to news reporting: either I saturated myself in stories as they developed, or I cut myself off from them entirely. While away, I had been content to let a vacuum of non-interest develop around me. From the paper I discovered that most of the news was the same as always: a new round of pay talks with the unions, fears of an IRA bombing campaign in London, tension in the Middle East, rumors of an upcoming general election, a political scandal in the U.S.A., drought and famine in East Africa.

I called the producer again and this time got through to him. He was pleased to hear from me: one of the American networks wanted documentary footage of

U.S. military involvement in Central America, and because of political sensitivity an American crew could not be used. He had been trying to find a camera operator all week, but no one wanted the job. I thought about it while we talked, and then said yes.

The evening drew on, and I felt increasingly restless. I knew I was waiting for Sue to call me as she had said she would. I had been out of the flat for an hour and a half and she might have called then, but surely she would try again later? I could easily have telephoned her, but she had said she would call me and there was a sort of emotional protocol involved. I was still feeling the effects of the day before.

I waited for her, feeling tired, and after about ten o'clock more and more irritated. I had a feeling in my bones about it, the familiar dread of Niall's intrusion. If he could mysteriously follow us to Biarritz, it would not be beyond him to have followed us home. More likely, though, there had been a message for her at the house—a letter, a telegram, a phone call.

I stayed up until I could hardly keep my eyes open. I went to bed still irritated with her, and so fell into an unpleasant state of exhausted but restless sleep. At one dark low point of the night I resolved never again to have anything to do with her. If this resolve survived until morning, it was broken by her telephoning me before I was out of bed. I picked up the receiver and heard the sound of pay-phone pips.

"Richard? It's me, Sue."

"I thought you were going to call me last night. I waited up for you."

"I rang an hour or two after you left, but there was no answer. I was going to try again later, but I fell asleep."

"I thought something might have happened."

She said nothing for a moment. Then: "No. I was exhausted. How are you?"

"You woke me up, so I'm not sure yet. What about you?"

"I've got to visit the studio. I'm more broke than I thought . . . there was a pile of bills waiting for me."

"Are you going to be at the studio all day?"

"I think so."

"Shall we meet this evening? I'd like to see you."

We made the practical arrangements as if we were fixing up a business meeting. Sue sounded cool and distant, and I was making an effort to keep a querulous tone out of my voice. I was still deeply suspicious of why she had not telephoned.

"By the way, your card was here in the mail."

"Card?"

"You sent me a postcard from France . . . at least I think it was you. It wasn't signed."

"Oh yes."

Old Saint-Tropez—fishermen, nets and a warehouse. It reminded me of being alone while she was with Niall, and it reminded me of how things had become since. My suspicions and her evasiveness, all about Niall.

"I'll see you later, then," she said.

"All right. Goodbye."

The call was over before the time pips could intervene. I went through the day trying not to think about her, but she had become so bound up in my life that I could not disregard her. She still informed everything I did or thought. Yet I knew my love of her was founded on two brief periods: a few days before she went to see Niall, a few days that had followed. I still loved her, but it was based on the past.

XVI

Full of forebodings, I walked down to Finchley Road underground station to meet her as planned. She was already there when I arrived, and as soon as she saw me she ran toward me, kissing me and holding me tightly. Forebodings dispersed.

She said, "You live somewhere around here, don't you?"

"In West Hampstead."

"Can I see your flat?"

"I thought we'd go for a drink now, and I've booked a table for later."

"Good, we'll go later. I want to see where you live."

She led me off, hurrying along. As soon as we were inside she started kissing me again, more affectionately than I could ever remember her. I felt emotionally detached, so hard had my defenses built up during the day. But there was no question of what she wanted, and soon we were in bed. Afterward she left the room and walked around the flat, looking at everything, then returned to me. She sat on the bed, cross-legged and naked.

"I'm going to make a speech, and I want you to listen," she said.

"I don't like speeches."

"This one's different. I've been working on it all day, and you're going to like it."

"Are you intending to read it to me?"

"Don't interrupt. The first thing I want to do is say I'm sorry I saw Niall without telling you. It's never going to happen again, and I'm sorry if I hurt you. The second thing is that Niall's going to be back in London any day now, and I can't stop him finding me. He knows where I live and he knows where I go to work. What I'm saying is, if I see Niall it's not going to be my fault, and I'll tell you immediately. The third—"

I said, "But what happens if you *do* see him? It'll be the same all over again."

"No, it won't be. You interrupted. The third thing is that I'm in love with you, you're the only person I want to be with and we must never let Niall interfere again."

I felt relaxed after the lovemaking, felt fond of her, felt the warmth radiating from her, but there was damage that had been done. Only that morning it had seemed to me that we had been broken apart irreparably by events, but now there was yet another reversal, Sue saying the very words I wanted her to say. What she did not know, and what I was only beginning to sense, was that it was the reversals themselves that did the harm. Each time I accommodated the change, something of the past became lost.

"What we have to do is see Niall together," I said. "I don't trust what he might do if he saw you alone. How do I know he won't beat you up again?"

Sue was shaking her head. "You can never see him, Richard."

"But if we're together, he would have to accept the situation for what it is."

"No. You don't understand."

"Then make me."

"I'm *scared* of him."

I suddenly thought of the job I had been offered, and how I was due to leave London in two days' time. For a moment I regretted having accepted, thinking of Niall's imminent return, the likelihood that he would see Sue while I was away. Knowing how he could influence her when I was there, I could imagine the worst. Yet to do so was to disbelieve her sincerity, her own freedom to act for herself. I had to trust her.

We eventually dressed and went to the restaurant, and while we were there I told Sue about having to go away. I said nothing of my fears, but she sensed them at once.

She said, "The worst thing about it is not seeing you until you get back. Nothing else will happen."

She stayed with me in my flat for the next two days, and then I left.

XVII

It was ten days before I returned, red-eyed and exhausted from the thirteen-hour flight, still irritated by the shooting delays we had encountered and still oppressed by the memory of the heat and humidity. It had been difficult work, constantly hampered by lack of cooperation and bureaucracy. At every new place we went to film we had to be approved by the local officers in charge, all of whom were suspicious of us or hostile to us. In the end the work had been done, the money had been paid. I was glad it was over.

I went back to my flat, and although I was tired I was restless and discontented. London felt cold and damp, but after the shanty towns and slums of Central America it looked tidy, prosperous, modern. I stayed in the flat long enough to look through my mail, then collected my car and drove over to see Sue.

One of the other people in the house opened the door to me, and I went straight to her room and knocked. There was a delay, but I could hear movement inside. In a moment the door opened, and Sue stood there with a dressing gown held around her. We stared at each other for a moment.

Then she said, "You'd better come in."

As she said this she gave a half-look over her shoulder as if someone was there, and when I walked in I was braced for a confrontation. Dread filled me.

The room smelt musty, and was in semidarkness. The curtains were closed, but daylight filtered through the thin material. Sue crossed the room and pulled them open. Outside was a brick wall forming a small drainage well, and bushes and overgrown grass stood in the garden above this, shading the room. The air had a faint blue haze to it, as if someone had been smoking, but I could not smell tobacco.

She had been in bed when I arrived, because the covers were thrown back and her clothes were draped over a chair. On the bedside table was a small, shallow dish, and lying in this were three cigarette ends.

I glared around suspiciously, looking for Niall.

Sue walked past me and closed the door. She stood by it, leaning her back against it and holding the gown wrapped over her body. She would not look at me, and her hair, untidy and tangled, concealed most of her face. I could see, though, that her mouth and chin were reddened.

I said, "Where's Niall?"

"Can you see him here?"

"Of course I can't. Is he in the house?" She shook her head. "Why are you still in bed?"

I glanced at my wristwatch, but it was still set on Central American time. The plane had landed in London soon after dawn, so I guessed that by now it must be nearly midday.

"I'm not working today—I was having a lie-in." She crossed the room and sat down on the bed. "Why are you here, anyway?"

"Why? Why the hell do you think? I just arrived back, and I came to see you!"

"I thought you'd telephone first."

"You promised me this wouldn't happen."

She said quietly, "Niall found me. He followed me home from work one evening, and I couldn't argue with him."

"How long ago was this?"

"About a week. Look, I know what this means. Don't make it any worse than it is. I can't go on being torn between the two of you. Niall isn't going to leave me alone as long as I'm with you, so it will never work, whatever you make me promise."

"I never extracted a promise from you," I said.

"All right, but it's finished now."

"You're damned right it's finished!"

"Let's leave it at that."

I could barely hear what she said. She was huddled on the bed, her arms folded in her lap, leaning forward so that all I could see of her was the top of her head and her shoulders. She had turned slightly to one side, facing the table. I noticed that the ashtray was no longer there, that somehow she must have moved it. I knew by this guilty concealment that Niall had been there just before I arrived.

"I'll go now," I said. "But tell me one thing. I don't understand the hold Niall has over you. Why do you let him do this to you? Is he going to run your life forever?"

She said, "He's glamorous, Richard."

"You said that before. What's glamour got to do with it?"

"Not glamour, *the* glamour. Niall has got the glamour."

"This is what's so ridiculous! You can't be serious!"

"It's the most important thing in my life. Yours too."

She looked up at me then, a thin, sad figure, sitting

in the mess of crumpled sheets that were heaped across the mattress. She had started crying, silently, hopelessly.

"I'm going," I said. "Don't contact me again."

She stood up, uncoiling stiffly as if in pain.

"Don't you know you're glamorous, Richard?" she said. "I love you for your glamour."

"I don't want to hear another word!"

"You can't change. The glamour will never leave you. This is why Niall won't let me go . . . when you understand the glamour, you'll know that's true."

Then, somewhere in the room, somewhere behind me, I heard the sound of a male laugh. I saw that the full-length door of the wardrobe had been open all along, that there was space behind it for someone to hide. Niall was there, he had been there all along! Heady with anger I lunged at the door of the room, wrenched it open, saw the bright glint of the stainless-steel bolts. I went outside, slamming the door behind me. I was too angry to drive so I hurried down the road, moving away from her as fast as I could. I walked and walked, heading home, wanting only in the blackness of rage to get away from her. I went up the long hill toward Archway, crossed the viaduct into Highgate, then started down toward Hampstead Heath. My anger was like a narcotic, turning my brain in a relentless swirl of vicious resentments. I knew I was tired from the long flight, that jet lag was no condition in which to be rational about anything, least of all this. London seemed like a hallucination around me; the glimpse from the Heath of the tall buildings to the south, the old red brick terraces on the far side, the people in the streets and the endless noise of traffic. I cut through side streets lined with Victorian villas; plane trees and ornamental cherries and crab apples now tired at the end of summer; cars parked on both sides, wheels up on the pavements. I pushed past people, hardly seeing them, ran across Finchley Road, dodging traffic. It was downhill to West Hampstead, long straight roads with cars and trucks, people waiting for buses or moving slowly from one shop to another. I shoved past them all, thinking now only of getting home, going to bed, trying to sleep off my anger and my jet lag. I turned into West End Lane, almost home. The walking had clarified my mind: no more Sue, no more Niall, no more raised hopes or broken promises or evasions or lies. From now I was going to live only for myself, never fool myself that love was simple. I hated Sue, everything she had done to me, regretted everything I had said to her and done with her. I passed West Hampstead station, passed the twenty-four-hour supermarket, passed the police station—all familiar landmarks, all part of my life in London before Sue. I was making plans, thinking of a job the producer had mentioned on the flight back—not news, but a documentary for the BBC, a long project, much travel. When I had recovered from this I would call him, get out of the country for a while, sleep with foreign women, work at what I did best. Something hit me low in the back, and I was hurled forward. I heard nothing, but crashed into the brick surround of a shop window; the glass shattered around me. Some part of me was rolling along the ground, twisting my back, while great heat scorched my neck and legs. As I came to a halt the only sound I could hear was of glass breaking and falling, slabs of it slicing down on top of me, an endless tormenting rain, and somewhere an immense and total silence out and around me, beyond my unseeing eyes.

Part IV

I

For the first few miles after leaving the hospital the roads were narrow and twisty, leading between the high Devon hedges. Because of the number of farm tractors that regularly used these lanes the road surface was muddy and slippery in the rain. Sue drove nervously and hesitantly, braking sharply as they approached corners, and steering around them with elaborate caution, craning her neck to see ahead. It was always dangerous for her to drive, demanding constant concentration, but these lanes presented an extra hazard to her. Fortunately the few oncoming cars they met were being driven slowly, so there was never any real danger of a collision, but the car felt large and unfamiliar and she wished they could reach the main road.

Richard was sitting beside her in the passenger seat, staring ahead and speaking hardly at all. He held the crossover seat belt with one hand, keeping it from pressing against his body, but whenever she braked for a corner he jerked forward with the momentum. She knew that he was tense because of the way she was driving, and that the lurching of the car was probably painful, but trying to compensate for this only made her more nervous.

A few miles beyond Totnes they came at last to the main A38 road, a modern two-lane highway with no sharp corners and only gentle gradients, and almost at once she felt more confident. She accelerated to a comfortable cruising speed of around sixty miles per hour. A fine drizzle was falling, and whenever they overtook a truck or some other large vehicle the windshield was blurred with a muddy spray. Once past Exeter the road joined the M5 motorway, leading directly via a link with the M4 to London.

At her suggestion Richard leaned forward and switched on the radio, tuning it to a number of stations before finding one they agreed on.

"Let me know if you'd like to stop somewhere," she said.

"I'm all right for the moment. I think I'll have to get out and walk around in about an hour."

"How do you feel?"

"Fine."

Sue felt fine too, glad to be returning permanently to London. She was exhausted by the frequent journeys to Devon in recent weeks. Richard had been walking unaided for almost a month now, and they had both grown impatient for his discharge. It was Dr. Hurdis who had delayed matters, saying he was unconvinced that the traumas had been dealt with. There had been several more sessions of hypnotherapy, but these, like the first, had been inconclusive. Richard himself was apparently untroubled, and anxious to be finished with the treatment.

Sue's own dilemma was that she agreed with Hurdis; she knew for her own reasons that Richard had not yet come to terms with his past, but she was convinced that nothing more could be gained from conventional therapy. She had her own indecisions on this, a reflection of her personal needs. Richard had lost his glamour, and knew nothing of hers.

Adding to their wish to leave had been the practicalities of seeing him at Middlecombe. The deception of Middlecombe was that it looked like and felt like a hotel, but was of course a hospital. The comfortable surroundings, the discreet furnishings, the steward service, the *haute cuisine* food raised hopes of privacy and personal freedom, but the reality was that they rarely had a chance of being alone together. Walking in the grounds was the only time they had to themselves, but they could not do too much of this. And for the same reasons, Sue could not actually stay at Middlecombe and had always had to find lodgings outside, sometimes in Kingsbridge, once or twice in Dartmouth, and this had added to the expense of the visits and made further inroads into their time together.

In all her several visits, they had been alone in his room just once. Then, very tentatively, they had tried to make love. It was a failure; they were both too aware of their surroundings, the bed was functional hospital apparatus, and his body was still sore and stiff. Through the thin partition wall they had been able to hear two of the other patients speaking in the next room, and the need to be quiet became another inhibition. In the end they had settled for lying naked in each other's arms for a few minutes. Even that had provided her with shocks: until then she had no notion of the extent of his injuries, and she was horrified by the scars from burns and operations. It marked a fresh phase in her feelings for him: the sheer scale of the hurt he had suffered awakened a new tenderness.

But now Middlecombe was behind them, and her own personal dilemma about Richard became pressing. What she wanted most was a clean start, a second chance, and on the surface there seemed no reason why this should not be. She still loved and needed him as much as ever, and simply because Richard had no memory of what had torn them apart before, the best thing she could do would be to build slowly from here.

She was rid of Niall at last. The accident had apparently destroyed Richard's glamour. The emotional turmoil of finally breaking with Niall and of hearing about the car bomb had shocked her out of her own glamour.

Everything she had hoped for in the old days was now hers.

Richard, though, was intent on rediscovery. He wanted to know what had happened, how they had met, how they had loved, what had pulled them apart. She was terrified of his finding out, and had no idea what to do.

In this sense the glamour still united them, and still threatened them.

"I'm beginning to feel stiff," Richard said, shifting in the seat and trying to readjust the position of the safety belt. "Shall we stop soon?"

They had been silent for most of the journey, listening to the classical music on Radio 3. She wondered what music he liked best, whether it was just classical music or if his taste extended to pop too. There were so many small things they did not know about each other, swept aside by the urgencies of love. What she remembered most about him was his passion, his exciting declarations, the impromptu of his feelings. In the hospital all this had been restrained by the conditions, but once they were home would she see this side of him again?

They were approaching Bristol, and just before the Avon Bridge she turned off the motorway and drove into the service area. After parking the car she went around to the passenger door and stood by it while Richard climbed out. He was able to do this on his own, insisted on it, but she wanted to be close by him. She reached into the back of the car for his walking stick, then locked up.

It had stopped raining, but the tarmac of the parking area was wet and scattered with puddles. A cool wind blew in from Wales, just across the Severn estuary.

She bought two cups of tea and some biscuits, and took them to the table where Richard was waiting. The cafeteria, brightly lit and garishly colored, was crowded with other motorists. She had never seen one of these places empty. From outside they could hear the electronic groans and whines of the video machines.

"Are you looking forward to being at home?" she said.

"Of course I am. But it's been a long time. I keep thinking about what the flat was like when I bought it. It had just been modernized, and it was empty. It's difficult to imagine it with furniture."

"I thought you said you could remember it?"

"My memories are all mixed up. I keep thinking of the day I moved in. I'd put the carpets at the back of the van, so I had to move all the furniture again. And I can remember later, when you were there, but it doesn't feel like the same place. I can remember them simultaneously, one on top of the other. Do you know what I mean?"

"Not really," she said.

"You haven't been back there, have you?"

"No." It had actually occurred to her once that she ought to call in to see if everything was all right, but she had never done so.

Since making her visits to Richard in Devon her life had been afflicted by two mundane problems: lack of time and lack of money. He actually knew very little of this, because in the early days he had been so suspicious of her excuses. Since then she had tried to minimize her problems to him, in the greater cause. He paid for everything he knew about: her travel expenses, the lodgings in Devon, car rental, meals whenever they were together, but these had very little to do with the central problem. She still had to find the rent, she had to eat, pay for heating, had to move around London, clothe herself.

Her working life had been thrown into chaos by her frequent absences from London. The studio seemed less and less inclined to commission work from her, because she had become unreliable, and she had no time to go out and look for alternatives.

The fact that she had supported herself for some years was a matter of considerable importance to her. It had always been precarious, but she had survived somehow. Independence and honestly earned income were identified in her mind with her growth away from Niall's influence, three or four years ago, when she had started to reject his way of life.

But the temptations were constant because the solution was within reach. Niall had taught her the techniques of shoplifting, and she knew she could still use them. Her glamour was much weaker, but it was there to be used if she needed it. So far she had resisted it, and Richard knew nothing of the struggle she had waged.

When she told herself that her past was behind her, this was exactly what she meant. Petty crime was a negative function of the glamour, and it was the negatives that had ruined everything before.

They left the cafeteria and returned to the car. Richard carried his stick rather than used it, but he was walking with a limp. She watched over him protectively as he lowered himself backward into the passenger seat, then swung his legs one at a time into place. These efforts at normal movements touched her, and after she had closed the door on him she stood for a moment, staring vacantly across the car's metal roof and remembering, briefly, a moment from their first affair when she had seen him running.

Soon they were back on the motorway, heading for London.

II

She found his apartment with some difficulty, in spite of his directions. She had always been scared of driving in London. After a wrong turn into a one-way system and several near misses with oncoming cars in the narrow back streets, she found the road and parked the car not too far from the front of the house.

Richard leaned forward and peered up through the windshield at the houses.

"It doesn't seem to have changed much," he said.

"Were you expecting it to?"

"It's been so long since I was here. I somehow imagined it would look different."

They left the car and went to the house. The main door led to a tiny hall with two more doors, one for the ground-floor flat and one for his own upstairs. As he fumbled with the key ring Sue watched his face, trying to judge his feelings. He revealed no expression, perhaps deliberately, and slipped the Yale key into the lock and pushed the door open. There was a rustling, scuffing sound and the door jammed briefly. He pushed again, and this time the door opened fully. On the floor at the bottom of the stairs was a huge pile of letters and newspapers, mostly newspapers.

He said, "You go first. I can't step over those."

He moved back to make room for her and she went in first, pushing the papers to one side against the wall. She scooped up as many of them as she could, and cradled them in her arms.

Richard led the way up the stairs, taking the steps slowly and carefully. She followed, thinking how strange it was to be here again, when for a time she had thought she would never even see Richard again. The place had memories for her.

At the top of the stairs he halted unexpectedly, and because she was right behind him she was forced to take a step down.

"What's the matter?" she said.

"Something wrong. I can't tell what it is."

There was a frosted-glass window built into the wall beside the stairs, but because all the room doors were closed the landing at the top was in semidarkness. The flat felt chilly.

"Would you like me to go first?" she said.

"No, it's all right."

He moved on, and she followed him onto the landing. He opened one door after another, peering inside, then moving to the next. Apart from the kitchen and bathroom, immediately to the right of the top of the stairs, there were three main rooms. The doors were old-fashioned and paneled, stained dark brown, giving the apartment a dinginess that reminded her of childhood. She remembered his saying once that one day he would get around to stripping the doors and repainting them.

She went into the living room and dumped her armload of newspapers and letters on one of the chairs. The air in the room had that indefinable smell of someone else's home, but there was also a sense of neglect, that the air had not changed in a long time. The curtains were half drawn, so she pulled them back and opened one of the windows. Street noises came in. On the sill in front of the main window was a sad row of house plants, all now dead. One of them was one she had given him as a present, *Fatsia japonica,* the castor-oil plant, but most of the leaves had fallen off and the single remaining one was brown and brittle. She stared at it, wondering whether to touch it and make it fall.

Richard walked in from the landing, looked around at the furniture, the bookshelves, the dusty television set.

"Something's different," he said. "It's been moved around." He swept his hand through his hair, lifting it away from his eyes. "I know it sounds crazy, but that's what's happened."

"Everything's the same."

"No. I knew it was different as soon as we walked in."

He swiveled around quickly, balancing his weight on his good hip, and went out again. Sue heard his irregular pace as he went down the thinly carpeted landing.

She was thinking about the first time she had been here, soon after they met. Because it was summer the

room had been full of light, and the newly painted walls
had seemed bright and refreshing; the same walls now
looked drab and cold, needing some pictures or wall hang-
ings to cheer them up. The whole flat wanted cleaning and
reviving. It brought out domestic instincts in her, but the
thought of doing housework for someone else was daunt-
ing. She was tired from the long drive, and felt like going
out for a drink.

She heard Richard moving around in the next
room, where he kept his pieces of antique film equipment,
and she went in to talk to him.

"There's a room missing, Sue!" he said at once.
"Down at the end, next to the bathroom. There used to be
a spare room!"

"I don't remember that," Sue said.

"I always had four rooms! This one, the living
room, the bedroom and a spare. Am I going mad?" He
went down the corridor and gestured at the blank wall at
the end.

"That's an outside wall," she said.

"You've been here before . . . don't you remember
it?"

"Yes. But it was just like this."

She went to him and squeezed his arm gently.
"Your memory's playing you tricks. Don't you remember
this morning, on the motorway, you said you were remembering the flat in two ways?"

"Yes, but now I'm *here.*"

He stumped away from her and limped down the
landing. Sue wondered what she could say. Unknown to
Richard she had had a private meeting with Dr. Hurdis
the day before. The psychiatrist had gone to some pains to
warn her that Richard's restoration of memory might be
only partial, in spite of what he claimed. Hurdis believed
that there were still gaps, and that some misremembered
details might be thought of as actual memories.

"But what am I to do?" Sue had said.

"Use your judgment. Most memory loss concerns small, irrelevant matters, but they can be very perplexing."

As perplexing as a room missing from a flat he thought he remembered?

Sue walked into the bedroom. Another room that smelled musty. She opened the curtains but the windows here were swollen, or seized with paint, and she could not shift them. A small fanlight opened for her. The bed stood against the wall, just inside the door. Someone had made it up, far more neatly than either she or Richard would have done it. Who could it have been? She knew the police had visited the flat after the car bomb, and suddenly she had a bizarre mental image of two uniformed policemen in helmets, painstakingly smoothing the sheets and pulling up the covers, tucking in the blankets. She smiled.

She pulled back the bedclothes, and found that the sheets were far from fresh. While Richard moved around in the other rooms she stripped the bed and struggled to turn over the mattress. This too smelled stale, but there was nothing she could do about that. She remembered there was a small airing cupboard in the bathroom, over the hot-water tank. In this she found a complete set of sheets and pillowcases, none of which smelled of damp. While she was there she switched on the electric immersion heater, thinking how, piece by piece, a home was brought back to life. With the same thought she plugged in the fridge, but nothing happened. The compressor did not start and the interior light would not come on. She went out to the landing, found the fuse box, and turned on the mains supply. The overhead light came on.

In the kitchen the fridge was whirring, but when she looked inside she discovered the white insulated walls had grown large areas of spotty black mold. A bottle of milk had separated out into a yellow liquid and a foul-smelling brown scum. She poured it away, and rinsed the bottle under the tap. She was kneeling on the floor, wiping away the mold with a damp cloth, when Richard came in.

"I suppose we ought to buy some food," he said. "Or shall we eat out this evening?"

"We could do both." She rinsed the cloth in clean water, then wiped the surfaces of the fridge once more. She stood up. "Let's get some food in for tomorrow, but eat in a restaurant tonight."

"Does that mean you're going to stay?"

"Probably." She kissed him lightly. "We ought to get your stuff into the flat. I've got to return the car this evening."

"While it's still ours, why don't we drive over to collect mine?"

"Where is it?"

"The last time I used it I parked it in the road outside your place. Unless it's been stolen, it should still be there. The battery's almost certainly dead."

"I don't remember seeing it." She frowned. "It's bright red, isn't it?"

"It was. It's probably covered in leaves and dirt now."

She said no more, but she was certain his car was not there. It had figured large in her life, and she would recognize it anywhere. He normally kept it in a rented lock-up, and she had been assuming it was there.

"Are you able to drive?" she said.

"I don't know until I try, but I think so."

The next hour was occupied with domestic tasks, and after they had returned to his flat and put away the groceries they set out on what she was convinced would be a wasted journey to find his car. The evening rush hour had begun, and driving across north London was a minor nightmare for her. At last they escaped the crush of traffic in Highgate and crossed the Archway into Hornsey. She drove slowly down her street, bringing the car to a halt outside the house.

"It's farther down," Richard said. "On the other side."

"I can't see it." But she drove the length of the street, and at the end executed an awkward turn.

As she drove back, Richard said, "I distinctly remember that I left it here. Under that tree, where the Mini is. And when I left I was too upset to drive, and walked home."

"Could you have come back for it later?"

"No, that was the day of the car bomb."

They reached her house again, and because there was a parking space opposite she pulled in and switched off the engine. Richard was obviously confused by the absence of his car, because he turned in his seat and was looking along the row of parked cars.

"Let's go back and at least look in your garage," Sue said. "It might have been moved by the police. They had all your papers, didn't they?"

"Yes. Maybe you're right."

She opened the driver's door. "I'm just going to go inside and see if there are any messages for me. Do you want to come in too?"

"I think I'll stay here."

A sudden tension in his voice made her glance at him, but his expression revealed nothing. He was scanning the parked cars that could be seen. She left the car and went to her house, searching for the keys.

Inside, she found two scribbled messages on the communal notice board beside the phone; one was from the studio, and her immediate instinct was to call them back at once. She looked at her wristwatch and realized they would have left by now. The message was undated, so it could be up to four days old. When she went into her room she found everything as she had left it. She was hardly ever here now. She took a change of clothes and underclothes from the wardrobe and thrust them into her

holdall. She had everything else she needed in her overnight bag at Richard's flat.

Alone for a few moments, she stared around the old
familiar room remembering how it had felt when she first
moved in, three years earlier. That had been her first real
attempt to reject Niall and the way of life into which he
had led her. By then she had already made the decision
which was only implemented when she met Richard, allowing Niall to hover around on the fringe of her life all
that time. She knew when she moved in that there was
more to life than Niall's way. The art-school education her
parents had given her was being wasted; she was growing
up and wanted more than a life of petty crime and useless
drifting. This room, legally rented, and paid for with
work professionally earned, had marked a new turning.
But with time it had simply become the place she lived in,
symbolic of nothing.

She returned to the car. They drove back to West
Hampstead; the traffic was lighter now, and she was beginning to learn the way, but he had to direct her to the
exact location of his garage. When he unlocked the door
they found the car inside. Two of its tires were flat and the
battery was dead, but otherwise it was just as he must have
left it, all those months ago.

III

They went to a Chinese restaurant in Camden High
Street, then returned to his flat. Using jump leads from
the rental car, they had managed to start Richard's and he
had tried driving it. He took it as far as the nearest filling

station, where they pumped up the tires, but after that he had been too fatigued for more driving.

This aside he seemed relaxed and happy, and for the first time since leaving Middlecombe he became talkative. He said he wanted to get back to work, perhaps overseas; he had always enjoyed travel. When they were back in the flat they watched the evening news on television, and he talked interestingly about the style of television reporting and how there were subtle differences between the British and American ways. He had had to learn the American style while working for the agency. After the program he even talked about trying to find a full-time job once more.

Then they went to bed, and of course she could not help thinking about the past. The physical act of love was a reminder for them both: how long ago it had been, how good it could be, how much it mattered. Afterward she lay close against him, resting her head on the side of his chest. She could see none of his scars from this position—an illusion of the past, because his injuries affected everything in the present. It had been here, in this bed and possibly in the same sheets, that they had first made love.

Neither of them was sleepy, and after a while Sue left the bed and made some tea for herself and took a can of beer from the fridge for Richard. Because the room was chilly in spite of the electric heater, she pulled on a sweater and sat facing him while he propped himself up against the pillows.

"You never did redecorate this place," she said, looking around at the room in the low light from the bedside lamp. "You said you were going to."

"Did I? I don't remember that."

"You said you'd put up some wallpaper. Or paint the walls a better color."

"Why? They look all right to me."

She smiled at him, half sitting, half lying, the beer

can held in his fingers. There was a pink latticework of graft tissue around his neck and shoulder.

"Don't you remember this?" she said.

"Have we talked about this before? The color of my walls?"

"You said you had regained your memory."

"I have, but I can't remember every tiny detail."

"This isn't a detail."

"But it can't *matter*, Sue!"

"How many more tiny details have you forgotten?" She said the words, not thinking of the warning from Dr. Hurdis until too late. And not thinking either of her own resolve to let the past lie.

"The main thing was for me to remember you. That's all that counted."

"We've got to put the past behind us."

"I can't, because I fell in love with you then and I want to remember how."

She felt again the familiar perverse excitement of their previous affair, knowing how dangerous it was to go back, yet still fatally drawn to it.

She said, "I just want to start again."

"That's what I want too. But remembering how we met, what we did together, that's crucial to me."

"You've got to let it go." He had already finished the beer, and he put the empty can on the tray she had brought for herself. "Do you want another?" she said.

"I'll get it."

"No, stay there."

She walked into the kitchen and took two more cans from the fridge. She had had to get away from him for a moment, because she felt the rapture in her, the risky thrill of wanting to try again. She stared blankly into the interior of the fridge, holding on to the open door, feeling the refrigerated air circulating down and around her naked legs. Maybe she was fooling herself to think they could be together without the glamour to link them. It had always been the condition of them, intrinsically fascinating. Richard had lost the glamour, or it had been forced out of him by the shock of his injuries; would knowledge of it now restore him to her?

She closed the fridge, went back to the bedroom. She put the two beer cans on the table next to him and sat again on top of the bed, crossing her legs and pulling down the front of the sweater into her lap.

She said, "Do you remember everything about me?"

"I thought I did. You're making me wonder."

She moved closer to him and took his hand. "You haven't really got your memory back, have you?"

"Yes I have. Most of it . . . the important events. I remember that you and I fell in love, but you had a boyfriend called Niall who wouldn't let you go, and in the end he split us up. That's what happened, isn't it?"

"That was the result, yes. Maybe that's how you remember it now."

"I remember being with you in France."

That startled her. She said, "But I've never been to France. I've never even been out of Britain. I don't have a passport."

"That's where we met . . . in France, on a train going to Nancy."

"Richard, I've never been to France."

He shook his head and drank more of the beer. "I've got to have a piss."

With some caution he swung his legs out of the bed, then limped from the room. She stared after him, trying to understand. He left both doors open, and while she waited she could hear him in the bathroom. After the toilet flushed there was just the sound of the water. At last he came back into the room, and returned to his position leaning on the pillows.

"Is that true—you've never visited France?" he said.

"I've never lied to you, Richard."

"All right, then where did we meet?"

"Here in London. A pub in Highgate."

"That *can't* be true!"

He had closed his eyes, and turned his face to the side. She felt a sudden fright, thinking how unqualified she was to cope with something like this. The doctor had been right: he had been discharged too soon; his memory was permanently affected. She looked at his scarred body, his trunk and arms not only stouter than before, but weaker too through lack of exercise. Was she wrong to challenge his memories? Were they as valid in their own way as hers? Why should he think they had met in France? It was a shock to learn this, something she could not even begin to work out.

All she knew was her own truth, the one dominant influence on her, and, in the end, on him.

She said, "Richard, do you remember the glamour?"

"Not that again!"

"So it means something to you. Do you remember what it is?"

"I don't know, and I don't want to know!"

"Then I'll show you."

A decision made, and she scrambled away from the bed, charged with purpose. The rapture of their past together had fixed itself on her, and she knew everything had to wait until this was settled. It was their condition.

"What are you doing?" Richard said.

"I want something bright-colored. Where do you keep your clothes?"

"In the chest of drawers."

But she already had one of the drawers open and was hunting through it. Almost at once she found a woolen sweater, a rich royal blue. She pulled it out. He must have used it for jobs about the house, because one of the elbows had frayed away and there was a smudge of dirt across the front. It gave her a strange, dangerous feeling to hold it, knowing that it was a dark color, something she would never choose for herself. It had a sexual quality, like picking a dress that was cut too low, or a skirt that was too short. She felt giddy.

"Look at me, Richard. Watch everything I do."

She pulled off the beige-colored sweater she was wearing, and tossed it on the bed. For a few seconds she stood naked, turning out one of the sleeves of the blue sweater so she could put it on. She pulled it over her head, wrestling her arms against its weight. As it passed over her face she briefly smelled him in it, his body, overlaid with the faint mustiness of months untouched inside the drawer. She brought her head through, and pulled the sweater down over her breasts. It was too large for her, and reached to her thighs.

"I preferred you naked," Richard said, but it was a weak joke. He was avoiding the truth of what she was about to do; he knew what was going to happen, he *knew*. It was too important for him to have forgotten. He blocked it in his mind, he somehow forced it out of his memory, but Sue knew he would remember again. Already he felt the same rapture. The peril of what she was doing coursed through her, exhilarating her.

"Look at the sweater, Richard." Her voice had thickened with her excitement. "See how dark and strong it is. Can you see?"

He was staring at her, and he nodded almost imperceptibly.

"Watch the color, don't lose sight of it."

She concentrated, thinking of the cloud, recalling the glamour to her. Once it had always been there, but now she had to force it. She felt the cloud gathering around her.

She became invisible.

Richard continued to stare at the place she had been as she moved away, unseen by him, walking to the other side of the bed.

It was always thus, like stripping in front of strangers, like those dreams of nakedness in public places. The half-guilty surge of sexual arousal, the sweet desire of becoming vulnerable. The first time you showed your glamour was always like first sex, a sudden revelation of a new self, a sacrifice, a loss of defense. Yet invisibility was secure, a concealment and a hiding, a power and a curse. Once before there had been a first time with Richard, but because he had forgotten, because his mind had been changed, there was this second first time, and the heady, sensual abandonment was there again.

She said, "Do you remember the time you saw Niall?"

And Richard turned his head sharply, a shocked expression on his face, and he looked toward the place where now she stood, invisible to him.

Part V

I

I thought I had seen you first, but Niall was always quicker than me. He had said nothing, but the moment I noticed you he was aware of that.

He said, "Come on, let's find another pub."

"I want to stay here."

It was a Saturday evening and the pub was crowded. All the tables were occupied, and many people stood in the spaces between, clustering around the bar itself. The room had a low ceiling, and cigarette smoke was thick in the air, blending with your cloud. If I had seen you earlier I had not actually noticed you, and in your seeming normality you had been paradoxically invisible to me.

I watched you from our table with all the fascination that like has for like. The woman you were with must have been a girlfriend, one you had not known long. You were trying to please her, making her laugh, paying her attention, but never touching her. She appeared to like you and smiled a lot, nodding whenever you spoke. She was a normal, and did not know what I already knew. In a sense I felt I already possessed a part of you, even though you were unaware of me. I felt predatory and excited, and waited for you to see me and recognize me.

Niall and I were both invisible that night, sitting at a small table just behind the main door, sharing it with two normals. They had not noticed us. Earlier, before I saw you, Niall and I had been arguing about his behavior. There was always something immature about him, and he had stolen a cigarette from the man's packet and used his matches to light it. It was a petty, stupid thing to do, the sort of casual trick Niall played as a matter of habit. He also insisted on getting all the drinks at the bar, going behind the counter and helping himself. He knew that if I went for the drinks I would make myself temporarily visible, wait with everyone else, and pay for them. He always interpreted this, rightly, as a gesture of resistance to him, a way of showing that for me the glamour was a partial option.

Watching you, I was wondering if you would see me. You were wholly preoccupied with your girlfriend, though, and if you glanced around the bar you did so with general eyes, looking without seeing. I thought you were very handsome, very attractive.

Niall said, "He's only incipiently glamorous, Susan. Don't waste your time."

I could not stop watching you, because it was that incipient quality that interested me. It seemed possible that you did not know, that you were only partially invisible. Your confidence in yourself was unlike any I had ever seen in an invisible, with the possible exception of Niall.

He was drinking heavily, and was pressing me to keep up with him. He relished drunkenness, lapsing into it like all the others. Sometimes when Niall was very drunk even I could barely see him. His cloud became dense, impenetrable, obscuring him.

I continued to stare at you. You were drinking moderately, obviously wanting to keep your wits about you, saving yourself for later in the evening when you would be alone with her. How I envied the woman you were with! Your cloud was thickening as the drink made you relax.

I said to Niall, "I'll get the next round."

Before he could argue I walked across to you and stood deliberately between you and your girlfriend, pretending to wait to be served by the bartender. You shifted your position to see around me, knowing subconsciously that I was there but failing to notice me. I was invisible to you, but standing so close I could feel my cloud mingling with yours, a deeply sensual imagining.

I moved away, satisfied for the moment, then went behind the counter to help myself to drinks. When I had poured them I put the money in the till, then carried the glasses back to our table.

"What were you doing, Susan?"

"I wanted to know if he could see me."

"You took too long."

"I'm just going to the Ladies'."

I left him again, thinking of the dullness in his eyes after so many pints of beer. As I crossed the room I made myself become visible, and went into the Ladies'. When I came out I walked across to you and stood beside you. Now that I was visible I could barely see your cloud, but I was almost as close as before. Then you noticed me at last, and eased back slightly.

You said, "Sorry . . . are you trying to get to the bar?"

"No. It's all right. I just wondered if you would have change for the cigarette machine?"

"The bar staff will change it for you."

"Yes, but they're busy at the moment."

You reached into your pocket and brought out a handful of coins, but there were not enough to exchange for a pound. I smiled at you and walked away, knowing you had seen me properly. Still visible, I sat down next to Niall.

"Will you quit doing this, Susan?"

"I'm not doing anything wrong."

I felt defiant. I was looking across the bar at you, hoping you would look in my direction. I was excited and nervous, feeling like a teenager again. For the first time since I had met him I did not feel intimidated by Niall. He always took me for granted, knowing that I disliked most of the other invisibles, that meeting a normal person was virtually impossible. But I had never made secret my wish for something better, and seeing you made me reckless.

I felt myself slipping back into invisibility, and as the change was completed Niall said, "Finish your drink. We're leaving."

"I'm going to stay a bit longer."

"You're wasting your time. He's not one of us."

Niall had already finished his drink and was anxious to get away and take me with him. He knew I often saw other men I found attractive, but because they were normals he felt safe from them. You were less clouded than any other invisible I had ever seen; Niall called you incipient, but I knew you simply weren't *aware* of the glamour. You appeared to be integrated into the real world, and it was this that excited me.

I too was then only partially invisible, just under the surface of normality, able to rise to visibility if I made the effort. Niall had no such choice: he was deeply invisible, profoundly lost from the world of normal people, and so he would have known immediately what you represented to me. You were the next transitional stage.

Concentrating, I forced myself into visibility again, deliberately challenging him.

"Come on, Susan. We're leaving."

"You go," I said. "I'm staying here."

"I'm not leaving without you."

"Then do what you like."

"Don't fuck around with me. There's nothing you can do about him."

"You're just scared of me meeting someone else."

"You can't do it without me," he said. "You'll revert."

I knew this was true, but stubbornly I refused to accept it. Only after meeting Niall had I perfected the technique of forming or unforming the cloud, and it was only when he was present that I could do it effortlessly. When I was alone, visibility was a constant strain and it always exhausted me. I knew that this was because my cloud had become linked with his; we had become interdependent, each of us holding on to the other long after we should have parted.

"I'm going to try anyway," I said. "If you don't like it, you can leave."

"Fuck you!"

Niall stood up suddenly, clouting the edge of the table and slopping the drinks that were standing on it. The two people opposite looked at me in surprise, thinking I had done it. I muttered an apology and slid one of the cardboard beer coasters across to soak up the splashes. Niall had gone, shoving through the crowd; the people made way for him, stepping back automatically as he elbowed past. None of them reacted, none of them really noticed him.

I stayed visible when he had left, proving to myself that I could do it. While the emotional charge was in me I found it fairly easy to sustain. I had never stood up to Niall like this before, and was amazed at my determination to do so. I knew there would be reprisals from him eventually, but at that moment I hardly gave them a thought. You were more important.

I considered carefully what to do, then got up from the table with my drink and moved to stand in the crowd around you. Now you had turned so your back was toward the rest of the people in the pub, and you were leaning with both elbows on the bar, turning your head to speak to your girlfriend. Hovering around, almost within touching distance of you, I felt predatory again, as if moving in on a victim. Because you were so unaware of me you seemed defenseless, and this gave me an extra edge of guilty excitement. I could sense your cloud, pale and incomplete, drifting around you without shape. Tendrils of it seemed to waver toward me.

I waited, and then one of the bartenders rang the bell for closing time. Several people moved toward the counter to buy their last drinks but you talked on to your friend, absorbed by her.

Then she said something to you, and you nodded and turned to your drink. She moved away from the bar, pushing past me and heading toward the Ladies'. I stepped forward and touched your arm.

I said, "I know you, don't I?"

You looked at me in surprise, then smiled. "Are you still looking for change?"

"No. It's all right. I just thought I knew you."

You shook your head slowly, and I saw in your face an expression I had sometimes seen in men when they meet a woman for the first time. It was curiosity mixed with a wish to be found interesting. I guessed that you knew many women, were always meeting more, and you did not always stay with the same one. This simple male reaction, in which you treated me as one more chance encounter with a member of the opposite sex, gave me a thrill I had not known before: you saw me as noninvisible, a normal.

"I don't think we've met," you said.

"You're here with someone, aren't you?"

"Yes."

"Do you ever come here on your own?"

"I could do."

"I'll be here next week. On Wednesday evening."

"All right," you said, and smiled. I backed away from you, feeling embarrassed by my brazenness. I had hardly known what I said, motivated only by the urgency of getting to know you better. I couldn't imagine what you were thinking, approached by a stranger in a pub, a straightforward pickup. I walked through the crowd to the door, still visible, wanting to run away from you because of what I had said, yet at the same time hoping fervently that enough had indeed been said, that you would want to see me, that you would, if only out of curiosity, come to the pub again next week.

I went outside and stood in the street. I expected to
find Niall waiting for me, but there was no sign of him. I
breathed deeply, making myself calm down, letting myself
revert naturally to invisibility. I could hear the noises
from the pub: conversation, music, and the clink of glasses
being collected. It was warm in the open air, because it
was summer, but also, because it was London, a light drizzle was falling. I was tormented by the discovery of you,
thrilled that you had treated me as normal, elated and yet
wincing inside at the directness of my approach to you. I
wondered if this was what normal people went through
when they tried to meet someone.

The pub customers were leaving, sometimes in
groups, sometimes in couples. I watched carefully for you,
hoping there was no back exit from the pub so that I
would miss you. I wanted to see you once more before you
went away, in case we never met again. At last you appeared, walking with your friend and holding her hand. I
followed you closely, hoping I would hear her say your
name or that I would pick up some other clue about you.

You walked to a side street, and I saw you go to
your car. I noticed that you held the passenger door open
for her, and closed it gently when she was seated. When
you were inside you kissed her before starting the engine.

As you drove away I memorized the number on the
license plate, thinking that if I lost you it might help me
find you again later.

II

I was born in a suburb of Manchester in the south of the city, close to the countryside of Cheshire. My parents were Scots, originally from the west coast, but they had lived for some time in Glasgow before moving farther south to England. My father worked as a payroll clerk in a large office near our house, and my mother did part-time work as a waitress. When I and my sister Rosemary were very young, she stayed at home to bring us up.

As far as I know or can remember, my childhood was normal with no hint of what I was to become. I was always the healthy one of the two girls, but my sister, three years older, was often ill. One of my clearest memories is of being told to be quiet, to tiptoe around the house so as not to disturb my sister. Silence became a habit, because I was not a rebel. I always wanted to please, and was, or tried to be, a model daughter, every mother's dream. My sister, between illnesses, was the opposite: she was a tomboy, a risk taker, a noisy nuisance about the house. I cringed and crept, wishing not to be noticed. With hindsight, it seems that it might be part of a pattern, but at the time it was only one aspect of my personality. I did the normal things of childhood: I went to school, I made friends, I had birthdays and parties, I fell down and grazed my legs and arms, I learned to ride a bicycle, I wanted to own a pony, I pasted up photographs of popstar idols.

The change in me came with puberty, and it developed gradually. I cannot remember exactly when I was aware I was different from the other girls at school, but by the time I was fifteen a distinct pattern had emerged. My family took no notice of what I was doing; teachers at school usually ignored any contributions I tried to make in class. They were all aware of me, but as I grew older it took increasing effort to impose myself on my surroundings. One by one, I drifted away from my earlier friendships. I always did well in class, and my marks were generally good, but the term-end reports talked of average ability, quiet working, steady progress. The only school subject in which I excelled was art, and this was partly from an innate ability, and partly because the art mistress made a special effort to encourage me out of school hours.

All this sounds as if my teenage years were quiet and meek, but the opposite was the case. I discovered I could get away with bad behavior. I became a talented troublemaker in class, emitting rude sounds at teachers or throwing things across the room or playing stupid pranks on the other kids. I was almost always undetected, and used to enjoy the reactions to my misbehavior. I started to steal at school, petty objects of no value, just for the sheer kick of getting away with it. And yet for all this I remained an averagely popular girl, never close to anyone but accepted by everyone.

My growing invisibility became a danger to me. When I was fourteen I was knocked down by a car, the driver claiming he had not seen me on the pedestrian crossing. I came close to being badly burned one day at home when I was leaning against the mantelpiece over an unlit gas fire and my father came in and lit the fire without realizing I was there. I remember my feelings of disbelief as it happened, being sure that he was not going to do it; I just stood there while the flame popped into life, and my skirt caught fire. My father only realized I was there when I shouted and leaped away, beating at the smoldering cloth.

Because of these incidents, and others less serious, I developed a phobia about objects and people that could hurt me. Even now I hate walking in crowded streets, or crossing roads. Although I learned to drive a few years ago, I dislike driving because I can never throw off the uneasy feeling that my driving it will make the car itself become unnoticeable. I never swim in the sea, because if I got into difficulties I might not be able to make myself seen or heard; I am nervous on the Underground, in case I am jostled on a crowded platform; I haven't ridden a bicycle since I was twelve; I've always steered clear of people carrying hot liquids since the time my mother spilled boiling tea on me.

Being unnoticed so much began to affect my health. Throughout my teens I was debilitated. I suffered one headache after another, fell asleep at inopportune moments, was prone to every infectious disease that went around. The family doctor attributed it all to "growing up," or congenital susceptibility, but I now know the real cause was my unconscious attempt to stay visible. I *wanted* to be noticed, to be thought the same as everyone else, to live an ordinary life. The wish manifested itself by forcing me into visibility. Throughout those late school years I must always have been sliding into and out of invisibility, impinging in varying degrees on the people around me.

The only relief from this strain was solitude. During the long school holidays, and sometimes on weekends, I frequently went off by myself into the countryside. The suburbs were spreading out from the city, but even so it was only a short bus journey south, past Wilmslow and Alderley Edge, to a still undeveloped landscape of farmland and woods. Out there, away from the main roads, I could draw a quiet strength from being on my own, from not having to force myself to be noticed.

It was on one of these trips, when I was about sixteen, that I met Mrs. Quayle.

It was she who first saw me, and she who made the approach. I was only aware of a pleasant-looking middle-aged woman walking along the lane toward me, a small

dog running at her heels. We passed each other, smiled
briefly as strangers sometimes do, and went on in our separate directions. I thought no more about her, but then
her dog ran past me, and I realized she had turned around
and was following behind.

We spoke, and the first words she said to me were,
"Dear, do you know that you have glamours?"

Because she was smiling, and because she looked so
ordinary, I felt no alarm, but I suppose that had I known
what she was I would have been frightened and hurried
away. Instead, the oddness of her question interested me
and I walked along with her, chattering inanely about the
countryside. I somehow never answered the question
then, nor did she repeat it. She shared my love of the
country, the wild flowers and the peacefulness, and that
was enough. We came eventually to her house, a cottage
set well back from the lane. She invited me in for a cup of
tea.

Inside, the house was pleasant and well furnished,
with central heating, a television set, a stereo, telephone,
and other modern fittings. She sat down on the sofa to
pour the tea, and her dog curled up beside her and went to
sleep.

Then the conversation returned to where we had
begun, and she asked me again about my "glamours." Of
course I had no idea what she was talking about, and being
the age I was I said so. She asked me if I believed in magic,
if I ever had strange dreams, if I could sometimes tell what
other people were thinking. She had become intent, and
this scared me. As soon as she saw me, she said, she had
known that I was possessed of glamours, that I had
psychic powers. Was I aware of this? Did I know anyone
else like me?

I said I wanted to leave, and stood up. Her manner
changed at once, and she apologized for frightening me.
As I left she told me to call again if I wanted to know
more, but outside in the lane I ran and ran, full of fears of

her. The following week, though, I returned to her cottage, and over the next two years I made repeated visits to see her.

I now know that what Mrs. Quayle told me was only a part of the story, and that it was influenced by her own special interests. She once described herself as a psychic, but never fully explained. I sometimes thought she might be a witch, but was always too scared to ask. It was she, though, who awakened me to the true nature of my special condition, and who gave me some idea of the extent and limitations of inherent invisibility.

The glamours she had seen around me, she said, were a kind of psychic aura emitted by those in touch with natural powers. She told me that I could instinctively intensify or weaken this "cloud," and within this projection from the astral plane my glamours could be worked. She told me of Madame Blavatsky, the spiritualist and Theosophist, who recorded many accounts of productions and vanishings through use of the cloud, and who claimed to be able to make herself invisible. Of the Ninja sect in medieval Japan, who made themselves invisible to their enemies by use of deception and distraction. Of Aleister Crowley, who declared invisibility a simple doctrine, one he claimed to have proved by parading around the streets in a scarlet robe and golden crown while no one noticed him. And of the novelist Bulwer Lytton, who believed himself capable of invisibility and tried to surprise his friends by moving among them before revealing himself. She taught me folklore, such as collecting the spores of ferns, possession of which was supposed to impart invisibility.

I only half believed what she told me, even then. I knew I was not psychic, that I was incapable of magic, but Mrs. Quayle would admit of no other possibility. Because I knew no better I accepted that at least some of it was true.

It was Mrs. Quayle who showed me, with a mirror, that I was invisible.

I had always been able to see myself in mirrors because I looked for myself, as everybody does, and in looking I noticed and *saw*. But one day Mrs. Quayle tricked me, placing a mirror in an unexpected position beyond a door and following me as I walked toward it. Before I realized what it was I saw the reflection of her behind me, and for two or three seconds, while I wondered at what I was seeing, I noticed no reflection of myself. Then I saw, and understood at last: I was not invisible in the sense that I was transparent, or that I could not be seen, but that the cloud somehow obscured me, made me difficult to be *noticed*. The effect was the same, explaining to me why most people reacted as if I were not there.

Mrs. Quayle could always see me, even when I was invisible to others—even, that time with the mirror, when I was briefly invisible to myself. She was a funny, single-minded woman, plain and ordinary in every way but the one she claimed. She was a widow, living alone, surrounded by prosaic snapshots of her family, by artefacts of the modern consumer society, by souvenirs of Italy and Spain. Her son was in the Merchant Navy, both her daughters were married and lived in another part of the country. She was a practical, down-to-earth woman who helped me a lot, and who filled my head with ideas and gave me a vocabulary for what I am and for what I can do. We became friends in an odd, unequal way, but she died suddenly, of angina, a few months before I moved to live in London.

My meetings with her were occasional, and sometimes separated by several months. I was finishing at school during the time I knew her, creeping almost unnoticed through "O" and "A" levels, passing my subjects with medium marks, gaining a distinction only in art. The strain to stay visible continued, and my last year at school was punctuated by fainting attacks or bouts of migraine. I was completely relaxed only when I was with Mrs. Quayle, and her death, just before I sat my "A" level exams, made me feel isolated and helpless.

On my eighteenth birthday my parents produced a surprise. They had taken out a small endowment policy for me when I was born, and now it had matured. I had been offered a place at an art college in London, but the only grant I qualified for would cover just the fees, not living expenses. The endowment policy was almost enough, and my father said he was prepared to make up the rest. At the end of the summer I left home for the first time in my life, and traveled to London.

III

Three years. College is a time of transition for every student: the growing away from school friends and family, mixing with an entirely new group of people of your own age, acquiring skills or knowledge for use in adult life, taking shape for the first time as an independent human being. All these happened to me, but something unique to me also changed. I came to terms with the fact of my invisibility, knowing that it was a part of me and would not go away.

I shared a flat with two other girls from the college. Although I made myself visible to them when I had to, for most of the three years they took for granted that I was somewhere around, closed away inside my own room, separate from them. This was the first change forced on me, because through them I learned that an invisible person is simply ignored, accepted as being there but not somehow *functioning.* They noticed me when I wished them to, and the rest of the time they acted as if I were not there.

College itself was more difficult. I was required to attend, and to be seen to attend, and to complete my courses and submit work and in general make my presence felt. I survived the first year by extending myself and establishing myself with the tutors, but at the expense of my health. From the beginning of the second year the strain was in theory eased, because we were encouraged to work alone more. I chose a large but general course in commercial art, because here, when working with others, I could blend with the crowd. Even so, the strain of being visible was continual and my exhaustion was a major problem. I lost weight, suffered recurring headaches and was frequently nauseated.

Living in London brought another change. At home I had grown used to eluding authority. At school it was the stupid pranks, the meaningless thievery, but away from school I had learned that I could get away with not paying fares, that if I used shops I never had to spend money unless I chose to. Now that I was in London and surviving on a tiny and fixed income, it soon became a habit to avoid payment. From there it became a way of life.

Living in a big city was a part of this corruption, because in London it is possible even for normal people to lose themselves in the crowd. After the first few weeks, in which I was psychologically adjusting to life in a major city, I felt more at home than I would ever have thought possible. London is made for invisibles; it deepened my state of anonymity, made my condition a natural means of survival. No one has identity in London unless it is claimed.

I bought a ticket the very first time I used the Underground, not knowing how the system worked. That was, literally, the last time I paid my fare. After that, swallowing my fear of the crowds, I used the trains and buses as my free taxi service, the cinemas and theaters for my free entertainment. None of this took anything from anybody: public transport would run whether or not I used it, the shows would be on regardless of my presence. I never took a seat that should have been occupied by someone who had paid, so kept my conscience clear. But these were still the early days.

A combination of need and opportunity took me farther into the state I thought of as the shadow world. Unless I had taken a part-time job, as one of the girls I shared with was forced to do, I could not have survived without stealing. Because of my constant debilitation, a job was never a real option anyway.

And invisibility refreshed me. A day in my shadow world, drifting unnoticed along streets and through buildings, gave me a feeling of power. To extend that and quietly steal whatever I needed made me feel vindicated. This was the function of invisibility, to move on the outer limits of the real world undetected, unseen. It always gave me a thrill to steal from out of the shadows, knowing that I was doing wrong, that I could never be caught. I never tired of this, and fled into the shadows as a cure for the emotional and physical drain caused by trying to be real.

Invisibility fitted me like old, familiar clothes.

Because I did not know how to see, and was concerned mostly with my own readjustments, it took me several months to realize I was not alone. There were other invisibles in London.

The first one I noticed was a girl about my own age. I was waiting for a train in an Underground station. As I glanced along the platform I saw her sitting on a bench, leaning back against the tiles of the curving tunnel wall. She looked tired, dirty and distraught. As I looked at her I felt there was something familiar about her without understanding why. The tube stations have many down-and-outs moving around them, usually in winter, and by her appearance she was one of these.

She moved, and sat up to look around. She saw me, and stared at me in momentary surprise. Then, losing interest, she looked away again.

My first reaction was terror. She had *noticed* me! But I was invisible, secure in my shadow world! I hurried away into one of the access tunnels, frightened at the ease with which my cloud had been penetrated. I reached the concourse at the bottom of the escalators, where dozens of people were moving about, heading up to the streets above, riding down to catch one of the trains, all of them moving past me as if I were not there. The renewal of my anonymity reassured me, and I became more interested than frightened. Who was she? How could she see me?

Sensing the answer I went back to the platform, but a train had been in and out and she was no longer there.

The second time it happened, the invisible was a middle-aged man. I saw him in Selfridges department store in Oxford Street, moving quietly around with a plastic bag in his hand. I sensed the same aura about him, and recognized the calm, unfurtive way he was stealing the goods. His condition was the same as mine. When I was sure I moved around so that I was in front of him, and walked directly toward him.

His reaction appalled me. He looked surprised, not because I was another invisible but because he interpreted my smile and my open expression as a sexual advance. He looked me up and down, then to my horror raised his bag and crammed it under his arm and moved toward me with a dreadful leering smile. What I remember is the sudden sight of his teeth: they were black and broken. I backed away from him, but his eyes were fixed on mine. He said something, but in the clamor of the store I could not hear what it was; there was no need, because I could guess what he said. He looked huge. All I wanted was to correct my blunder and get away from him. I turned to run and collided with someone, another man, but he was unaware of me. The invisible man was almost on me, reaching out with his free arm, the hand clawing to grab me. I knew that being in a public place offered no safety, that if he caught me he could do anything he liked in full view of everyone. I had never been so frightened. I rushed away, dodging between the shoppers, knowing he was behind me. I wanted to scream, but no one would hear me! It was lunchtime, there were hundreds of people in the store, and none of them moved to get out of the way. In a crowd like that there was no help, only obstacles. I looked back at him once again: he was running with terrifying agility, his face violently angry, a predator deprived of his prey. This glimpse of him so scared me that I nearly fell. My legs were weak, and the fear almost paralyzed me. I knew I was plunging deeper into invisibility—my instinctive defense, but useless against this man. I pushed through the crowd, aiming for the closest exit.

When I next looked back I was in the street, and the man had given up. I saw him by the entrance to the store, leaning against the wall, winded, watching me flee. Even then he was still utterly menacing, and I continued down the street, running until I could not keep going. I never saw him again.

These two encounters were my introduction to the larger shadow world of the invisibles. After the incident in Selfridges I began to notice more and more invisibles around London—as if seeing one or two had opened my eyes to the rest—but I kept out of their way. I learned the places where they generally gathered, somewhere that food could be stolen or a bed found or crowds tended to congregate. I usually saw at least one other invisible person whenever I went to a supermarket, and department stores were frequent haunts. Some invisibles lived permanently in large stores; others drifted around, sleeping in hotels or breaking into people's houses to borrow unused beds or stretch out on furniture. Later I discovered that this underground network had a semblance of organization: there were known meeting places, even a particular pub where some of them gathered regularly.

Inevitably I was drawn to them. I learned that the man who had attacked me in Selfridges was not typical of them, but neither was he all that unusual. As male invisibles grew older they became loners, moving on the periphery of society, uncaring of how they acted. Normal friendships were impossible except with other invisibles, forcing abnormal behavior. Lonely outcasts, thinking themselves above the law, are dangerous in any form.

The typical invisible would be young, or youngish. He or she—the sexes were more or less evenly divided—would have had an isolated adolescence, and been drawn to London or one of the other big cities out of a need to meet others.

Collectively the invisibles were a paranoid group, believing themselves rejected by society, despised, feared, and forced into crime. They were terrified of normal people but envied them profoundly. Most of them were frightened of each other, but when in each other's company would brag about their individual achievements. There were even some who took the paranoia to the other extreme, attempting to make claims for the inherent superiority of invisibles, the power and freedom of their condition being paramount.

The invisibles seemed to have two traits in common. In the first place, almost every one I met was a hypochondriac, and with good reason. Health was an obsession, because illness was incurable except by nature. Many of the invisibles had VD, and all of them suffered with their teeth. Life expectancy was low, partly because of the risk of illness and partly because of the vagrant lifestyle and irregular diet. A large number of them were alcoholics or incipient alcoholics. Drug taking was not, in general, a problem, because of the difficulties of supply. Most of the invisibles dressed well, because clothes were easy to steal, but few cared about their appearance. What they most cared about was their health, and many of them carried about with them large quantities of patent medicines, the only ones they could steal with any regularity.

The second unifying factor was the cloud. Meeting other invisibles, I began to understand what I had thought was Mrs. Quayle's mysticism. Each invisible person is surrounded by an aura, a certain density of presence, and this can be detected by the others. It was what I had instinctively recognized in my first two encounters, and what Mrs. Quayle, in a different way, had noticed about me. Her talk of ectoplasm and spiritual auras had confused me, but I realized now that this was simply her way of describing it.

Interestingly, though, the invisibles had picked up the same vocabulary and incorporated it into their slang. They all knew about the cloud, and called it that. Ordinary people were fleshers; the real world was hard. To themselves, they were the glams. It was part of their defensive but bragging paranoia to think of themselves as glamorous.

IV

I was not one of them. I knew it and they knew it. From their point of view I was only half-glam, able to enter and leave their world at will. I was never trusted, never accepted, always betrayed by my clean clothes, my equanimity about illness, by my cared-for, unhurting teeth. I had an identity in the hard world, a place I lived in, a college course to attend. I went home to my parents at Christmas and Easter, escaping, as the invisibles saw it, to the world of the fleshers.

Even so, entering the glamorous world was important to me. For the first time since my early teens I was meeting people like myself. That to them my invisibility was a question of degree made no difference to me. I was more invisible than visible, and this constantly affected me. The glams tried to reject me, but only because for most of them there was no escape.

There was another attraction too. I had always found invisibility refreshing, making the next return to the hard world that little bit easier. Once I met the real invisibles—pathetic, frightening and isolated as I found them to be—I discovered that the option of visibility was more accessible. At first I was repelled by their hopelessness and paranoia, but later I found them a source of strength.

Contact with their clouds gave me the energy to reenter the real world, and knowing them gave me the thrill of the glamorous life. I was still very young, and I was attracted to both.

Then, in my last term at college, when I knew I was going to have to make new decisions, and when I was less certain than ever of how I wanted to live, I met Niall.

V

Niall was different from any other invisible I had ever met. He was profoundly glamorous, completely unnoticeable by anyone who was not another invisible, his cloud a dense screen against the world. He was more deeply embedded than any of the others, more remote from reality, a thin wraith in a community of ghosts.

But his separateness was also in his personality.

While most invisibles lamented their lack of identity, he relished his.

He was the only invisible I ever found physically attractive. He was fit, handsome, elegant. He was at ease in his body, and worried no more about illness than I ever did. He dressed rakishly, choosing the most modern clothes and the most flowery colors. He smoked Gauloises cigarettes and traveled light; the average glam worried too much about his health to smoke, and carried vast amounts of belongings wherever he went. Niall was funny, outspoken, rude to people he disliked, full of ideas and ambitions, and completely amoral. While I and some of the other glams had scruples about our parasitic lives, Niall saw invisibility as freedom, an extension of normal abilities.

Something else I found attractive and different about him was that he was *doing* something. Niall wanted to be a writer. He was the only invisible who ever stole books. He was always in and out of libraries and bookstores, borrowing or stealing poetry, novels, literary biographies, travel books. He was always reading, and when we were together he would sometimes read aloud to me. Books were the only part of his life where he was not amoral: when he was finished with one he would leave it somewhere it could be found, or would even return it. Paddington Library was the one he frequented, conscientiously returning what he had borrowed, and sometimes pretending guilt to me if he thought the book was overdue.

When he was not reading he was writing. He filled innumerable notebooks with his work, writing slowly in his ornate and flamboyant handwriting. I was never allowed to see what he had written, nor did he read it to me, but I was supremely impressed.

This was Niall when I first met him, and I fell under his spell at once. He was a few months younger than I, but in every other way he was wiser, more exciting, more experienced, more stimulating than anyone I had ever

known. When I finished at art school and came away with
my diploma, I no longer had any doubt about what I
wanted to do. The glamour had become a sanctuary from
the hard world, and I fled into it.

The sheer excitement of being with Niall swept
aside any doubts. Everything we did was enhanced by ir-
responsibility, and because I admired him I tried to im-
press him by being like him. We brought out the worst in
each other, his amorality satisfying my wish for a better
life.

I became thoroughly assimilated into the glamorous
world. We lived nowhere, and drifted from one overnight
stay to the next; we slept in the spare room in someone's
house, or went to a department store or hotel. We ate well,
having nothing but fresh food stolen as we needed it.
When we wanted cooked food we went to the kitchens of
hotels or restaurants. We always had as many new clothes
as we wanted, we were never cold, never hungry, never
forced to sleep outdoors.

It was Niall who showed me how to break into
banks and steal from post offices, but money was something we never needed. A bank robbery was always a dare,
done for the sheer fun of it, entering the staff area in full
view of the employees, taking a handful of bank notes
from the cash drawers, riffling them unnoticed in front of
their faces. Sometimes we would steal only a few coins or
a note or two, just to prove we could do it. We were never
silent during a robbery, talking to each other as we went,
sometimes laughing aloud or singing with the glee of being unseen and unheard.

I feel guilty about this now, looking back. I was
easily impressed, and Niall was awakening the restlessness
in me, the last stirring of immaturity.

In time I grew less dazzled by him. I saw that he
was not so original after all, that many people in the real
world affected bright colors, unusual hairstyles, French
cigarettes. Niall was different only in comparison with the

other invisibles, and they no longer mattered to me. His interest in books and in becoming a writer was still admirable, but I was always held at arm's length from this. I continued to find his personality attractive, but with increasing familiarity I realized most of what impressed me was superficial.

Even so, our reckless life as invisibles carried on for about three years. It all runs together now in my memory, blurring into what I would like to think of as an adolescent escapade. But I still often remember specific incidents, when the heady feeling returns to me of how clever and superior we thought we were. It was an ideal life; everything we wanted was literally within our grasp, and we never answered to anyone.

Internal changes were taking place too. Because of my constant closeness to Niall, I drew strength from his cloud. I found it increasingly easy to move into visibility, and it was this that started to erode our relationship.

Niall hated it when I was visible. It gave me an advantage over him. If he ever saw me visible, and he always knew when I had made the change, he would claim that I was endangering us both, risking discovery. The reality was that he was deeply resentful of his condition, and his bravado was a front. He was jealous of me, and my ability to move in the real world was a freedom from him.

Or that's how he saw it. The paradox was that this very strength came from him. I needed to be close to him to gain the normality I had always craved, and which he so feared, but the closer I drew the more dependent on him I became.

Other needs were surfacing. As I grew older I began to develop a conscience about the money and goods we were stealing. A culminating incident occurred in a supermarket: as we were leaving I saw an open till full of cash, and on an impulse I took a handful of five-pound notes. It was a foolish and needless theft, because money was superfluous. A few days later I found out that the woman on the checkout had lost her job as a result, and this was the first time I realized that other people were being hurt. It was a sobering realization, changing everything.

More subtly, though, I was hungering for an ordinary way of life; I wanted the dignity of a real job, the knowledge that I earned what I lived by. I wanted to pay my way, buy food and clothes, pay to see movies, pay to travel on buses and trains. Above all I wanted to settle down, find somewhere I could call home, a place that was mine.

None of this was possible unless I was prepared or able to be visible for substantial periods of time. While I lived the rootless life with Niall, that was out of the question.

Then these stirrings took a positive shape. I wanted to go home, see my parents and sister, wander around in places I remembered. I had been away too long, because I had not been back since meeting Niall. My only contact with home was the occasional letter I wrote to my parents, but even this had been taken by Niall as a breach of our compact of invisibility. In the last twelve months I had written home only once.

I was growing up at last, and it was taking me away from Niall. I wanted something more than he was giving me; I could not spend the rest of my life in the shadows.

Niall sensed the change, and he knew I was trying to break away from him.

We reached a compromise about my parents, and one weekend went to see them together. I cannot imagine what I had hoped this would achieve, because I knew in my bones that it would lead to disaster.

Everything started to go wrong from the moment we arrived. I had never before seen at close hand how normal people react to the presence of an invisible, and the fact that these were my parents, from whom I was already partly estranged, only added layers of emotional complexity. I was visible throughout my stay, able to maintain it without much effort because Niall was there, but Niall remained unnoticed. I was trying to cope with three different problems simultaneously: I wanted to behave toward my parents in a natural way, relax with them, tell them something of my life in London without revealing the truth; I was constantly aware that they could not see that Niall was with me; and Niall himself, no longer the focus of my interest, began to behave badly.

Most of all it was Niall. He callously exploited the fact that they did not know he was there. When my parents were asking how I lived, who my friends were, what work I was doing, and I was attempting to answer with the bland lies I had been using in the few letters I had written, Niall was beside me, talking across me, giving them (unheard) the answers he felt they should have. When we sat down in the evening to watch television, Niall, bored with their choice of program, started touching my body to distract me. We drove over to see my sister so that I could meet her new husband, but Niall, getting into the back seat beside me, whistled loudly and talked across my parents, infuriating me but leaving me helpless to do anything about it. All through that weekend I was never allowed to forget Niall was there: he stole drinks and cigarettes, yawned boredly whenever my father spoke. He lounged around, used the toilet without flushing it, objected to every suggestion anyone made about where we could go or who we might see—in short he did everything in his power to remind me that he was the true center of my life.

How could my parents not have known he was there? It was the most uncanny and disturbing sensation because even setting aside Niall's abominable behavior, it seemed impossible they could not be aware of him. Yet I was greeted and he was not; they spoke only to me, looked only at me; no place was set for him at mealtimes; I was given the single bed in my old room; even in the cramped

confines of my father's car, no acknowledgment was made
of his presence. Trying to cope with this—the blatant contradiction between what I knew was happening and how
my parents were reacting to it—was my major preoccupation. I knew how they had reacted to my own invisibility
in the old days, but then there had always been ambigu-
ities. This was different: Niall was emphatically there, but
somehow they could not see him. Even so, I was convinced that on some deeper level they were aware of him.
His invisible presence created a vacuum, a silent nexus of
the whole weekend.

For me it made real the fact that my life in London
was a rebellion against my background. I found my father
dull and inflexible, my mother prissily concerned over details that did not interest me. I loved them still, but they
could not see that I was growing up, that I was not, and
never would be again, the child-daughter they had
glimpsed a few years before. This was Niall's influence on
me, of course, and his sardonic interjections, heard only
by me, were a continual counterpoint to my own
thoughts.

As the visit progressed I felt more and more isolated—cut off from my parents by misunderstandings,
alienated from Niall by his behavior. We had been planning to stay for three nights, but after a blazing row with
Niall on the Saturday—invisible together in the bedroom,
shouting at each other in cocoon of our protective clouds
—I could stand the strain no longer. In the morning my
parents drove me, us, to the station, and there we said
goodbye. My father was stiff and white with suppressed
anger, my mother was in tears. Niall was jubilant, dragging me back, as he thought, to our invisible life in London.

But none of that could ever be the same. Soon after
we reached London I left Niall. I made myself visible, I
integrated with the real world. I was escaping from Niall
at last, and I tried to make sure he would never find me.

VI

He found me. I had been living in the glamorous world too long, and didn't know how to survive without stealing. Niall knew our haunts better than I did, and one day two months later he was there.

I had had enough time, though, and something had changed. In my two months of solitude I had rented a room, the place I still live in. It was mine, and although it was not yet earned it was full of stuff I thought of as mine, it had a door and a lock, and it was a place I could *be*. It meant more to me than anything else in my life, and nothing would make me relinquish it. I was still surviving by theft, but I was full of resolve. I was slowly working up a portfolio of drawings, I had contacted one of my old tutors, and had already visited one editor in the hope of getting commissions. A free-lance life, with all its difficulties, was my only real hope of independence.

But Niall walked back into my life assuming we would continue as before. He understood better than anyone what the room signified to me, but I made the mistake of letting him in. I showed it off to him proudly, thinking that he would have to accept that I had changed, that by showing it to him I was implying that he could be included in my new life.

What it really meant, I quickly discovered, was that he always knew where to find me when he wanted me. This was the worst of it: he would turn up at any time of the day or night, wanting company, wanting reassurance, wanting sex. My independence made him change, and I saw a new side of him: he became possessive, sulky, bullying.

I held on, knowing that the room and what it stood for were my only hope of a better life.

Through my tenuous contacts I started to sell a little work: an illustration for a magazine article, some layout work for an advertising agency, some lettering for a firm of management consultants. The fees were small to begin with, but one piece of work led gradually to another, and I became known for what I could do. Commissions started to turn up without my seeking them, I was recommended by one editor to another, I made contact with a small independent studio that gave me free-lance work. I opened a bank account, had some letterheads printed, bought a proper desk, and by such tokens felt I was establishing myself in the visible world. As soon as I started earning money I cut my stealing back to the absolute essentials, and when the checks began arriving with reasonable frequency I stopped altogether. It became an article of my faith in myself that I would never go back, and although there were difficult times I never weakened. I derived real pleasure from making myself visible to cash a check, to line up with everyone else at supermarket checkouts, to try on dresses in clothing stores and produce my checkbook for payment. As a final gesture I took driving lessons, and passed the test at the second attempt.

The strain of being visible was also less. By working at home I could relax inside the glamour as long as I wished, only becoming visible if I went out. I achieved an emotional stability I had never known before.

Even Niall began to accept that it was permanent. He knew that the old days were gone for good, and he adjusted to that, but he also had a claim on me he could always exploit. Only I understood the profundity of his invisibility, how impossible it was for him ever to become normal. He played on my sympathy for this, blackmailing me with it. If I tried to cut myself off from him, he pleaded with me not to abandon him. He pointed out the advantages I had over him, the stability I had achieved, hinting at the misery and loss he had always to endure. I invariably capitulated. I saw him as a tragic figure, and even as I knew he was manipulating me I let him get away with it.

He would not let me grow away from him, and used his invisibility against me. When I started a tentative friendship with one of the young illustrators at the studio and fixed up an evening with him, Niall put on such a display of recriminations and wounded jealousy that I almost canceled the date. I had never had a real boyfriend, though, and was determined to stand up for myself. I went on my date, an evening of total innocence, but it was ruined by Niall. Niall followed, Niall hung around, Niall interfered. It led to a furious row that night, back in my room, and the seedling romance was crushed. I never tried again.

This was the worst of Niall, but it was not all of him. So long as I remained sexually faithful to him and was available whenever he chose to see me and did not make any more overt gestures toward the hard world, then he left me to live and work as I chose.

He was not always around me; sometimes he would vanish for a week or two at a time, never explaining where he had been. He told me he had found a place to live, although how he managed it or where it was I never discovered. He claimed to have friends, never named, who owned property where he could come and go as he pleased. He told me he had started writing in earnest, and was submitting his work to publishers. He dropped hints about other women, presumably hoping to arouse my possessiveness, but if they were true nothing would have pleased me more; anyway, in Niall's amoral world view, sexual fidelity was a one-sided matter, and I had always assumed he slept with other women when he felt like it.

Above all, he allowed me to work, to live on the fringes of the real world, to develop self-respect. In my

distorted life, cursed by natural invisibility, it seemed to
be the best I could hope for.

Then, that night in the pub in Highgate, I saw you.

VII

After the excitement of talking to you, my preoccupation
was Niall and what he would do in revenge.

Your glamour was so faint that you were probably
unaware of it. It was like an aura of sexuality, the more
potent for being unconscious. I had felt the touch of your
cloud, and the stimulus of it made me dizzy. It was un-
shaped, unused; invisibility was an option—you were the
converse of me.

What Niall and I both knew was that you could
lead me to the real world. I could draw strength from your
cloud, make myself visible with ease and permanence, pass
for normal.

You were to Niall more potentially threatening
than even a fully visible man; you could take me from him
for good.

I dreaded what Niall would do, because I thought I
knew him. I expected his bullying, his blackmail, his usual
tears, the self-pitying but contrived pleas about his hopeless invisibility. I braced myself against his violence. Yet in
the pub he had left us alone, freeing me to approach you.

After you had driven away with your girlfriend, I
walked back to Hornsey in the light rain, joyful at the
meeting but terrified of its consequences with Niall. I was
ready for the worst.

But Niall was not waiting for me. He was not in
the street outside, not hanging around in the hall. I let

myself into the room, convinced that he had used his copy key to enter it—but he was not there either, and nothing had been disturbed.

I was awake most of the night, certain he would turn up in the end. I waited through Sunday, trying to get on with some work. Niall made no contact with me then, nor on Monday, nor on Tuesday. I managed to complete the commission I was working on and took it into the West End to deliver it, again expecting Niall to contact me.

I wanted to get it over with. I hated his blustering threats, but at least I was used to them and within certain limits could deal with them. Whether by instinct or planning, Niall had hit on the perfect way of making his feelings known. By leaving me alone and making me wonder what he would do, he succeeded in getting my full interest.

And inside that, a moment of panic. Suppose Niall could make himself invisible even to *me!*

The thought had never occurred to me before. I could always see Niall, even when his cloud was densest, but then how would I know? Had there been times in the past when he had concealed himself from me? I was halfway in the real world; suppose Niall could move below my threshold of sight? He had often revealed an uncanny knowledge of me, an almost supernatural degree of insight. Did he watch me when I thought I was alone? Niall was clever and unscrupulous. How far would he go to protect what he saw as his interests?

Suppose he had not actually left the pub? He might have been there when I spoke to you, followed me as I followed you, haunted me as I walked home in the rain.

He could be with me now! In my room, even as I thought of it!

Truly terrified, I sat at my drawing board, head bent and eyes closed. I knew then the primal fear of ghosts, the terror of the invisible, of the concealed

watcher. I listened for his breathing, for the faintest movement of his clothes. The room was silent, and when I
turned my head, fearful of both seeing and not seeing, I
formed my cloud more densely than ever before, hoping
to know the truth.

There was nothing I could see.

The telephone rang late on the Wednesday afternoon. I was not expecting to hear from anyone so I let it
ring, thinking someone else would answer it. After a long
time it was still ringing, so I went into the hall and picked
it up.

It was Niall, speaking from a private phone. I felt a
surge of relief, because only then was I certain he was not
invisible somewhere around me.

"I'm going away for a while," he said. "I thought
you'd like to know."

"Where are you going?"

"Some friends of mine own a house in the South of
France. I thought I might stay with them for a week or
two."

"All right," I said. "That's a good idea."

"Don't you want to come with me?"

"You know I'm working."

"You're seeing that man, aren't you?"

"I might be."

"When is it? This evening?"

"I haven't arranged anything yet."

Silence from Niall. I waited, staring at the wall
with its notice board full of old messages for the other
tenants. Their lives always seemed so straightforward to
me, so uncomplicated by unseen matters. Anne, please
phone Seb. Dick, your sister called. Party at No. 27 on
Saturday night, all invited.

I said, "How long did you say you'd be gone?"

"I haven't decided yet. A couple of weeks. Maybe
longer. I'll call you when I get back."

"When will that be?"

"I've told you, Susan, I don't know. It shouldn't matter to you now, should it? You're going to be busy."

"I'm going to be working."

"I know what you'll be doing."

The conversation was a fraud. It was completely unlike Niall to go away, especially if he knew I had met someone else. He was planning something, and we both knew it.

"Where exactly are you going to be?" I said.

"I'll call you when I get there. Or send a card. I don't know the exact address. It's a house somewhere near Saint-Raphaël."

"But who are these people you'll be staying with? Do I know any of them?"

"Why should that matter? You'll be having fun without me."

"Niall, you're jumping to conclusions. I just want to talk to him, that's all. I don't know anything about him."

"I can tell you something. His name's Richard Grey."

"How the hell do you know that?" Suddenly, my heart started thumping.

"I make it my business to find things out."

"What else do you know?"

"That's about all. I'm going to hang up now. We're leaving in an hour."

"If you're thinking of interfering, Niall, I'll never speak to you again."

"You've nothing to worry about. You won't see me for a while."

"Niall! Don't hang up!"

"I'll send you a card from France."

He put the phone down. I stood in the hallway, fuming with anger and fear. How had he found out your name? What had he been up to? What was he doing now? I *knew* he was lying to me about going away, because his voice had a familiar threatening tone. In this mood he was capable of anything. He never ran away from me when he wanted to control me.

Back inside my room, I sat on the edge of my bed and tried to calm down. There were only another two hours before I was due to meet you, and Niall had succeeded in driving you from my mind. I loathed his cleverness: he knew that I would stand up to him somehow, but appearing to relent was a deliberate new tactic. I was thinking about him, not about you.

It was hopeless trying to get any more work done, so I showered and changed, then spent some time tidying up my room. I had nothing to eat, because Niall had ruined my appetite.

I set off for Highgate far too early, walking quickly to burn off my nervous energy. When I reached the High Street I started to dawdle, looking in the shop windows, staring without seeing. I was invisible, saving myself for later. I was trying to concentrate on you, remember what you looked like, recall that feeling of excitement when I had seen you. I knew in my heart that this would mean the end of Niall, and even though I knew nothing about you the risk and novelty were preferable to the past.

After eight o'clock I made myself visible and went into the bar where we had met. You were not there. I bought myself a half of bitter, then sat alone at one of the tables. Because it was midweek and still relatively early, the pub was less than half full. I let myself sink into invisibility.

You arrived a few minutes later; I saw you enter the bar, look briefly around it, then go to the counter. What struck me first was how normal you looked, just as I remembered you. I became visible, and waited for you to see me.

Niall slipped from my mind.

You walked over, smiling, and stood by the table.

"Can I get you another drink?" you said.

"No, thanks. Not at the moment."

You sat down, across the table from me. "I was wondering if you'd be here."

"I can't imagine what you must have thought," I said. "I don't normally approach strange men in pubs."

"It's all right," you said. "I don't—"

"You see, I thought I recognized you." I wanted to get through my explanation, the only one I had been able to invent. "You look like someone I used to know, but once I'd spoken to you I knew I was wrong and I didn't know what to say next." It sounded lame, but you were still smiling.

"Don't explain any more. I was glad to meet you."

I had reddened, remembering my clumsy approach to you. We talked for a while about the mythical friend you were supposed to resemble, and then at last we exchanged names. I was both pleased and irritated to learn that Niall had been right about your name. I told you I was called Sue; everyone I had ever known called me Susan, but I liked the idea of becoming Sue to someone I had newly met.

We had a few more drinks, talking about the sorts of things I had always presumed normal people discussed when getting to know each other—what we did for a living, where we lived, places we both knew, possible mutual friends, anecdotes about ourselves. You told me frankly about the woman you had been with, that her name was Annette, that she was an occasional girlfriend, that she had gone away for a month to visit relatives. I said nothing about Niall.

You suggested a meal, so we crossed the road to an Indonesian restaurant. I was hungry, and glad of the idea. You appeared to be liking me, and I started being worried in case I was being too eager. I knew I should act more coolly, maintain a slight distance from you to keep your interest alive—I had read about this in magazines! But I was excited. I found you more likable than I had dared hope, and it had nothing to do with that first attraction. All the time we were together I was aware of your cloud, its slight exhilarating haze just touching on mine. I was drawing from it, holding myself visible without any strain, finding how easy it was to relax with you and be normal. But aside from this I found you amusing, intelligent, interesting. When you left the table to visit the men's room I had to close my eyes and breathe steadily, force myself not to overdo it. I was trying to imagine how you must be seeing me, and I did not want to appear too interested or gushing. I was painfully aware how inexperienced I was: twenty-seven, and still a virgin in matters of normality!

At the end of the meal we shared the expense, conscientiously dividing it between us. I was wondering what was going to happen next. From my restricted viewpoint you were such a man of the world, talking lightly of past girlfriends, of having traveled to the States, Australia, Africa, of not having ties or any intention to settle down. Were you taking it for granted we would go to bed together? What would you think of me if we didn't? What would you think of me if we *did?*

We walked to your car, and you offered to run me home. I was silent in the car, watching the way you drove, thinking how self-confident you were. Niall was so different, and so was I.

Outside my house you switched off the engine, and for a moment that seemed to say you expected to be invited in. Then you said, "Can I see you again?"

I couldn't help smiling, hearing the unconscious irony of the phrase. This was what I found so refreshing after years of Niall: all your assumptions about me were entirely new. You saw me smile, but of course I was unable to explain. We sat there in the darkened car for several minutes, making plans for a second date on Saturday evening. I wanted more and more to invite you in for a drink, delay you, but I was scared you would tire of me. We parted with a light kiss.

VIII

A heat wave broke over London that week, making it difficult to concentrate on working. All incentive to work declined in the summer anyway, as many of the firms I dealt with slowed down their output, and hot weather always distracted me. Bright sunshine emphasizes London's inherent scruffiness, the old buildings showing their cracks and weathering faults. I liked the city under gray cloud, the narrow congested streets closed in by dark stone and low roofs, softened by rain. Summer made me restless, thinking how much I should like to be on a beach or cooling down in mountain passes.

Now I had you to distract me even more. The morning after our date I lay in my bed, musing contentedly and staring up through the window at the tops of the trees in the adjacent gardens. It was all right to indulge myself when you were not there to see me. I knew I was acting like a teenager, but I was happy. Niall had never made me happy.

The three days passed slowly again, and I had plenty of time to indulge my fantasies. Although I was worried about seeming too keen on you, I was also wondering how long Niall would be lying low. It was so important to know you well before he returned. I thought about him briefly, away on his mysterious trip to France, wondering if he was really there.

I was getting ready to go out on the Saturday evening when I was called to the telephone. It was Niall—of course it was Niall. His talent for sensing the most inconvenient and intrusive moment was almost psychic. I was expecting you to pick me up in less than half an hour.

"How are you getting on, Susan?"

"I'm fine. What do you want? I'm just about to go out."

"Yes, that'll be Grey again, won't it?"

"It doesn't matter what I'm doing. Can you call back tomorrow?"

"I want to talk to you now. This is long-distance."

"It isn't convenient now," I said. His voice was clear and loud in the earpiece, making me suspicious. There was none of the usual quiet electronic noise on the line, the sense of intervening miles. He sounded as if he was in London.

"I don't care about that," he said. "I'm lonely, and I want to see you."

"I thought you were with friends. Where are you?"

"In France. I told you."

"You sound very close."

"We've got a good line. Susan, I made a mistake coming here without you. Why don't you come and join me?"

"I can't. I've got a lot of work to do."

"You always say there's not much in summer."

"It's different this time. I've got a pile of stuff to deliver next week."

"Then why are you going out this evening? It wouldn't take you long to get here, and you needn't stay more than a few days."

"I can't afford it," I said. "I've run out of money again."

"You don't need money to travel. Get the first train."

"Niall, this is ridiculous! I can't just drop everything!"

"But I *need* you, Susan."

I was suddenly less sure he was lying to me. Niall's fits of introspection and loneliness were real enough. If he really had been in London, as I still half suspected, he would have abandoned the pretense of being away and come to see me. It made me feel hard and unsympathetic to hear the self-pity in his voice, because it was a naked appeal to my better nature, one that had usually worked in the past. I wished he would leave me alone! I was staring again at the notice board by the telephone; the same messages were there, unanswered.

"I can't think about this now," I said. "Call me tomorrow."

"You think I don't know what you're up to. You're with Grey, aren't you?"

"No, I'm not." The truth was temporary, but it was still a truth.

"Well, you will be seeing him. I know what you're doing."

I said nothing, turning away from the wall and the phone, the coiled cable of the receiver stretching across my throat. A telephone conversation has an unseen quality, each speaker invisible to the other. I tried to imagine where Niall was: a shuttered room in a French villa, bare polished floorboards, flowers and sunlight, different voices in another room? Or some house in London, one he had broken in to so he could use the phone? His voice sounded so close it was impossible to believe he was in France. If he wanted me to visit him, why did he not tell me where he was? If he was paranoid about you, why had he gone away and left me?

He was still crowding me; it was just a new way of doing it.

"Why aren't you saying anything?" Niall said.

"I've nothing to say that you would want to hear."

"I'm only asking you to see me for a few days."

I said, "You're interfering because you know I've

met someone else. If you must know, I'm going out with Richard tonight."

Niall broke the connection immediately, hanging up on me. The line clicked, went clear, and then I heard a whining sound. I was left standing there with the thing in my hand, still tangled up in the cable, listening to the petulant noise. No one had ever hung up on me before, and it had an instant effect. I felt angry, humiliated, repentant and alarmed, all at once. I wanted to call him back directly, but I had no idea how to do that.

You arrived a few minutes later, and I was still upset by the call. I was relieved, just then, that we were still relatively unknown to each other, because I was able to conceal this from you. We saw a film that evening, then afterward went for a late supper. That night, when you ran me home in the car, I invited you in. We stayed up talking very late, and at the end of it our kisses were lingering and intimate. We did not sleep together. Before you left we made plans to go for a walk the following afternoon.

Shortly before you were due to arrive, I finally admitted to myself that I was in a jumpy state. It had been growing in me all morning, and I had tried to ignore it. A few minutes before you arrived I could hardly keep still for the tension, knowing that Niall was going to ring.

When the telephone went I was almost relieved. I ran to it before anyone else in the house could get to the hall, and picked it up. How did he *know?*

This call was different. Niall was in, or sounded as if he was in, a suppressed mood. He apologized for hanging up on me the day before, and said he had been upset.

"When I saw you in the pub with Grey, I knew you preferred him to me. I had to go away. I knew this would happen one day."

His voice was clear and close, almost as if he were in the next house. I was trembling.

"I want to lead a normal life," I said. "You know that."

"Yes, but why are you doing *this* to me?"

"Richard's just a friend." It was a lie, because already you had become more than that. Perversely, I wanted Niall to be angry, because that would be easier.

"Then if he doesn't matter to you, come and see me."

"I'll think about it," I said, wondering if by appearing to go along with what he wanted I would find out what he was doing. "I don't even know where you are."

"If I tell you, will you promise to visit me?"

"I said I'll think about it."

"Just a few days, so we can be together."

"Then tell me how to find you. No, wait a minute—"

The doorbell had rung, and I could see your shape through the frosted and stained-glass window built into the front door. While the receiver swung on its cable I opened the front door. I explained I was in the middle of a conversation, and showed you into my room. I made sure the door was closed so you would not hear, and cupped my hand over the mouthpiece.

"Go on, Niall."

"He's there, isn't he?"

"Tell me where you are."

He started detailed instructions which I barely heard: a train to Marseilles, a bus along the coast, the village of Saint-Raphaël, a white-painted house. I was thinking: it's a lie, he's making it up, he's somewhere close by and watching me, in a house across the road, standing by the window and seeing you arrive, following me whenever I meet you. How else does he know to call just before I see you?

I let him finish, then said, "Why are you telling me all this, Niall?"

"I want to see you. When will you leave? Tomorrow?"

"I'm going to have to go now."

"Not just yet!"

"I've got to. Goodbye, Niall."

I put down the phone before I heard anything else. I was still trembling because I knew he was in London and the story about France was untrue. He knew I would know, but we both maintained the lie. What was he up to?

I was too upset to see you straight away, so I walked to the front door and leaned against it for a few moments, trying to steady myself. Something moved outside, vaguely blurred through the translucent glass. I started with alarm, and backed away. I think it was only a bird, or someone walking down the road. I thought of you, waiting inside my room, just a few feet away. All I wanted was to be with you, but Niall intruded at every step. He must know our plans! I remembered the terrible dread that Niall could achieve a level of invisibility which even I could not detect. He could be with me every moment I was with you!

It was madness to think he was capable of such deviousness.

But how else? As I stood alone in the bare hallway, plucking up the courage to go in and see you, I wondered, not for the first time, whether invisibility itself was a form of madness. Niall himself had once described it as the inability to believe in oneself, a failure of identity. The glams led a mad life, riddled with phobias and neuroses, paranoiac in their creed, parasitic on society. Their perception of the real world was distorted, a classic definition of insanity. If so, then my wish for normality would be a quest for sanity, a search for belief in myself and a sense of my own identity. Niall's hold on me was the desperate clutching of a madman who sees a fellow inmate open the outer door of an asylum, yet who knows he cannot follow.

To escape I had to put the madness behind me. Not

just cure myself, but change my whole knowledge of the invisible world. While Niall made me believe he was haunting me, his grip was still tight around me.

My only hope of normality was to disbelieve in him.

You were standing by the window in my room, looking out at what could be seen of the overgrown garden. You turned as soon as I walked in, and came smiling across the room to kiss me.

"Sorry about that," I said. "Just a friend."

"You look a little pale. Is everything all right?"

"I need some fresh air. Where shall we go?"

"What about the Heath?"

I made a perfunctory effort to tidy the room, realizing I had left a pile of unwashed clothes on the floor and half-finished work scattered across my desk, then collected my bag and we drove to Hampstead. It was another hot afternoon, and there were people all over the Heath, enjoying London's unreliable summer. We strolled around all afternoon, arms linked, talking and looking at the other people, sometimes kissing. I loved being with you.

That evening we went to your flat and there we made love for the first time. I felt secure in your flat, believing that Niall could not find it, and so I was more relaxed with you than I had ever been. A summer storm blew up while we were in bed, and we lay there in the sultry evening, the windows open, while the thunder rolled across the roofs. It felt delicious and illicit to be curled up naked with you, listening to the weather.

IX

You dressed and went out to buy some Greek take-away food, and when you returned I put on your dressing gown and we sat side by side on the bed, chewing our way through chunky kebabs. I was very happy.

Then you said, "Are you busy at the moment? I mean, do you have a lot of work on?"

"Not really. In fact, there's hardly anything. Everyone's away."

"I'm at a bit of a loose end myself. What I'd planned to do was lounge around for the summer, but I'm getting rather bored. And it's difficult finding free-lance work at the moment." You had told me earlier why you had given up your job. You said, "There's something I've always wanted to do, an idea I had for a film. I don't think it'll amount to anything, because it's really just an excuse for a trip. I was wondering if you'd like to go with me."

"A trip?" I said. "When?"

"Whenever you like. We could leave more or less straight away, if you're not busy."

"But where would we go?"

"Well, that's the idea for the film. Have I told you about my postcards?"

"No."

"I'll show you." You left the bed and went into the room you called your study. You returned a few moments later carrying an old shoe box. "I'm not really a collector . . . I just hoard. I bought most of these a year or two ago, and I've added a few since. They're all prewar. Some of them go back to the last century."

We pulled some of the cards out and spread them on the bed. They had been sorted into groups by countries and towns, with neat labels for each section. About half of all the cards were British, and these were unsorted. The rest were from Germany, Switzerland, France, Italy, a few from Belgium and Holland. Almost all of them were black and white or sepia-tinted. Many of them had handwritten messages on the back, conventional greetings from holidaymakers to people still at home.

"What I've often thought I'd like to do is go to some of these places. Try to find the views as they are today, compare them with these old photographs, and see how places change in half a century. As I said, it might be the basis for a film one day, but all I'd really like to do is go and have a look. What about it?"

The cards were fascinating. Frozen moments of a lost age: city centers almost free of traffic, travelers in plus fours parading on foreign seafronts, cathedrals and casinos, beaches with bathers in modest costumes and strollers in straw hats, mountain scenery with funicular railways, palaces and museums and broad deserted plazas.

"You want to go to all of these places?" I said.

"No, just a few. I thought I'd concentrate on France, in the south. I've got a lot of cards from there." You took some of the postcards from me. "It's really only since the war that the Riviera has been intensively developed for tourism. Most of these cards show the places before that."

You started going through them, pulling out a few examples to show me. I saw familiar names, unfamiliar views. One of the sets of cards was of the coastline around Saint-Raphaël. The coincidence was striking, and my fear of Niall suddenly hit me.

"Couldn't we go somewhere else, Richard?" I said.

"Of course we could. But this is where I'd *like* to go."

"Not France—I don't want to go to France."

You looked so disappointed, the cards spread out on the bed around us.

I said, "What about some of the other places? Switzerland, for instance?"

"No, it's got to be the south of France. Well, we could leave it."

I found myself going through the same excuses I had used on Niall. "I'd love to go, really I would. But I'm broke at the moment."

"We'd go in my car . . . I could pay for everything. I'm not hard up."

"I haven't got a passport."

"We could get you a Visitors' Passport. You buy those over the counter."

"No, Richard. I'm sorry."

You started picking up the postcards, keeping them in their meticulous order. "There's another reason, isn't there?"

"Yes." I could not look at you. "The truth is there's someone I know, someone I don't want to see. He's in France at the moment. Or I think he is, and—"

"Is this the boyfriend you've gone out of your way never to mention?"

"Yes. How do you know?"

"I always assumed there must be someone else." The postcards were all put away now, restored to their neat row in the shoe box. "Are you still seeing him?"

Again, your unconsciously ironic choice of words. I started telling you about Niall, trying to translate the reality into terms you would accept. I described him as a long-time lover, someone I had known since I was young. I said that we had grown away from each other, but that he was reluctant to let go. I characterized him as possessive, childish, violent, manipulative; Niall was all of these, of course, but that was only a part of it.

We discussed the problem for a while, you putting the reasonable case that we were most unlikely to run into him, and anyway if we did that Niall would be forced, by seeing us together, to accept that I had left him. I was adamant, saying that you could not conceive the influence he had over me. I wanted to run no risk of meeting him.

Even as I was saying this I was remembering my own doubts about where Niall might actually be, and the way I knew I had to deal with this. To believe that Niall was anywhere *other* than Saint-Raphaël was to accept the madness.

"But if you're finished with him," you said, "he's going to have to live with the idea sooner or later."

"I'd rather it was later. I want to be with *you*. We could go somewhere else."

"All right. It was just an idea. Any suggestions?"

"What I'd really like is to be out of London for a while. Couldn't we just get in your car and drive somewhere?"

"In England, you mean?"

"I know it sounds very dull . . . but I've never seen some parts of Britain. We could tour around. Wales, or the West Country, just on our own."

You seemed surprised, the French Riviera exchanged in favor of Britain, but that was what we agreed. When you took the cards back to your study I went with you, looking at the oddments of film equipment you had bought up. You seemed a little embarrassed about them, saying they took up space and collected dust, but for me they were an insight into you before we met. Your awards were in the study too, half hidden behind a stack of film cans.

"You didn't say you were famous!" I said, taking down the Prix Italia and reading the inscription.

"Come on . . . that was luck."

" '. . . extreme personal danger'," I read. "What happened?"

"Just the sort of thing news crews get into from time to time." You took the trophy from me and put it back on the shelf, even farther out of sight. You led me back into the bedroom. "It was a riot in Belfast. The sound recordist was there too. It was nothing special."

I was intrigued. Suddenly I was seeing you as I had not seen you before: a cameraman with a reputation, a career, awards.

"Please tell me about it," I said.

You looked uncomfortable. "I don't often talk about it."

"Well, tell me."

"It was just a job—we all took it in turns to go to Northern Ireland. You get paid extra, because it's fairly difficult work. I don't mind that sort of thing. Filming is filming, and you get different sorts of problem on every job. Well, there had been a Protestant march during the day and we'd covered that, and in the evening we were back in the hotel having a few drinks. Then word came round that the army were going in to sort out a few kids who were throwing stones in the Falls Road. We talked about whether we should go down there, we were all tired, but in the end we decided to go and have a look. I loaded the camera with night stock, then we hitched a ride with the army. When we got down there it didn't look like much—about fifty teenagers hurling stuff around. We were behind the troops, fairly well shielded, and nothing much seemed to be about to happen. These things generally fizzle out around midnight. But then suddenly it got worse. A few petrol bombs were thrown, and it was obvious that some older men were joining in. The army decided to break it up, and they fired a few plastic bullets. Instead of scattering the kids carried on, slinging rocks and bombs. A couple of Saracens were called in, and the soldiers charged. Willie and I—Willie was the soundman —went forward with them, because it's generally the safest place, behind the troops. We ran about a hundred yards and came straight into a sort of ambush. There were snipers in houses, and one of the side streets had a whole gang of people waiting with bombs and rocks. Everything went mad. Willie and I were separated from the reporter and didn't see him again until later. The soldiers were dashing in every direction, and petrol bombs were going off all around us. I suppose I got a bit carried away, and went on shooting film—right in the middle of it all. Nothing hit us, but a couple of bullets were quite close. We got in among the people who were stoning the troops, and somehow they never seemed to notice us. Then the soldiers started firing plastic bullets again, and this time we were on the receiving end. Well, we got away in the end, but the footage was pretty good."

You grinned, trying to minimize the story. It suddenly struck me that I might have heard about the incident somewhere, one more horrifying night in Northern Ireland.

I said, "When you were there filming, what did it feel like?"

"I can't remember much about it now. It just happened."

"You said you got carried away. What did you mean?"

"It was like flying on autopilot. I went on filming and didn't take too much notice of what was going on around us."

"Were you excited?"

"I suppose I was."

"And the people didn't notice you?"

"Not really, no."

I said nothing more, but I knew then what had happened. I could see it in my mind: you and the soundman, running and crouching, linked by the equipment, right in the thick of the action, filming by instinct. You said you had had a few drinks, that you were tired, that no one seemed to notice you. I could sense the feeling, imagine exactly how you had felt. For those few moments your cloud had thickened around you and the other man, and taken you through the danger invisibly.

X

We spent three more days in London, ostensibly preparing for our holiday but in practice using the time to get to know each other better, and to spend a lot of time in bed. Your bachelor existence made me feel domestic. We talked about redecorating your flat, I made you buy a lot of cookware and household goods, and as a present I gave you a huge houseplant for your living room. You seemed bemused by all this, but I had never felt more blissful.

We left London on a Thursday morning, driving north on the M1 motorway with no particular route in mind, just a shared wish to be on our own together.

I was still nervous that Niall might be somewhere around, in spite of my self-declared belief that he was in France. Only when we were in your car, speeding away, did I feel finally safe from him.

We stopped for the first night in Lancaster, checking in to a small hotel near the university. We rested after the long drive, feeling happy, anticipating the holiday together. That evening we made plans for the next day, touring around the Lake District.

We discovered we were both lazy about sightseeing. We were content to drive to a place, walk around briefly, perhaps have a meal or a drink, then drive on to somewhere else. I liked being driven by you, and found your car smooth and comfortable to sit in. With our things in the luggage space at the rear, the back passenger seat was empty, and so we used it as a dump for the tourist guides and maps, the food we bought to eat on the way, a bag of apples and chocolate, and all the other accumulated litter of traveling.

For three days we followed an erratic route, crossing and recrossing the north of the country: from the Lakes we went to the Yorkshire Dales, then briefly visited the hills of southern Scotland before returning to the northeast coast of England. I loved the contrasts in the British scenery, the swift transitions from low to high ground, from industry to open countryside. We left the north and headed down the eastern side. You said you had never seen this part of the country before, so it was new to both of us. The longer we were together like this the more I felt I was leaving my old, inadequate life behind me. I felt free of cares, happy, loving, and above all assimilating at last into a normal life.

But then, on the fifth day, there came the first of the intrusions.

X I

We had arrived in a village called Blakeney, on the north coast of Norfolk, and were staying in a bed-and-breakfast private house in the narrow street leading down to the shore. I had disliked the look of the village as soon as we arrived, but we had been driving all day and all we really wanted was a place to stay for the night. We planned to visit Norwich the next day. The woman who owned the house told us the restaurants closed early, so after a brief rest in our room we went straight out, leaving our bags unopened.

When we returned, all my clothes had been removed from my suitcase and were laid out in neat piles on
the bed. Each garment had been carefully folded.

"It must have been the woman downstairs," you
said.

"But surely she wouldn't come in and interfere
with our stuff?"

I went downstairs to find her, but the lights in the
rooms were out, and to judge by the gleam under one of
the doors upstairs, she had already gone to bed.

The following night, in a hotel in Norwich, I was
awakened in the small hours by the sudden and unpleasant sensation of having been hit by something. You were
asleep. I reached over to switch on the bedside lamp, and
as I did so something moved quickly down the pillow and
onto the mattress. It was hard and cold. I sat up in fright,
moving away from it, and got the light on. What I found
in the bed beside me was a cake of soap, quite dry, per-
fumed, the brand name engraved into its surface. You
stirred but did not wake up. I climbed out of bed, and
almost at once discovered the colored-foil wrapper. It had
been neatly opened, and laid flat on the carpet. I climbed
back into bed, switched off the light, then lay deep under
the covers, holding on to you. I did not sleep again that
night.

In the morning you suggested driving westward,
right across the widest part of the country, and visiting
Wales. I was deeply preoccupied with the event in the
night, and simply agreed. We realized we had left the road
map in the car, so I offered to go down and collect it.

The car was where we had left it the night before,
in the hotel park. There was a key in the ignition, and the
engine was running.

My first thought was that it must have been running all night, that you had accidentally not switched off,
but when I tried the door I found it was locked. The same
key was used for both. Trembling, I opened the driver's

door with the key you had given me, and reached in for the one in the ignition. It was brand-new, as if recently bought, or stolen.

I hurled it as hard as I could into the shrubbery surrounding the car park. Back in the room, when I gave you the road map, you asked me what the matter was. I did not know what to say, so I told you my period was due to start, as in truth it was, but the real reason was my growing dread of the inevitable.

I was silent all through breakfast, and stayed deep inside my terrified introspections as we drove along the straight roads that crossed the Fens.

Then you said, "I'd like an apple. Do we have any left?"

"I'll look," I managed to say.

I turned around in my seat, pulling against the restraint of the seat belt, something I had done many times in the last few days, but this time I was shaking with fear.

The paper bag containing the apples was on the part of the passenger seat directly behind you. Everything else was there, heaped into a pile on that side: the maps, your jacket, my holdall, the shopping bag with the food for our picnic lunch. It was all on the one side of the bench seat: every time we put the stuff behind us we instinctively placed it there, leaving the other side empty.

There was room for a passenger.

I forced myself to look at the place, behind my seat. The cushions were slightly indented, bearing weight.

Niall was in the car with us.

I said to you, "Can you stop the car, Richard?"

"What's the matter?"

"Please—I'm feeling sick. Hurry!"

You pulled the car over at once, running it up on the verge. The moment it stopped I scrambled out, still holding your apple. I staggered away from the car, feeling weak, shaking all over. There was a rising bank, a low hedge, and beyond was an immense flat field with crops. I leaned forward into the hedge, the thorns and sticks prodding into me. You had switched off the engine, and you came running to me. I felt your arm around my shoulders, but I was shuddering and crying. You were saying soothing things, but the horror of what I had just discovered was throbbing through me. As you held me I thrust myself forward and down against the hedge, and vomited.

You brought some tissues from the car, and I wiped myself clean with them. I had moved back from the hedge, but I could not turn to face the car.

"What shall we do, Sue? Do you want to find a doctor?"

"I'll be all right in a few minutes. It's my period. It sometimes happens like this." I couldn't tell you the truth. "I just needed some air."

"Do you want to stay here?"

"No, we can drive on. In a while."

I had some magnesia tablets in my bag, and you brought me those. They helped settle my stomach. I sat down in the dry grass, staring at the stalks of cow parsley nodding around and above me, insects drifting in the heat. Cars rushed by on the road behind us, their tires making a sucking sound on the soft tarmac. I could not make myself look back, knowing Niall was there.

He must have been with us from the start. He had probably stayed to overhear me speak to you in the pub, had been with us on our first dates, had been with us in the car from the time we left London. He had been there, silent behind us, watching and listening. I had never been free of him.

I knew that he was forcing me to act. To have for myself the normal life I craved, I had to put Niall behind me forever. I could not go back to that morbid, vagrant life of the glams. Niall wanted to drag me back; he sought nothing less. Niall was the worst of that past, hopelessly and despairingly holding on to me.

I had to fight him. Not at that moment—the shock

of discovery was still too fresh—and probably not alone. I would need you to help me.

I waited in the grass while you crouched beside me. A few minutes earlier the thought of getting back in the car, knowing Niall was there, would have been out of the question, but now I knew it would be the first necessary stage.

"I'm feeling a little better," I said. "Shall we drive on?"

"Are you sure?"

You helped me up, and we embraced lightly. I said I was sorry to cause a fuss, that it wouldn't happen again, that as soon as the period actually started I would feel a lot better . . . but over your shoulder I was looking at the car. Reflected sunlight glinted from the rear passenger window.

We walked back to the car, took our seats and strapped ourselves in. I tried to listen for the sound of the door behind me, in case Niall too had been outside while we halted, but an invisible can use a door without being detected.

When we were back on the road, I steeled myself and turned to look at the back seat. I knew he was there, could feel the presence of his cloud . . . but it was impossible to *see* him. I could look at our untidy pile of maps and food, could see to the luggage compartment behind, but when I tried to look at the seat directly behind mine, my eyes would not settle, my sight was diverted away. There was just the unseen presence, the suggestion of weight compressing the seat cushion. After that I stared straight ahead at the road, constantly aware of him being there, looking at me, looking at you.

XII

We stayed overnight in Great Malvern, the hotel built in a beautiful position on the side of the hills overlooking the town. The Vale of Evesham spread away beneath us. I had said and done nothing about Niall all day, trying to establish my priorities. I came back time and again to you, who had so suddenly become the most important person in my life. How could I ever begin to tell you about Niall? And what future would we have if he continually followed us?

The decision I came to was to act as if Niall were not there, suppress the thoughts of him. But it was impossible to act on such a decision: all through the evening as we walked on the hills, then drove into the town for a meal, I instinctively steered the conversation away from anything personal. Of course, you were aware of this.

Later, when we went up to the hotel bedroom, I took the room key away from you and opened the door myself. You walked in first, and I followed quickly, pushing the door closed suddenly. I was rewarded with the feeling of weight pressing against it from outside, but I shoved the door into place and locked it. There was no bolt. Locked doors presented no barrier to Niall: he could steal a master key, and later enter the room without either of us noticing. But that would take him several minutes, which was all I needed.

I said, "Richard, I've got to talk to you about something."

"What's going on, Sue? You've been acting strangely all evening."

"I'm upset, and I've got to be frank with you. I told you about Niall. Well, he's here."

"What do you mean, he's here?"

"He's in Malvern. I saw him this evening when we were walking."

"I thought you said he was in France."

"I never know where he is. He told me he was going to France, but he must have changed his mind."

"But what the hell is he doing here? Has he followed us?"

"I don't know . . . it must be a coincidence. He's always traveling around to see friends."

"I don't see it makes any difference," you said. "What are you saying, that he should join us for the rest of the trip?"

"No." It was painful having to lie, but how could I tell the whole truth? "He's seen us together. I'll have to talk to him, tell him what's happening with you and me."

"If he's seen us he'll already know. What's the point of saying any more? We're leaving in the morning, and won't see him again."

"You don't understand! I can't do that to him. I've known him for too long—I can't just walk out on him."

"But you already have, Sue."

Trying to see it from your point of view I knew I was being unreasonable, but the only way I could present Niall to you was as a possessive former lover, accidentally encountered. We argued on for an hour or more, both of us getting depressed and entrenched. Niall must have entered the room at some point during it all, but I could not allow the fear of him to influence me. At last we went to bed, worn out by the impasse. I felt safer in the darkness, and we held on to each other under the sheets. Because my period had actually started in the afternoon we did not make love, nor did we wish to.

I had another restless night, the problem churning away in my mind. Like all obsessive thoughts that keep

you awake, no solution presented itself beyond the resolve
to confront Niall as soon as possible.

I was awake at half-past six, and I decided to act. I
left you asleep in bed, got dressed, then walked quickly
from the hotel.

It was already a fine, warm morning. Knowing it
made no difference where I went to find Niall, I walked
up the hill, following the long straight road as it climbed
away from the town. At the top there were a few houses,
then the road turned sharply to cut between two steep
cliffs to the other side of the hill. I scrambled up one of the
mounds and walked across the broad summit. Rocks pro-
truded from the grass. It was utterly still and quiet.

I found a flat rock and sat down on it, staring across
Herefordshire.

I said, "Are you there, Niall?"

Silence. Sheep grazed on the slopes beneath me,
and a solitary car drove up the road then cut through the
gap toward Malvern.

"Niall? I want to talk to you."

"I'm here, bitch." His voice came from a short distance away, somewhere to my left. He sounded out of
breath.

"Where are you? I want to see you."

"We can talk like this."

"Make yourself visible, Niall."

"No . . . *you* make yourself invisible."

He made me realize that I had been continuously
visible for more than a week, the longest time since puberty. It had happened so naturally that I had simply not
thought about it.

"I'm going to stay like this," I said.

"Suit yourself."

He had moved; his voice came from a different
place each time he spoke. I was trying to see him, knowing
there was always a way to find the cloud if only I knew
how to see. But I had been with you too long, or Niall had

retreated too far into his glamour. I imagined him prowling around, circling as I sat on the rock. I stood up.

"Why won't you leave me alone, Niall?"

"Because you're fucking with Grey. I'm trying to make you quit."

"Leave us alone! I'm finished with you. I'm never going to see you again."

"I've already arranged that for you, Susan."

He was still moving around, sometimes behind me. If only he had stayed still I would not have grown so frightened.

I said, "Don't interfere, Niall. It's over between us!"

"You're a glam. It'll never work with him."

"I'll never be like you! I hate you!"

It was then that he struck me, a hard fist coming out of the air, banging against the side of my head. I lurched backward gasping, trying to keep my balance, reaching behind me as my foot struck a rock and I fell heavily on the ground. An instant later Niall kicked me, high up on my leg by my hip. I shouted with the pain and curled up desperately in a fetal position, my arms over my head. I braced myself against more pain.

But I heard him right beside me, leaning down so that his invisible mouth was close by my ear. I smelt the sourness of old tobacco on his breath.

"I'm never going to leave you, Susan. You're mine, and I'm helpless without you. I'm not going to leave you until you finish with Grey."

His hand thrust roughly into the front of my blouse, and he tore and scratched at my breast. I hunched myself tighter and squirmed away from him, forcing him to remove his hand but ripping the fabric at the front.

He said, still by my face, "You haven't told him about me yet. Tell him you're an invisible, tell him you're mad."

"No!"

"If you don't, I will."

"You've done enough harm already."

"I've hardly started. Would you like me to grab the steering wheel when he's driving?"

"You're crazy, Niall!"

"No more than you are, Susan. We're both mad. Make him understand that, and if he still wants you then maybe I'll leave you alone."

I sensed him move away from me, but I stayed huddled on the ground, terrified of more blows. Niall had often hit me in the past when he was angry, but never like this, never from within the cloud. I was still dazed from being hit on the head, and my leg and back were aching. I let more time pass and then sat up slowly, looking around for him. How close was he?

I was desperate to talk to you, wanted your comfort, but what would you say? Sitting on the ground I explored the damage to me: there was a sore area on my lower back and a bruised lump on my thigh. I had a grass graze on my elbow. The front of my blouse was hanging open, and two buttons were missing.

I wandered around on the hill for a while, but soon my need to be with you became all-important. I limped slowly down the road toward the hotel, holding my blouse together with my hand. It was uncanny how Niall could voice my worst fears: never before had he described invisibility as madness. It was as if he had read my mind.

I saw you the moment I entered the hotel grounds. You had opened the rear hatch of the car and were putting your suitcase inside. I called out to you, but you did not hear. Then I realized that in my misery I had slipped back into invisibility—another of Niall's achievements. I forced myself out of the cloud and called to you again. This time you heard me, straightening by the car and turning toward me, and I ran sobbing into your arms.

XIII

You knew I had seen Niall; I could not conceal it from you. I tried to minimize what he had done, but I could not hide my torn clothes and bruises. In the end I admitted he had struck me in jealousy, and that the problem was not solved. I think I would have been ready for you too to have been angry, but you were as upset as I was. We stayed on all morning in the Malvern hotel discussing Niall—but always in your terms, not mine.

We left the hotel after an early lunch and drove into Wales. Niall was in the car, sitting behind us silently.

We stopped on the way to buy petrol, and for a few moments I was alone in the car with Niall.

I said, "I'll tell him tomorrow."

Silence.

"Are you there, Niall?"

I had turned around to look back at the empty half of the rear seat, but again I was unable to see. Outside, the petrol pump whirred, electronic digits flickering orange in the sunlight. You were crouching over the filler, looking back at the pump, just a few inches behind Niall. You saw me apparently looking at you, and you smiled briefly.

When you turned away again I said, "It's what you wanted . . . I'll tell Richard tomorrow."

Niall said nothing, but I knew he was there. His silence intimidated me, probably on purpose, so I opened the door and got out of the car. I leaned on the front wing while you paid the cashier.

We arrived in the village of Little Haven, on the far westerly coast of Dyfed. It was a small and pretty place, not crowded with visitors, and had a long rocky shoreline. In the evening we walked on the beach to watch the sunset, then called in at the local pub before returning to the hotel.

There was now a distance between us. You could not understand why I had agreed to meet Niall, nor why, after he had beaten me up, I would not renounce him. I knew you were hurt, puzzled and angry. I was desperate to mend everything. Niall's way, to tell you of my invisibility, was the probable solution: it would satisfy him, and explain myself to you.

But I was exhausted by the subject. I wanted time to sort things out, so that anything I said came from *my* needs, and was not simply a way of appeasing Niall. I resolved to tell you in the morning, but in the meantime I had other plans.

When we were back in our room, I slipped away to the bathroom. Although my period was continuing, I put in my diaphragm to halt the bleeding temporarily.

In bed, you wanted to talk about Niall again, but I deflected you. There was nothing I could say to make amends. I held you, kissed you, tried to arouse you. At first you resisted me, but I knew what I wanted. The evening was warm again and we were lying on top of the covers, the elderly double bed creaking as we moved around. You responded at last, and I felt my own arousal growing. I wanted to make love to you more excitingly than ever before, and I kissed and fondled you with great intimacy; I loved your body, the solidity of it and its hard curves.

We rolled over so that you were above me, and now you were caressing me with your hands and tongue. I raised my parted knees, ready for you—but you appeared to change your mind, and rolled to the side. I felt your hands pulling me around against you, pushing my shoulders down against your chest. I wanted you inside me, but your hands pulled my rear away from you, twisting my haunches awkwardly. We were kissing mouth to mouth, and I could not understand what you were wanting to do. Your fingers were digging into the flesh of my hips, thrusting me away. Then I realized that both your hands were on my breasts, lightly fingering my nipples. *Other* hands were reaching from behind, pulling at my hips! Suddenly, with a pushing intrusion, I was entered from behind. Pubic hair prickled against my buttocks. I gasped, turned my head, felt an unshaven chin beat into the curve of my neck, and knees kicked into the crook of mine. The weight of the man behind me thrust me forward against you, and one of your hands slipped down towards my crotch. I grabbed your wrist to stop you finding what was already there, and in desperation brought your hand up to my mouth to kiss it. Niall's sexual pushing against me was violent, making me gasp in outrage. You were growing more excited, wanting to enter me. I had to stop you somehow, and so I curled away from the man behind me, pushing my backside more acutely against him in a desperate effort to twist free, and at the same time took you into my mouth to suck. Niall shifted position, moving forward so that he was kneeling between my legs, his hands under my belly and holding me while he rammed. His movements grew more urgent, and he put one of his hands on my head, taking a handful of my hair and wrenching it painfully, pushing my mouth farther down on you. I began gagging. You were lying back, your arms somewhere away from me, while the rape went on. I could barely breathe, but I was swinging my elbows upward and back, trying to beat Niall away from me. I managed to get you out of my mouth, but my face was still being pushed into your groin. I heard you groaning with pleasure, while Niall hammered unrelentingly at me. I felt him climaxing, and he grunted audibly, expelling breath noisily. You said my name, your voice full of desire for me. Niall slumped forward across my back, releasing my hair and playing his hands across my breasts. As he relaxed I was able to shift my weight, but I couldn't wriggle him out of me. He was still there, monstrously possessing me, his weight forcing my face down against you. You said my name again, wanting to make love. I managed to turn my face to see you; your eyes were closed, your mouth was open. I had to get Niall out of me, but I was pinned beneath him. Jabs with my elbows had no effect; his frantic breathing was close by my ear. I could feel him softening inside me, so I made another effort to twist my hips, raising my body as I did so. This time I managed to slide away from him, but he was still there holding on to me. I elbowed him again, and he loosened his grip on me. As soon as I could I crawled across your body, hugging your chest, bringing my face to yours. You kissed me with great passion, and pulled me over you. I could feel Niall beside us on the bed, some part of him pressing against my side.

You entered me at last, and we made love. There was no pleasure in it for me, just relief that it was you, not Niall. Because I was squatting above you, we were looking at each other. I kept my face rigid, knowing that if I tried to respond to you my true feelings would be revealed. All I could do was move my body with yours, hoping it would be enough. Niall was still there; I could feel the warmth of his body against my lower leg.

How could you not be aware of him? Was Niall so profoundly invisible to you that you could not hear him, smell him, not feel his weight on the bed, not react to the violent contortions he had forced on me?

As soon as you had finished I lay beside you, and we pulled the sheet over us. I whispered that I was tired, and we lay in each other's arms with the light out. I waited and waited as your breathing steadied and you fell into sleep. When I was sure I would not disturb you, I slipped out of the bed and went to the bathroom. I showered as quietly as I could, scrubbing myself clean.

When I returned, the room smelled of French tobacco smoke.

XIV

In the morning, I said to you, "Do you remember the puzzle that used to be printed in children's books?"

I took a piece of paper, and made two marks:

X   O

"If you close your left eye," I said, "and look with your right eye at the cross, then move your face closer to the paper, the nought seems to vanish."

You said, That's a physical failure of the eye. The retina has only a limited amount of peripheral vision.

I said, "But the brain compensates for what the eye cannot see. It's not as if the nought has *actually* been removed—there's no hole in the paper. You think you can still see the paper where the nought was."

You said, What are you getting at?

I said to you, "Imagine that you are invited to a party where almost everyone else is a stranger. You enter the room where they are standing around. The people are drinking, smoking, talking. No one greets you, and you feel self-conscious. Your main awareness is the sense of a crowd. No one person stands out from the others. You take a drink and stand at the edge of the room, looking at the people, hoping to see a familiar face. You see someone you recognize, and although he or she is talking to someone else and doesn't come over to you, you notice them in preference to anyone else.

"You are still on your own, so you look at the other people. The ones you notice now are probably the women, making quick judgments of their appearance and whether or not they are alone. If they are with men, you will notice them too. Eventually someone speaks to you, and that person then becomes the center of your attention. Later on you will single out other people for closer notice, and then you will concentrate on each of them in turn. There might be a man who is very drunk, a girl in a sexy dress, someone who laughs too loudly. As you speak to other people, they enter your sphere of immediate awareness. The other people, the ones you have not yet spoken to or specifically noticed, will remain in your awareness, but only in a general or peripheral sense.

"During this, you will gradually become aware of other things in the room: the food and drink, obviously. There might be a domestic animal, which you see. You will notice houseplants. You will see the furniture and carpet. In the end, you might even notice how the room itself has been decorated.

"Every object and every person in the room is visible to you, but there is an unconscious order in which you become aware of them.

"Always, at every party, there will be someone you *never* notice."

I said to you, "Now, suppose you are at another gathering of people you do not know. There are ten men and one woman. As you enter the room the woman, who is beautiful and voluptuous, starts to dance and remove her clothes. As soon as she is naked you leave the room. How many of the men would you be able to describe afterward? Would you even be sure there were ten of them, and not nine, or an eleventh you did not notice at all?"

I said to you, "Richard, suppose you are walking down a street and two women approach you. One of them is young and pretty and is wearing attractive clothes. The other is an older woman, perhaps the girl's middle-aged mother, and she is wearing a plain, shapeless coat. As you pass, they both smile at you. Which one do you notice first?"

You said, But these are sexual responses.

"Not always," I said. "Suppose there is a group of ten people, five men and five women. A sixth woman approaches the group. What she will notice first is the other women, and will look at them in preference to the men. Women notice women, just as men notice women. A child will notice other children before seeing the adults. Women notice children before they notice adults. Men see women before they see children, and then they notice the other men.

"There is a hierarchy of visual interest. In any group of people there is always someone who is noticed *last.*"

I said to you, "You are walking down a busy shopping street, looking for someone you know. Let us assume it is a woman. Crowds of people, all of them strangers to you, are pushing past. You see them all, because you are searching for your friend. You constantly scan faces, looking for the one you recognize. You look at men as well as women. Some of the faces interest you, most of them do not. The time passes, and you begin to wonder if you might have missed seeing your friend. You know what she looks like, you saw her only yesterday, but you begin to wonder if you will be able to spot her in the crowd. Perhaps she is wearing different clothes? Or has done her hair differently? You continue to look at the people, more intently, no longer sure of what you are looking for. You notice one or two other women who look like your friend, and for a moment you wonder if you have found her. Then at last she appears, and the problem is over. She looks exactly like she did the last time you saw her, and all you are aware of is the relief of finding her. Now you notice no one else in the street, although the crowds continue to surge past.

"Afterward, if you think about it, you will be able

to recall several of the faces you saw while you were searching. Yet in those few minutes you looked directly at possibly hundreds of faces, and were aware of thousands of others. You looked at most of them and you thought you saw them, but in fact they did not register on your mind."

You said, But there's nothing unusual in that.

I said to you, "The point I'm making is that it's normal *not* to notice everything around you. What you see is what you choose to see, or what interests you, or anything that is drawn to your attention. What I'm trying to tell you is that there are some people whom you will *never* see. They are too low in the hierarchy. In any group, they are the ones who are noticed last. Ordinary people do not know how to see them. They are people who are naturally invisible, who do not know how to make themselves noticed."

I said, "*I* am naturally invisible, Richard, and you only see me because I want you to see me."

You said, That's ridiculous.

I said, "Watch, Richard."

And I stood before you and let myself slip into invisibility, and when you could not see me I hid from you until I saw how upset you were.

X V

I said to you, "Richard, you are naturally invisible too. You do not know it, but you have the power to make glamours around you. I can teach you how to use that power."

You said, I can't believe I'm hearing this.

I said, "Then you are halfway to invisibility, because disbelief is part of it. Let me show you how to intensify your cloud."

We were sitting on the rocks of the shore near Little Haven. The sea was at low tide, and the sands were glistening in the sunlight. Holidaymakers were all around us, and far away a number of children were splashing in the shallows. I tried to explain the technique of intensifying the cloud, keeping away from the jargon used by the glams. For me, invisibility was a way of making myself *see* or *not see*, and in seeing or not seeing becoming unseen or seen.

I said, "You have to relax, develop a mental attitude of disbelief in yourself."

You said, It's impossible.

I thought about your story of filming the riot. I said, "Remember how you felt when you were filming. Imagine you have a camera here. Suppose you wanted to film some of these people, say those two girls sunbathing. If you walked up to them with a camera they would *notice*, they would become self-conscious, they would start seeing themselves through you. How would you avoid that?"

You said, I'd use a telephoto lens.

"No, go in close. Think of yourself crouching beside them, the camera right on them. How would you do it?"

You said, All right. I'll try.

You walked across the beach, not directly toward the girls but seeming to amble accidentally in their direction. I saw you pause, look out to sea, stare down at the sand, thinking. The two girls were teenagers, spread out on towels, wearing chain-store bikinis. They had a transitor radio playing pop music. They looked very young, rather plump, not yet suntanned. When you turned back to them I saw you straighten your back, and you shrugged one shoulder, as if imagining the weight of a camera. As you walked toward them, more confidently than before, I saw your cloud intensifying. You stood beside them, crouched down. Neither of them noticed you. There was a pause, and then you moved to the radio and pushed it to one side. Still they showed no response. One of the girls turned over and lay in the sun with one knee raised. You walked around to look down at her, blocking the sun and throwing your shadow across her face.

When you came back to me you were still invisible, laughing and laughing. We held each other and kissed, and you said, Now what else can I do?

I said to you, "First I must tell you about Niall."

XVI

We stayed in Little Haven for three days, then drove up the coast to St. David's. We were torn about what to do; we both felt we would like to go back to London, and yet we were reluctant to finish the holiday. Everything that stood between us before had now been cleared up, and we were in love. The words were exchanged regularly, and the feeling was constant.

When we arrived in St. David's, the little cathedral city was crowded with tourists and it was difficult to find somewhere to stay. The place we eventually found was in a narrow side street, with nowhere to park the car. I went up to the room while you took the car to a parking lot a short distance away.

As soon as I was inside the room Niall said, "You haven't done what I told you to do."

I turned around in horror; he was still invisible.

"Don't come near me!" I said. "I'll scream if you touch me."

"You said you would tell Grey about me."

"Where are you, Niall? Show yourself."

"You know where I am. Why didn't you tell him about me?"

"I *did* tell him. He knows everything now."

"I heard what you said. I was there. He still doesn't know about me, what I mean to you."

"You don't mean anything to me!" I said. "It's finished for good. After what you did to me, I'm never having anything to do with you again!"

"I need you, Susan. I can't let you go."

"You'll have to!" I went quickly across the room and opened the door. I wanted to find you quickly before Niall could say anything else. I heard him following me down the corridor, so I started to run. I hurried down the stairs and through the small hotel lounge, hoping desperately that you were returning. Outside in the narrow street, Niall caught my arm and turned me around. He had made himself visible to me at last.

I was shocked to see him. A week's growth of beard shadowed his face, his hair was uncombed and his clothes were dirty. I had never seen him like this; Niall had always been dapper. His eyes had a wild, desperate look, and all the self-confidence had gone from him. Suddenly to see him again brought an abrupt change in me. While he lurked invisibly around me he was an unseen threat, an intruder, a rapist . . . but now he was here he looked young, frightened, rather pathetic.

He said, "Please, Susan, I must talk to you."

"I can't. There's nothing more to say."

"I'd just like to be alone with you for an hour. Can't you manage that? Just for a while? I know you hate me now, but I'm desperate to be with you again."

"Richard's here, and I can't leave him."

"Tell him you want to be on your own for a while. He'll understand."

"I don't *want* to talk to you!" I said.

"Please . . . just to say goodbye?"

I saw you then, walking back toward the hotel. You saw me, and waved. As you strode toward me I thought how lithe and fit you were, so full of confidence, so unlike Niall.

"He'll see you!" I said to Niall.

"No, he won't."

You came up to us. "We've still got all afternoon. Why don't we find a beach? I feel like a swim."

"Tell him," Niall said.

"I think I'll walk around the shops for a while. You go on your own."

"Something's happened, Sue . . . what is it?"

"Nothing. I just don't feel like being on a beach."

"All right. We'll do it tomorrow. I'll come shopping with you."

Niall was standing back from us, his shoulders hunched. I said, "I think I'd like to be on my own for a while."

"What's up, Sue?" you said. "You weren't like this just now."

"Nothing's wrong. I'd like to be by myself."

You made an exasperated gesture. "If that's how it is, I'll find a beach and lie on it until you feel like being with me again."

Niall was watching as I took your arm and kissed you affectionately on your cheek. "I won't be long," I said.

"See you back at the hotel, then."

You stalked off quickly, obviously irritated with me. I stood with Niall until you had gone inside the hotel, then walked decisively away from him. Niall followed. I led the way out of the small town into the country lanes that surrounded it, and only then slowed the pace. I had been visible ever since Niall spoke to me in the room, and I was determined to stay that way. Niall too remained visible, if only to me.

I was with him for the rest of the afternoon, and into the early evening.

I heard him out. He said many of the same things I had already heard: that he still loved me, that he was lonely, that he was jealous of you. He said he was frightened on his own. I could harden myself against this, and nothing changed.

But we talked a long time. I began to learn things about him that made me realize I had been blocking him too long. He said that he was regretting his past, and, like me, wanted an end to the isolation of invisibility. He wanted somewhere permanent to live, an end to the constant petty crime and trespass. He said he was envious of the way I had been selling my drawings, and as a result had been writing more and more, trying to establish himself. His main problem was finding somewhere to work. Ironically, he was losing confidence in his invisibility and could never concentrate on his writing if he was in somebody else's house with people there.

And he was convinced that no one read the manuscripts he sent off. He never used the post office, because of the fear most invisibles had that their mail would be overlooked or lost, and so he always delivered to the publishers by hand. Even so, he felt certain the manuscripts were not being read. They were rarely returned to him, and more often than not he had to break in to the offices to retrieve them. Sometimes, he said, the manuscripts were still lying where he had left them. He spoke cynically of his conviction that even if his work somehow overcame this obstacle and was actually published, the printed books would not be noticed or bought.

I tried drawing him out on what he had been writing, but he would only describe the work as stories. He had always been secretive about his writing, but I wished I could read some of it. He made a vague promise to show me a manuscript one day, but I didn't press him.

Niall would not admit as much, but I interpreted his ambition to be a writer as a symptom of the larger problem. He repeatedly described himself as isolated or lost, comparing himself unfavorably with me. In the past he had usually treated my own wish for normality with contempt, but now he was different. He was frightened he would lose me. I was his link with the real world; he said I was like a guide dog for a blind person. He needed me to help him join the world. This was his real fear and dislike of you: that in losing me to you he would lose himself.

Niall was making a potent appeal to my loyalties. I knew the bitter truth of what he said, and I realized he was maturing at last. I could not harden myself against hearing this. I was not forgetting you, but I found myself forgiving him for the intrusions he had made on us, even apologizing to him for having been unsympathetic. I stayed silent when he tried to make me promise never to see you again, but later said I did not see why we couldn't remain friends.

I was acutely aware of how long I had been away from you, so I headed back to the town. The sun was lowering and had lost most of its heat, and I knew you would no longer be on the beach. Niall walked with me, urging me to confront you the moment I saw you.

We came across you unexpectedly, walking around in the small square near the cathedral. You saw me before I saw you, and my first reaction was that you must have seen me with Niall. I felt confused, and acted guilty.

You said, "I've been looking for you. Where the hell have you been?"

"Walking around the shops," I said, painfully aware of how few shops there were in the town. "What about you?"

"I lay on the beach for a while, then came looking for you."

I had glanced at Niall, convinced you could see him.

Niall said, "He doesn't know I'm here."

You had an angry look, and what I wanted to do

was put my arms around you and explain and try to put it right, but Niall was there.

"I'm sorry," I said, knowing how feeble it must sound.

"What would you like to do?" you said.

"I don't mind . . . anything you like."

"All right. I'll leave you to it. You obviously want to be left alone."

"I didn't say that."

You walked away without looking back. I started to follow you, but your shoulders had a determined set to them, and I knew it would have to wait until later. I turned back to Niall, but he had disappeared.

"Niall! Are you there?"

"I'm here." His voice was close beside me.

"Let me see you."

"Not now. You want to be with him."

"It's not possible at the moment, thanks to you." I looked around, realizing that to the other people in the street I would appear to be standing and talking to myself. I started walking, knowing that Niall would stay with me. I said, "Don't you see what you're doing to him?"

There was no reply. I carried on walking, thinking that Niall was just not answering, but after a few seconds I realized he had moved off and left me. I turned back. Why had he suddenly gone away from me? I went back to the place where he had last spoken to me, called his name. There was no sound of him.

One or two passers-by were glancing at me curiously, so I moved on. There was a small patch of grass in the center of the square, and I went over to it and sat down on a wooden bench. The air was still warm in the evening. I hated it when Niall suddenly left me. It confused me and made me feel uncertain, just as it had the time he hung up on me. It made me remember the awfulness of his intrusions, the neurotic state he could induce in me.

And worse than this, it made me question whether or not he had really been there. His sudden manifestations were those of a visitant, a voice striking out of the air, conscience of my past.

Until I met you, Niall had never used his profound invisibility against me. Why?

If he cannot be seen, is he really there?

When he materializes from nowhere, what is it I appear to see?

Such thoughts lay close to the madness I feared. To clear my mind of them I walked away from the center of the little town and headed for our hotel. I wanted to see you whatever the circumstances, and whatever the outcome might be. Only in you lay certainty and sanity.

XVII

You were sitting on the bed in the room, reading the morning's newspaper, and you pretended not to notice me.

I said, "I'm hungry, Richard. Shall we find a restaurant?"

"All right." Without another word you folded away the paper and stood up.

The only restaurant we liked the look of was crowded, and we had to share a small table with another couple. Conversation was impossible, beyond the barest exchange of formalities about ordering the food. We left as soon as we could, and returned to the hotel. I was feeling sweaty and dusty after my long afternoon, so I took a shower. When I came out you had undressed and were lying on top of the bed. I toweled my hair, then got in under the sheet.

I said: "I know you're angry, but if I tell you the truth, will you listen?"

"It depends what it is."

"It's Niall. He's here in town, and I saw him today."

I thought you would have guessed somehow, but I saw the surprise register in your face.

"What the hell's he doing here?" you said. "He was in Malvern. Is he following us around?"

"The only thing that matters is that he's here."

"Why should you want to see him? I've had enough of this. I'm going back to London tomorrow. If you want to be with your damned boyfriend, you can stay here."

"I had to see him," I said. "I wanted to tell him that everything between him and me is over."

"You said that before."

"Richard, I love you."

"I don't think that's true any longer."

"It is."

It threw me aside from what I wanted to say. Everything was too complicated and charged with emotion. I wanted to simplify it, start again from what I saw as the central truth: that you were the only one I wanted to be with. But you threw it in my face, and that made me angry too. The arguing became illogical, until we both abandoned it. An irreparable change had taken place.

In a period of quiet I started thinking about what Niall had said in the afternoon, his need for me to tell you why he still mattered to me. In the desperation we had reached it felt as if it would be the only way to make you understand. You had left the bed, and were pacing about the room.

Then you said, "There's something I want to know. Why did you come out with all that stuff about invisibility?"

"What do you mean? You know what happened."

"I know what you *said* happened. What was it all about?"

"We're both naturally invisible, Richard."

"No we're not. It's a lot of bullshit."

"It's the single most important fact in my life."

"All right—do it now. Make yourself invisible."

"Why?"

"Because I don't believe you." You were staring at me with cold dislike.

"I'm upset now. It's difficult."

"Then tell me why you came out with all that crap."

"It's not crap," I said. I concentrated on intensifying the cloud, and after a few moments' uncertainty felt myself slip into invisibility. "I've done it."

You were staring directly at me. "Then why can I still see you?"

"I don't know—can you?"

"Plain as daylight."

"It's because . . . you know how to *look*. You know where I am. And because you're an invisible too."

You shook your head.

I deepened the cloud, and within it I climbed out of bed and moved away to the side. It was a small room, but I stood as far away from the bed as I could go, pressing myself against the polished wood of the wardrobe door. You were looking at me.

"I can still see you," you said.

"Richard, it's because you know *how!* Don't you understand that?"

"You're no more invisible than I am."

"I'm scared to go deeper." But I tried again, staring back at your angry face from within my cloud, wondering how I could ever convince you. I was trying to remember the disciplines Mrs. Quayle had taught me. I knew how to intensify the cloud, but for many years my fear of the shadows had pushed me the other way. I always had the terror that once I entered the deepest levels of the glamour I would become, like Niall, stuck forever.

For a moment you frowned, looking away, as if watching me cross the room. I held my breath, knowing you had lost sight of me. But you looked back.

"I can still see you," you said again, looking me in the eyes.

The cloud dispersed and I slumped on the bed. I began weeping. There was a pause, and then you were sitting beside me, your arm around my back. You held me close, and neither of us said anything. I let the tension drain out of me, and I sobbed against you.

We went to bed at last, but there was no lovemaking that night. We lay beside each other in the dark, and although I was exhausted I found it impossible to sleep. I knew that you too were awake. How much could I tell you about Niall? If you disbelieved my invisibility, what would you say about his?

Like you, I knew we could not go on like this, but I was scared that if you knew the truth I would lose you. Niall would then haunt me for the rest of my life.

Out of the dark, you said, "When I met you in the square this evening, what were you doing?"

"Trying to work things out."

"You seemed to be acting strangely. Was Niall watching you?"

"I think so."

"Where is he now?"

"I'm not sure . . . somewhere around."

"I still don't understand how he found us," you said.

"When he wants something, he's persistent."

"He seems to have power over you. I wish to God I knew what it was."

I lay there silently, wondering what to say. Nothing made sense that was not *my* sense, but you would not believe that.

"Sue?"

"It's Niall," I said. "I thought you would realize . . . he's glamorous too."

XVIII

We spent the whole of the next day driving back to London. There was a barrier of resentment and misunderstanding between us, and I had no idea what I could do or say to retrieve the situation. You seemed hurt and angry, unapproachable by reason or lovingness. I still wanted only you, but no longer knew how. I was losing you.

Niall traveled back with us, sitting invisibly in the rear seat of the car.

We came into London during the evening rush hour, and after leaving the motorway it was a slow and tiresome drive to Hornsey. You took me to my house, and parked the car outside. I could see the fatigue in your eyes.

"Would you like to come in for a few minutes?" I said.

"Yes, but I won't stay long."

We unloaded my stuff from the back of the car. I was watching to see some sign of Niall, but if he climbed out of the car he did so without my noticing. I let us into the house, closing the front door quickly, just in case. It was a senseless precaution, because he had had a key for years. I picked up the small stack of mail waiting for me on the hall table, then opened my room door. As soon as we were inside I closed the door quickly and bolted it, the only way I could be sure of keeping Niall out. You noticed this, but said nothing.

I opened a window at the top, and pulled back the half-drawn curtains. You sat down on the end of the bed.

You said, "Sue, we've got to sort this out. Are we going to go on seeing each other?"

"Do you want to?"

"I'd like to—but not with Niall hanging around."

"It's all over, I promise you."

"You've said that before. How do I know he isn't going to turn up again?"

"Because he told me that if I talked to you about him, so that you know what he thinks he's losing, then he would accept that."

"All right . . . what's the great sacrifice?"

"I told you last night. Niall is an invisible too."

"Not that again!" You stood up and moved away from me. "I'll tell you what I think of all that. The only invisibility I'm aware of is this damned ex-boyfriend who follows you around. I've never met him, never seen him, and as far as I'm concerned he doesn't exist! You've got to get rid of him, Sue!"

"Yes, I know."

"All right, we're both tired. I want to go back to my place and get some sleep. We'll probably feel different in the morning. Shall we meet for dinner tomorrow evening?"

"Do you want to?"

"I wouldn't suggest it if I didn't. I'll telephone you in the morning."

On that, after a brief kiss, we parted. I watched you drive away, and had a superstitious feeling I would not see you again. It felt as if we had reached a natural end, one which I had been incapable of preventing. I was helpless in the face of your doubts about invisibility. Niall had undermined everything.

I returned to my room and closed the door, bolting it behind me.

I said, "Niall, are you here?" A long silence followed. "If you're here, please tell me."

His absence unnerved me as much as his invisible presence. I walked around the room, thrashing my arms about, trying to find him in case he was staying silent to intimidate me, but at last I was sure I was alone. I opened my suitcase and hung up my clothes, making a heap on the floor of the ones that needed washing. There was no food in the place, but we had stopped for lunch on the way and I was not really hungry. I changed my clothes, putting on jeans and a clean shirt. Then I remembered the pile of mail, and sat on the bed to go through it.

In the middle of the stack of envelopes was a picture postcard.

XIX

The postcard was unsigned, but I knew the handwriting was Niall's. The message simply read, "Wish you were here," and underneath was an X. The picture was a modern reproduction of an old black-and-white photograph: a quayside in Saint-Tropez with a large warehouse in the background. I tried to decipher the postmark, but it was smudged and illegible. The postage stamp was French: the green head of a goddess, *France Postes*, f.1.70.

It was undoubtedly from Niall. He never signed his name, and anyway I knew his handwriting. Even the X was flamboyant.

I opened the other letters, skimming through their contents, barely registering them. When I had finished I tipped the envelopes into the wastebasket. The picture postcard lay on the bed.

I still had the bruise on my thigh where Niall had kicked me; I was still slightly stiff from the blow on my back. I vividly remembered the rape, the car with the engine running, the unpacked clothes, the bar of soap dropped on me in the night. I had *seen* Niall, had spent most of the previous afternoon with him.

How could he have been in France?

The postcard with its derisive message, its showy anonymity, denied everything I had experienced in the last few days.

Either Niall had been following me on my holiday with you, or he had been in France, where he had claimed from the outset he was.

Was I imagining everything?

I remembered the decision I had taken: Niall *had* to be in France, otherwise I was accepting the madness of the invisible world. I had wanted to act on that, but Niall had appeared in England.

Throughout our trip I had felt the fear of madness, the uncertainty of his visitations. I looked to passers-by as if I were talking to myself; you never saw him; he could rape me while I made love to you and you never knew. He entered and left rooms without my seeing the door open, he was in the car and not in the car, sitting behind us, invisible to us both.

But there were odd and authentic details: his being out of breath after we climbed the hill behind Malvern, the rasp of his pubic hair as he raped me, the clarity of those suspiciously close phone calls, the smell of Gauloises cigarettes in the room and on his breath.

The postcard was an objective disproof of this. It was there, and it had been mailed. It arrived in the impartiality of a bundle of letters.

I tried to think of explanations for the card, however wild. He had bought the card in England, and talked one of his friends into posting it to me from France. But where would you come across a card like this in England? Perhaps he had found it in a shop somewhere, and thought of sending it to me as a way of disorienting me? Niall was capable of something like that, but it was over-elaborate. Maybe he had indeed traveled to France when he said, sent the card, then returned? But why? It was implausible, too much trouble to go to when he had other ways of distracting me. And I was still sure those phone calls had come from London.

Anyway, I had *seen* him. He looked like someone who had been trailing us, unshaven, pale, wearing dirty clothes. He had seemed realistic in every way, bar the madness that kept him out of the real world.

Again the idea of madness. Was it me?

Had I imagined him into existence, an embodiment of guilt, or of my past, or of my conscience?

If I could make myself invisible to the world, was I equally capable of summoning another presence into visibility?

Had I produced Niall out of my unconscious, a visitation of what I wished on myself, what I expected, what I most dreaded?

As I sat there, these turbulent fears whirling through me, I realized I had slipped without noticing it into invisibility. My cloud had intensified because of my terror. I pushed the postcard under the covers of the bed, out of sight.

My invisibility—curse or talent, whichever it might be—was the only area of my life of which I was certain. I knew what I was, and what I could become. It might be my madness, but it was all mine.

I walked across the room and opened the long wardrobe door. I stared into the mirror inside. My reflection came back at me: my hair was untidy, my eyes were dilated. I swung the door to and fro, trying to confuse the image, trying to make myself not see—but I was always there. I remembered the trick Mrs. Quayle had played on me, concealing a mirror so that in my surprise I failed to see myself. Only Mrs. Quayle had believed in my talent more than I did.

Both Niall and you eroded my self-confidence, in different ways: Niall by his behavior, you by disbelieving. I had thought that by bringing you into the world of the invisibles you would see me as I really was, and by understanding would show me the way out of it. Niall, for converse reasons, held me back, or tried to. You were each the complement of the other, suspending me between you.

Whichever way I turned I seemed to be losing my mind.

I stared at the reflection of myself, knowing I could not trust even that. It made me look as if I were there, when I knew I was not.

You said you saw me, when I knew you could not.

Only Niall knew me for what I really was, and I could not trust him at all.

I ran out to the hall and picked up the telephone. I dialed your number and the ringing tone was sounding before I realized I had brought no coins. Anyway, there was no answer.

Back in my room, the postcard from Niall was still to be explained. I stared at it for a while, thinking of its consequences, then propped it up on the shelf over the gas fire. It was safest to treat it as just another postcard, sent by a friend on holiday.

I went through the rest of my mail again—one letter enclosed a much-needed check, and another a commission for some artwork—then I undressed and went to bed.

The first thing I did in the morning was to telephone you. After a few rings you answered, and I slipped in two coins before we spoke.

"Richard? It's me . . . Sue."

"I thought you might have called last night." Your

voice sounded husky, and I wondered if I had woken you up.

"I did try, but there was no answer." You said nothing, and I couldn't remember if we had made a firm arrangement that I would ring you. "How are you?" I said.

"Tired. What are you doing today?"

"I'm going in to visit the studio. There was a letter . . . there's a job for me. I can't afford to let it go."

"Will you be out all day?"

"Most of it," I said.

"Shall we meet this evening? I'd like to see you and I've got some news."

"News? What is it?"

"I've been offered some work. I'll tell you about it this evening."

We made arrangements about when and where to meet. Talking to you I had a mental image of you sitting on the floor by your phone. I imagined you with your hair mussed from the bed, your eyes still half closed; I wondered if you slept in pajamas when you were alone. The thought made me feel affectionate toward you, and I wished I could see you at once. I wanted to visit your flat again, be with you in your home, not always traveling around from one hotel to the next, never sure if Niall was watching. For some reason I thought of your flat as safe from Niall, although there was no reason why it should be.

Thinking of you there reminded me of the day of the storm, when we had planned our holiday. I remembered your collection of postcards.

I said, "While we were away, someone sent me a postcard. It wasn't you, was it?"

"Postcard? Why should I do that?"

"Whoever sent it didn't sign it." I thought of Niall's distinctive handwriting. "It was an old card . . . the sort you collect."

"Well, it wasn't me."

I said, "When I see you this evening, would you bring some of your cards along? The places you wanted to visit, in France—I'd like to look at them again."

XX

I visited the studio in town, and collected the work they wanted me to do. I made a start on it at home in the afternoon, but my mind was elsewhere. To meet you in the evening I had to take a bus across North London; when we had agreed on the place I had been thinking I would be coming straight from the West End. It was a tube station, fairly close to your apartment. I arrived before you, but as soon as I saw you, walking up from the direction of the flat, I was so glad and relieved to see you that all my worries vanished. I ran toward you, and we stood for a long time kissing and holding each other as the traffic went by.

We walked back to your flat, arm in arm, and we went to bed as soon as we were there. So much had happened since we last made love, but to be together again made everything right. Afterward we walked up the hill to Hampstead and found a restaurant.

Feeling relaxed with you, I talked about my day and the commission I had received. I deliberately did not think about or mention Niall.

Then you said, "Don't you want to hear my news?"

"You said you'd been offered some work."

"A camera job. I'm thinking of accepting it."

"Why shouldn't you?"

"Because it'll mean going away for a while. Maybe as long as two weeks." You explained about the political tension in Central America, the reason a British crew was wanted. You appeared to be doubtful about telling me this, and at first I assumed it was because the work would be dangerous.

"What about it, Sue? Should I accept?"

"Not if you think you might be killed."

You made a dismissive gesture. "I'm thinking about you. If I go away for a couple of weeks, will you be here when I get back?"

"Of course I will!"

"What about Niall, Sue? Is that all over?"

"I'm sure it is."

"Have you seen him today?"

"No, and I don't even know where he is."

"You'd better be sure of this. Niall and I don't mix. Either you put the past behind you, or we've had it."

I took your hand across the table. "Richard, I love *you*."

I meant it then, as I had always done, but I knew in my heart that the problem of Niall was not yet solved. I changed the subject. I told you to take the job, to be careful, and to come back as soon as you could. With that I implied what you wanted to hear, and sincerely meant to do so. You talked a little more about the work—the other men you would be working with, where you would be going, the sort of stories you were supposed to be covering. I wished it were possible for me to go with you.

You had brought some of your postcards to the restaurant, and you gave them to me to look at. I glanced through them quickly, trying to give the impression that my curiosity was idle. There were pictures of Grenoble, Nice, Antibes, Cannes, Saint-Raphaël, Saint-Tropez, Toulon, all of them depicting the places in their innocent past. There were only two of Saint-Tropez: one showed a beach near the village, the other was a view of one of the streets, with a glimpse of the harbor through the houses.

You said, "What are you looking for?"

"Nothing." I stacked the cards together and passed them back to you.

"You said on the phone that someone had sent you an old card. Was it one like these?"

"No . . . I think it's a modern reproduction."

"Who sent it? Was it Niall?"

I tried to laugh lightly. "Of course not. You know where Niall has been for the last few days."

"I know where you said he was. You also told me he was in France—that was why you didn't want to go there."

"Oh yes," I said.

"Come on, let's get the bill." You turned your head away with a sharp movement and I saw your angry expression. The waitress came over and you paid the bill. Moments later we were in the street, retracing our steps toward your flat. This time I was not invited in. We went straight to your car, parked outside. I saw you toss the postcards onto the back seat before you unlocked the passenger door for me.

We drove in silence to Hornsey. Outside my house, I said, "Would you like to come in for a while?"

"I know you probably think I'm being unfair, but you've got to quit deceiving me about Niall." I tried to say something, but you went on. "You're the only woman I've ever loved, but I'm damned if this is going to go on any longer. I'll be away for a couple of weeks. That should give you enough time to make up your mind what it is you want."

"You mean I have to choose between you and Niall."

"You've hit it."

"I've already chosen, Richard. It's just that Niall won't accept it."

"Then you'll have to make him."

As soon as I was back in my room I took down Niall's postcard and tore it into small pieces. I flushed the whole thing down the lavatory. The following day you telephoned to say you were flying out to Managua that evening, and promised you would get in touch as soon as you were home.

Two days after you left, Niall returned.

XXI

What then followed was my own doing, the result of a decision. You had given me an ultimatum, one that I knew you meant. You forced a choice between you and Niall, and I chose Niall.

I had been wrong to think I could start a new life and leave Niall behind me; the plain fact was that Niall was haunting me, and would go on doing so until he had his way. I could no longer stand the torment, the feeling of being torn between you. I had had enough.

Like you, Niall saw everything in terms of the other man. What I had to do was prove I had grown away from him, and to do that I had to be alone with him. I hoped all this could be accomplished before you returned, but if that was not to be, then I was prepared to lose you.

This was not a cold decision. When Niall turned up I was still holding on, waiting for you to come back, but as soon as I saw him I realized what I was going to have to do.

He arrived outside my door, having let himself into the house with his key. I slid back the bolts, and he walked in. He looked well. He was clean-shaven, wearing new clothes, and was exuding some of his old air of self-confidence. He was in good spirits, and when I told him you were away he said only that he knew it would never have worked out. He moved back in on me as if nothing had changed, and although I would not let him stay that first night, afterward we were sleeping together again.

Where had he been? I never asked him directly, nor did we refer to the afternoon in St. David's. Nothing was certain: if he had been in the South of France he had none of the suntan I would expect, but I noticed that the Gauloises he was smoking did *not* have the UK government health warning, as if they had been bought from a duty-free shop. He had brought me a liter bottle of Côtes-de-Provence, describing it as "the local plonk," but a few days later I noticed a local wine merchant was selling identical bottles.

I never asked him about the postcard, I never mentioned the intrusions, the beating he had given me, the rape. Frankly, I was scared of what he would say.

If he really had been in France, what had been happening to me while I was with you? If he had been following us around, who sent me the postcard?

I was glad of the mental respite, the freedom to concentrate on one problem which I knew could be solved in the end. I *would* convince him we were finished, and I *would* get him out of my life for good, but as the time passed I realized it was going to take longer than the few days remaining.

The worst possible thing happened. You returned from your trip two or three days earlier than I had thought, and came to the house without telephoning first. I was in bed with Niall when I heard the house bell ring. Someone else opened the door, and I heard your voice. In panic, I leaped out of bed and pulled on my dressing gown, remembering in time to make myself visible. Niall lay naked on the bed behind me, visible to me, invisible to you. As you knocked on my door I glanced back at him and saw how his expression had changed. Moments before, we had been lying sleepily together, chatting idly,

Niall smoking a cigarette; now he looked alert and frightened.

He said, "If that's who I think it is, get rid of him."

"Don't do anything, Niall," I said quietly. "Please don't let him know you're here."

I opened the door, and you were standing there. I was too shocked by your sudden arrival to know what to say, but backed guiltily into the room, clutching the untied dressing gown across my body.

"You're still in bed!" you said, and glanced at your watch. You looked tired and confused.

"I was having a lie-in."

"Are you on your own?"

"Can you see anyone?"

"Niall's been here, hasn't he?"

"Tell him I'm here now," Niall said. I looked back at him, and he was standing by the bed; his moment of fright had been replaced by a hard, determined expression. Knowing the worst of him, what he was capable of, I stepped between the two of you. Niall's temper was unpredictable.

"Richard, let me explain—"

"No, don't say anything—you don't have to. I suppose I asked for this. God, what's the bloody time? My watch is wrong."

"It's half-past eleven," Niall said, and took my clock from the shelf and shook it in front of your face. I moved again, trying to elbow Niall back.

"It's late morning," I said. "I was just about to get up."

"I was just about to get up *you* again," Niall said, crudely.

"But you have been seeing Niall again, haven't you?"

"I had to. You forced me to make a choice, and that's all there is to say."

"Then it's finished, Sue."

"You know what annoys me most?" Niall said, moving again. "It's when he calls you Sue. Get rid of him."

"Well?" you said.

"All right. Let's leave it at that."

"I just wish to God I knew what it is that Niall has over you. Is he going to run your life forever?"

"I told you," I said. "Niall's glamorous too."

You looked impatient. "Not that again!"

"What do you see in this cretin, Susan?" Niall said.

I could no longer attempt to control a three-way conversation. I retreated, and went to sit on the edge of the bed. I stared hopelessly at the floor.

"Sue, what has glamour to do with this?"

"Not glamour," I said. "*The* glamour. Niall has the glamour."

"You can't be serious!"

"It's the most important thing in my life, and in yours too if only you knew it. We're all invisible, can't you get that into your head?"

In my misery I knew I was sinking into invisibility. I no longer cared, no longer wanted anything but to be rid of you both. Niall was standing beside you, ludicrously naked, his face set in that unpleasant combination of arrogance and inadequacy that showed when he felt threatened. You had a stupid look, as you stared around the room.

You said, "Sue, I can't see you! What's happening?"

I said nothing, knowing that even if I spoke you would be unable to hear. You stepped back, placed your hand on the door and opened it a few inches.

"That's right, Grey. Time to fuck off."

I said, "Shut up, Niall!"

But you must have heard, because you looked sharply toward me.

"He's here, isn't he?" you said. "Niall's here now!"

I said, "He's been with us ever since I met you. If

you had learned how to look when I tried to show you, you would have seen him."

"Where is he?"

"I'm here, you stupid bastard!"

Niall's voice was suddenly stronger than ever before, and I realized that for the last few seconds his cloud had been thinning. It was more dispersed than I had ever seen it.

"I'm here, Grey!" Niall said, waving his arms, moving around. He kicked out at you with his foot, catching you on the shin. You reacted in surprise, and looked intently at Niall. He was closer to visibility than I had thought was possible for him, and I knew you could see him, or something of him. You whirled around, shoving Niall out of the way, snatched the door open and went outside, slamming it behind you. Moments later the street door slammed too. I sprawled across the bed and started to cry. I could hear Niall moving around, but I closed my mind to him. When I next looked, he was standing with his peacock clothes on, looking both defiant and shaken.

"I'll call in later, Susan," he said.

"Don't!" I cried. "I never want to see you again!"

"He won't come back, you know."

"I don't care! I don't want to see him, and I don't want to see you! Now get out of here!"

"I'll call you when you've calmed down."

"I won't answer. Just get to hell out of here, and don't come back!"

"I'm going to fix Grey . . ."

"Get out!" I ran from the bed, opened the door and shoved him through, pushing it against his weight and then bolting it. He banged on the door and called something to me, but I didn't listen. I lay on the bed and pressed the pillow over my ears. I was utterly sick of everything, blaming myself, blaming you, blaming Niall.

A long time later, when I dressed and went out for a walk, I discovered I had become visible.

I had grown used to being visible with you, and I was accustomed to the feeling, but now I was alone. There was no other cloud near me from which I could draw strength. My visibility had become my normal state. It felt odd, like new clothes.

When I was back in my room, I tried to make myself invisible. It was more difficult than I would have believed, a strain to sustain it. As soon as I relaxed, I slipped into visibility again.

By the time evening came I knew that everything I had sought was now mine. It seemed ironical, but deserved, that I had had to lose you to gain it.

That was the day of the car bomb, but I did not hear about it for some time. I had no television and read no newspapers, and anyway my interior preoccupations were flooding everything. I worked at my drawing board until late into the night.

I went into the West End the next day to visit the studio, and learned from newspaper placards and headlines that a bomb had been set off outside a police station in northwest London. Six people had been killed, and several more had been seriously injured. It did not occur to me that you might have been one of them.

I saw nothing of Niall for almost a week, then one day he turned up at the house. He rang the bell at the street door, and when I went out I found him in a subdued, defensive mood. I felt no shock at seeing him.

He said, "I won't come in, Susan. I wanted to see how you are."

"I'm fine. You can come in for a few minutes if you like."

"No. I was just passing." He was acting guiltily, avoiding my eyes. "I suppose you've heard the news?"

I shook my head. "I don't read the papers."

"I thought not. You'd better read this one." He passed me a copy of *The Times*, rolled up tightly. I started to unfurl it. "Don't look at it now," Niall said. "Read it inside."

I said, "Is it about Richard?"

"You'll see what it is. And there's something else. . . . You said you wanted to read what I've been writing. I wrote this for you—I don't want it back."

He passed over a manila envelope sealed with transparent tape.

"What's happened to Richard?" I said, the newspaper already half open.

"It's all in there," Niall said, and turned and walked quickly away.

I opened the newspaper as I stood in the doorway, and by reading the main story I found out at last about the car bomb, and what had happened to you. Most of the news was about the police hunt for the terrorists, with new security measures being introduced, but I learned that you and the other injured people were in intensive care, under police protection. It turned out that one of the terrorists had been injured in the blast, and the others had issued a macabre warning that "witnesses" would be eliminated. Even the hospital in which you were being treated was kept a secret.

I bought every newspaper I could find, and followed the story for as long as it was prominent. You were the worst injured of all the victims, and the last to be removed from the danger list. I know that if I had really tried I would have been allowed to visit you earlier, but I sincerely believed that seeing me might have done you more harm than good.

In the end only one newspaper carried occasional bulletins about your progress, following what they called your "story." From this paper I learned that you had been moved to a convalescent hospital, and at long last I plucked up the courage to try to see you. I telephoned the newspaper, and they arranged everything.

As soon as I saw you, that morning with the reporter, the first thing I noticed was that you had lost your glamour.

This is what happened to you, Richard, in the weeks before the car bomb. Do you now remember?

Part VI

Part VI

I

Three weeks after returning to London, Richard Grey was offered filming work in Liverpool. It was to be a four-day assignment, operating the camera for a television documentary about urban renewal in the wake of the Toxteth riots. It would be physically demanding on him, but the unit would be working with full union crew, including camera assistants, and after an hour's indecision he accepted. He caught the train to Liverpool the following day.

It temporarily solved the problem of what to do. He felt frustrated by the continuing stiffness in his body, and was restless to be working again. Anyway, his money was at last beginning to run low. There was talk of compensation being paid by the Home Office, and correspondence was going to and fro between a solicitor and his MP, but it was not something he was counting on.

Until the film work came along, Grey had been hobbling through his life, learning again how to go shopping, to the movies, to the pub. Everything had to be taken slowly. Once a week he went to the physiotherapy department at Whittington Hospital to be manipulated and exercised; he was improving, but it was very gradual. He walked as much as he could, because although immediately afterward he felt tired and uncomfortable, the long-term effect was a steady easing of his left hip. The stairs outside his apartment were a constant obstacle, but he found he could manage. Driving was difficult, because using the clutch pedal put a strain on his hip. What he needed was a car with automatic transmission, but this would have to wait until more money arrived.

Leaving London would mean a break from Sue,

something which a few weeks before he would never have dreamed he wanted, but which now seemed essential. He had to have time away from her to think about other things, clear his mind a little.

Grey wished fervently that she had turned out to be in reality what she had appeared to be at first: a girlfriend from his lost weeks with whom a relationship could be continued, renewed by the freshness of rediscovery. When he first met her he had found her oddness intriguing and winsome, hinting at layers of buried complexity which patience would release.

He still found her physically attractive, she interested him, and great tenderness existed. As his body healed, their physical relationship became more exciting and satisfying. But the difference was that she said she loved him, whereas in his innermost self Grey knew he did not feel the same. He liked her and he wanted to know her better and more intimately, but he did not love her. He was emotionally dependent on her, missed her when they were apart, felt protective of her, but still he did not love her.

The problem was their past together.

He did not *feel* about it. Memories of sorts now came from his lost weeks, but they were fragmentary and disconcerting, appearing from some subconscious or near-conscious level of his mind.

Real memories are a muddle of overlooked experience; odd and irrelevant facts lurk in the mind, stubbornly unforgotten after a period of years; snatches of forgotten tunes appear unsummoned in the head; strange associations exist—a smell will evoke a particular event, a color will be an inexplicable reminder of a place visited long ago. Grey had such normal memory capabilities concerning most of his past life, but his amnesiac period was still closed to him.

What memories he had of that time came to him with a superficial accuracy that he sensed was unreliable.

His mind told him stories, gave him anecdotes and se-
quences that had a shallow plausibility. The analogy he
made for it was a film that had been edited, so that narra-
tive continuity was already there.

The rest of his memories, his old life, were like un-
cut rushes, unsorted, unassembled, hanging around in the
can of his mind for order to be edited into them.

He now recognized that his memories of France
were mostly false, projected onto his mind from some
quirk of the unconscious. He knew he had not been to
France—or not, at least, at the time he remembered. Some
parts of the story were true: he had met Sue, there was the
business with Niall, there had been a holiday together, he
had been filming in Central America, there had been a
final row.

But then there was Sue's account of their past together, and here the real gap appeared.

While she indirectly confirmed his edited memories, her story was something he had only *heard*. He could
accept what she said in the way he might read and accept
something in a book or a newspaper. She obviously believed that once she told her story some buried unconscious memory would be triggered, and his real memories
of the same incidents would leap into his mind. He had
wanted to believe that too, and throughout had waited for
something he could identify, a resonant image, some moment of psychological conviction opening the way to the
rest. It had not come. Her story remained a story, and it
was as yet remote from him.

If anything, it had deepened the problem of his forgotten period. She had in a sense shown him another edited film, ready-made, complete in itself.

The muddle of reality still eluded him.

His present misgivings, though, centered on two
other areas. There was Sue's emphasis on her claims to
invisibility, and her obsessive and destructive relationship
with Niall.

Once before in his life Grey had been briefly involved in a triangular situation. Although he had genuinely cared for the woman at the center of that, and had tried not to put pressure on her, the constant indecision, the to-ings and fro-ings of loyalty and his own unavoidable feelings of sexual jealousy had ultimately poisoned the affair. He had sworn afterward never again to get involved with someone leading a double life, yet this was exactly what he appeared to have done with Sue. Something very powerful must have drawn him to her.

Sue said that Niall was no longer bothering her, and that she had not seen him since the day he gave her the copy of *The Times*. It certainly appeared to be true that there was no one else in her life at the moment.

Niall remained a factor, though.

It was as if she was holding something in reserve about him, as if, should he suddenly reappear, he would again demand a place in her life. Niall had become a subject neither of them raised, and by not being discussed he remained distant but omnipresent.

Invisibility deepened the division.

Grey was a practical man, trained to use eye and hand. His vocation was with visual images, lit and seen and photographed. What he saw he believed in; what he did not see was not there.

Listening to Sue's account of her life, he thought at first that her endless talk of invisible people was allegorical in some way, a description of an attitude to life. Maybe this was so, but he knew she also meant it literally and physically. She maintained that some people could escape being seen through the failure of others to notice them. That he, Grey himself, was of the same condition was frankly incredible to him.

Yet Sue's account of this was that she had awakened him to it, that she had demonstrated to him the talent he had. Now, she claimed, it was latent in him again, shocked out of him by the assault of his injuries. If he remembered *how*, she said, he would rediscover it.

Listening to her, the doubts she frequently expressed, the talk of madness and delusion, he wondered if the explanation lay there. The sheer obsession of Sue's insistence was itself close to delusion—a mad jargon, the desperation of persistent but illogical belief.

His was the sort of mind that demanded proof, and, failing that, evidence. It seemed to him that it would be simple to settle the matter one way or another, but Sue was maddeningly imprecise. Invisible people were *there*, they could be *seen*, but unless you knew how to see they would not be *noticed*.

They went out one day to Kensington High Street, mingling with the crowds of shoppers on a busy afternoon. Sue pointed out a number of people, claiming that they were invisibles. Sometimes Grey could see who she meant, sometimes he could not. He photographed them all. The results were inconclusive: when the prints came back from the processor, the crowds were just crowds, and he and Sue could only argue whether this person had been visible at the time, or that couple was invisible.

"Make yourself invisible," Grey said. "Do it now, while I watch."

"I can't."

"But you said you could."

"It's different now. It's not easy for me anymore."

"You can still do it, though."

"Yes, but you know how to *see* me."

Nevertheless, she tried. After much frowning and concentration she declared herself to be invisible, but as far as Grey was concerned she was still there, noticed in the room. She accused him of disbelieving her, but it was not as straightforward as that. He believed, for instance, in the fact of her appearance.

She had always attracted him with the neutrality of the way she looked. Everything about her was plain: her skin was fair, her hair was light brown, her eyes were hazel, her features were regular, her figure was slim. She was of average height, and her clothes sat naturally on her body. When she moved, she did so quietly. Her voice was pleasant but unremarkable. A disinterested glance at her might dismiss her as dull and mousy, but to Grey, interested in her and involved with her, she was unusually attractive. What he perceived in her was hidden by the plainness of the surface; something electric came from within. When they were together he was always wanting to touch her. He liked the way her face changed when she smiled, or was preoccupied. When they made love he felt that their bodies blended without touching, an imprecise sensation that he experienced every time but which he could never define. It was as if she were a complement to him, someone who responded to his immediate needs.

She claimed that by disbelieving her invisibility he was rejecting everything she had told him, but in fact this concealed quality of her intrigued him.

She was not invisible to him, or not in any way he understood the word, but she was for all that an *inexact* person. This did persuade him that her claims had an inner truth, and he believed he was a long way from rejecting her.

Even so, the trip to Liverpool gave him the opportunity to reflect.

II

The sea could always be felt in Liverpool; the great riverfront with the view across to Birkenhead, the glimpse of the Irish Sea to the west, the self-confident architecture of the Victorian shipping offices, the smell of water on the gusting wind. Away from the center, but not far away, where the buildings were meaner and the streets were narrower, the sea evidenced itself differently: a grim red-light district of slum houses, empty warehouses where bonded goods had once been stored, pubs with maritime names, cleared areas fronted with advertising posters selling Jamaican rum and airlines to America.

Here was Toxteth, where belated government intervention was trying to impose community spirit on a place where transience had always been the norm.

It was good to be working with an Arriflex again, feeling its lumpy weight on his shoulder, the molded eyepiece against his brow. Grey greeted the workaday camera with a sense of quiet reunion, amazed to discover how natural it still felt in his hands, how his vision was narrowed and sharpened by seeing and thinking through the viewfinder. But he was used to working with a smaller crew, and the large number of people around him disconcerted him at first. He felt he was on trial, that they were waiting to see if he still knew what to do, but within a short time of starting he realized that these were his own fears and everyone else was too busy with his own job to be thinking about him.

He settled to the work, glad to be doing again what he was best at. The first day's shooting exhausted him because he was out of practice in other ways, and the morning of the second day his leg and shoulders were painful. The work absorbed him, though, and he knew that these few days were worth a hundred hours of physiotherapy.

The director was an experienced documentary maker, and they kept easily to the schedule. They were always finished with filming by late afternoon, leaving the evenings free. The crew were staying at the Adelphi Hotel, a glorious Victorian extravaganza in the center of the city, and each evening most of the people stayed in to drink in the large palm-filled mezzanine bar. For Grey it was an opportunity to talk shop, swap stories about old assignments, catch up on gossip about people he knew. There was talk of more jobs coming up, a chance to work on contract in Saudi Arabia, a story developing in Italy.

It was all radically different from the last few weeks when he had been obsessed with himself and Sue, her bizarre story and claustrophobic relationships. He telephoned her from his room one evening, and hearing her voice, thin and faint down the trunk line, gave him the sense of drilling a long tunnel back to something he had already left behind. She said she was lonely without him . . . wanted him back with her quickly . . . sorry about everything . . . different now. He uttered reassurances, feeling glib, trying to make them sincere. He still wanted her, yearned for lovemaking with her, but while he was away it all felt as different as she said.

They shot the last footage on the fourth evening. The location was a workingmen's club, a smoky barn loud with music and raised voices. Grey arrived early with his assistants and set up the lights for the interviews, widened a few gangways for the camera to dolly along. To one side there was a small platform with a number of spotlights, musical amplifiers stacked unused under covers at the back. The acoustics were bright, and the soundman winced at the amount of echo when he took a level. Most of the club members were men, wearing suits without neckties, and the few women kept their outdoor coats on. Everyone drank from straight glasses, talking noisily over the recorded band music coming from the loudspeakers. As the place filled up and the bouncers took up their positions by the bar and the door, Grey was reminded of a pub in Northern Ireland where he had been filming a few years before. That had had the same spartan décor: plain tables and chairs, bare floorboards, beer-mats and ashtrays from breweries, overhead lights with cheap lampshades, the bar itself lit by fluorescent tubes.

They started filming: a few establishing shots of the

crowded room, close-ups on a few drinkers, and then a
number of interviews: how many people were unem-
ployed, what life was like, prospects of moving away, a
works closure impending.

The main entertainment of the evening was a stripper, who came onto the platform wearing a gaudy se-
quined outfit that had obviously seen much use. Grey took
the camera on his shoulder and moved in to film her act.
Seeing the camera, the woman put on an elaborate show,
grimacing sexily, grinding her backside, stripping off her
costume with exaggerated gestures. She looked to be in
her middle thirties—overweight, with a bad complexion
under her makeup, stretch marks on her belly, and pendu-
lous breasts. When she was naked she jumped down from
the platform. Grey followed her with the camera as she
went from table to table sitting on laps, spreading her legs,
letting her breasts be fingered, a look of grim gaiety on her
face.

When she had gone and the camera was being rein-
stalled on the dolly, Grey stood to one side, remembering.

There had been a stripper in that bar in Belfast. He
and the soundman had gone there in the middle of the
evening, after a sectarian shooting had taken place. They
arrived just as the ambulances and police were leaving,
and all there was left to film were bullet holes in the wall
and broken glass on the floor. Because it was Belfast the
blood was soon mopped up and the commotion died
down, and even as they were filming the drinking went on
and new customers arrived. A stripper came on and went
through her act, and Grey and the soundman had stayed
to watch. Just as they were about to leave, the gunmen
abruptly returned, pushing through the crowd near the
door and shouting threats. Both carried Armalite rifles,
pointed upward. Without thinking what he was doing,
Grey hefted the camera to his shoulder and started filming. He forced his way through the crowd, going right up
to the gunmen, filming their faces. He was there when

they opened fire, pumping a dozen rounds into the ceiling, bringing plaster down in flakes and lumps. Then they left.

Grey's film was never transmitted, but it was later used by the security forces to identify the men, and they were arrested and convicted.

Grey's reckless act of courage had been rewarded by a cash bonus from the network, but the incident was soon forgotten. What no one, including Grey, could understand was why the gunmen had let him film them, why they had not shot him.

Standing there in the racket of the drinking club in Liverpool, Grey was remembering something Sue had said. She had reminded him of the story he must have told her, of filming in the street riot. She said: in the heat of the moment you made yourself invisible.

Had that happened in the bar in Belfast too? Was there after all something in what she said?

He completed the rest of the filming in the club, now feeling self-conscious, thinking himself an intruder into the depressing lives of these people, and was glad when the equipment was packed up and they could return to the hotel.

III

As soon as he was awake in the morning, Grey telephoned Sue at the house. She came to the phone sounding groggy with sleep. He told her that the schedule had had to be extended, and that he would not be back in London for another two days. She sounded disappointed, but did not question him. She said she had been doing some thinking, and wanted to talk to him. Grey promised he would contact her as soon as he was back, and they hung up.

After breakfast the crew met in the lobby before dispersing. Grey noted down a few phone numbers, and provisionally arranged to meet the producer in London the following week. When they had all said their farewells, he hitched a lift in the car of the assistant director, who was driving to Manchester. Grey was dropped off a short bus ride away from the suburb where Sue had said she was born.

He located the address in a telephone directory and walked through the residential streets to find it. The house was a prewar detached villa, standing in a short cul-de-sac.

A woman answered the door, smiling at him but looking cautious.

"Excuse me, are you Mrs. Kewley?"

"Yes. Can I help you?"

"You have a daughter Susan, living in London?"

The smile disappeared. "It's not bad news, is it?"

"Not at all. My name's Richard Grey, and I'm a friend of Susan's. I've been working around here, and I thought I'd call on you and say hello."

"There hasn't been an accident, has there?"

"I'm sorry—I should have telephoned first. Susan's fine, and she sends her love. I didn't mean to alarm you."

"You said your name was . . . ?"

"Richard Grey. Look, if it's inconvenient, I—"

"Would you like to come in for a few minutes? I'll make some tea."

There was a long corridor inside, with a glimpse through to a kitchen at the far end. Carpeted stairs rose from the hall, with small framed paintings hanging from the wall. He was shown into the front room, where chairs and ornaments were set out with neat precision. Mrs. Kewley bent down to light the gas fire, and straightened slowly.

"Is it tea you would like, Mr. Grey? Or I could

make some coffee." Her accent was northern, with no detectable trace of the Scottish he had expected.

"Tea, please. I'm sorry to arrive without warning, but—"

"I'm always glad to meet Susan's friends. I won't be a moment."

There was a photograph of Sue on the mantelpiece: her hair was longer, and tied back with a ribbon. She looked much younger, but her awkward way of sitting when she knew she was being looked at was the same. The photo was mounted in a frame, and the name of the studio was inscribed in one corner. He guessed it had been taken shortly before she left home.

Grey prowled quietly around the room, sensing that it was not often used. He could hear voices and the movement of crockery at the distant end of the corridor. He felt like an intruder, knowing that Sue would be furious if she found out what he was doing. He heard voices coming down the corridor, so he sat down in one of the chairs by the fire. A woman said, " 'Bye now, May. I'll pop in again tomorrow."

" 'Bye, Alice." The front door opened and closed, and Sue's mother came into the room with a tray.

They were overpolite and uncomfortable with each other, Grey because of his uncertain motives for being there, and Mrs. Kewley presumably because of his unannounced arrival. She looked rather older than he would have expected Sue's mother to be, with hair already white and a slight stiffness in her movements. But her face was unmistakably like Sue's, and he was pleased at glimpsing little similarities in gesture.

"Are you the friend who is a photographer?" she said.

"That's right . . . well, I'm a film cameraman."

"Oh yes. Susan told us about you. You were in an accident, weren't you?"

They talked for a while about the bomb and his

spell in the hospital, Grey surprised to learn that Sue had
talked about him to her parents. Realizing that what people say to their parents is often a guarded form of the
whole truth, he was cautious about what he said of Sue's
present life, but Mrs. Kewley said that Sue wrote many
letters home. She knew all about Sue's career, and even
had a scrapbook of press clippings, many of which Grey
had never seen. It was a small insight into Sue, discover-
ing how much work she had sold and that she was obviously well established in her field.

When the scrapbook had been put aside Mrs.
Kewley said, "Is Susan still going out with Niall?"

"I'm not sure . . . I don't think so. I didn't know
you had met him."

"Oh yes, we know Niall well. Susan brought him
home with her one weekend. A very nice boy, we thought,
though rather quiet. I think he is some kind of writer, but
he wouldn't say too much about it. Is he a friend of yours
too?"

"No, I've never met him to speak to."

"I see." Mrs. Kewley suddenly smiled nervously
and glanced away, just like Sue. She presumably thought
she had made a gaffe, so Grey was quick to reassure her
that he and Sue were simply friends. This moment off her
guard broke the ice, and Mrs. Kewley became more talkative after it. She told him about her other daughter Rosemary, married and living a few miles away in Stockport.
There were two grandchildren, whom Sue had never
mentioned.

Grey was thinking about Niall, and the account
Sue had given him of the one occasion she had brought
him to this house. It had been very different from the
scene of indulgent parental approval that Mrs. Kewley implied, and according to Sue had led directly to her first
separation from Niall. He remembered her story of Niall
the invisible companion, distracting her and generally acting badly. Yet Mrs. Kewley had obviously met him, found

nothing unusual about him, and had even formed a favorable opinion of him.

"My husband will be home from work soon," she said. "He only works part-time now. You will stay and meet him, won't you?"

"I'd like to very much," Grey said, "but I have to catch a train to London this afternoon. Maybe I'll meet your husband before I leave."

She started asking innocent questions about Sue: what her room was like, the sort of people she worked with, whether she took enough exercise. Grey answered her, feeling uncomfortable, aware that he could easily blunder into some minor contradiction with Sue's own version of her life. The revelation about Niall underlined how little he really knew or understood about Sue. To avoid the problem he started asking questions of his own. It was not long before a photograph album was produced. Feeling more like a spy than ever, Grey looked with interest at pictures of Sue's childhood.

She had been a pretty child in little dresses with ribbons in her hair. The plainness that he found so intriguing developed later; in her teens Sue began to look gawky and sullen, standing obediently for the photographs but averting her face. These pictures were passed over quickly, Mrs. Kewley obviously remembering particular moments.

At the back of the album, not mounted like the others but slipped loosely inside the pages, was a color snapshot. It slid to the floor as Mrs. Kewley was putting away the album, and Grey picked it up. It was a more recent picture of Sue, looking very much as he knew her. She was standing in a garden next to a flower bed, and beside her was a young man with his arm around her shoulders.

"Who is this?" Grey said.

"That's Niall, of course."

"Niall?"

"Yes—I thought you knew him. We took that picture in the garden, the time he visited us."

"Oh yes, I recognize him now." Grey stared at the photograph. Until this moment his unseen rival had possessed minatory powers in Grey's mind, but to see him at last, even in a rather blurred snapshot, made him immediately less of a threat. Niall was young-looking, with a slight build, a shock of fair hair, and an expression that looked both surly and conceited. He was smartly dressed and had a cigarette in his mouth. His face was turned toward Sue and he held her possessively, but she was standing ill at ease and looked stressful.

He passed the photograph back to Mrs. Kewley and she slipped it back inside the album. Not realizing the effect the picture had had on him, she began talking about Sue and the years when she was growing up. Grey kept his silence and listened. What emerged was a story supported by neither the pictures he had just seen nor Sue's own version. According to her mother, Sue had been a contented girl, clever at school, popular with the other girls, talented at drawing. She had been a good daughter, close to her sister, considerate of her parents. Her teachers spoke glowingly of her, and friends in the neighborhood were still always asking after her. Until the girls grew up and left home they had been a happy, intimate family, sharing most things. Now they were very proud of her, feeling that she was fulfilling the promise she had always shown. Her parents' only regret was that she could not visit home more often, but they knew how busy she was.

Something was missing, and after a while Grey sensed what it was. Parents who spoke well of their children usually told amusing stories about them, harmless anecdotes about childish foibles. Mrs. Kewley spoke in generalizations and platitudes, reciting what sounded like a well-rehearsed eulogy. But her enthusiasm was genuine and she smiled often at her memories, a kind woman, a nice woman.

Just after half-past twelve her husband arrived home. Grey saw him on the path outside the window, and Mrs. Kewley went out to meet him. Moments later he entered the room, shook hands with Grey and smiled in an embarrassed way.

"I'd better put lunch on," Mrs. Kewley said. "Would you like to join us?"

"No thanks, I really must be going soon."

The two men were left together, standing facing each other, an awkward silence.

"Perhaps you'd care for a drink before you leave?" said Mr. Kewley, still with the morning's newspaper under his arm.

"Yes, thank you." But the only alcohol in the house turned out to be sweet sherry, a drink Grey disliked. He accepted it with good grace, sipping at it politely. Soon afterward Mrs. Kewley returned and the three of them sat in a semicircle in the little room, talking about the firm Mr. Kewley worked for. Grey finished his drink as quickly as he could, then said he really must be getting to the station. The other two seemed relieved, but they all went through the motions of renewed invitations to lunch and grateful refusal. Grey shook hands again with Sue's father, and Mrs. Kewley saw him to the door.

He had walked only a short distance from the house when he heard the door reopen.

"Mr. Grey!" Sue's mother came quickly toward him. In the daylight she looked suddenly younger, more like Sue herself. "Just something!"

"What is it?" he said, smiling to reassure her, because unexpectedly she had a different look, a new urgency.

"I'm sorry—I don't want to delay you." She glanced back at the house as if expecting her husband to be following. "It's Susan. How is she?"

"She's fine—really."

"No, you don't understand. Please tell me!"

"I don't know what to say. She's happy, working hard. Enjoying life."

"But do you *see* her?"

"Yes, from time to time. Once or twice a week."

Mrs. Kewley seemed close to tears. She said, "My husband and I . . . well, we don't really know Susan anymore. She writes to us, and sometimes rings us up, but . . . you know . . ."

"She talks about you a lot," Grey said. "You mean a great deal to her."

"I'd love to see her again. Please tell her that." She sobbed once but controlled it quickly, turning her head up and away, her chest heaving.

"I'll tell her as soon as I see her."

Mrs. Kewley nodded, then walked quickly back to the house. The door closed and Grey stood silently in the street, aware that Sue's account of her life had oddly been confirmed. He wished he had not called.

I V

Grey had promised Sue he would phone her as soon as he was in London, but he was tired when he arrived back from Manchester. In the morning he realized he had an extra day, and decided to contact her that evening.

He felt sorry he had visited her parents, particularly as he could not tell her what he had done. Nothing had been established by the trip. Now that it was over he acknowledged that his real motive had been curiosity about her invisibility—proof or disproof, whichever might have been produced.

All he had found were clues to a difficult adolescence, now remembered by her parents in a synoptic way, partially suppressed, accounted for normally. If she had been invisible to them it was failure of vision of another kind: an inability to see her growing up and changing, rejecting her parents' lives and background.

The pressure of domestic needs grew on him. Returning home from a trip always involved the same routine: a backlog of mail, a shortage of clean clothes, food to be bought. He was out most of the morning attending to this, and while he was around the shops he called in at the newsagent who was still delivering the tabloid newspaper every weekday morning. He loathed the paper for what it was, with its emphasis on royal visits, gossip about film stars, photographs of seminude models and salacious reporting of sex crimes, but in addition it was a daily reminder of his long stay in the hospital. Grey was told that the paper was being delivered on the instructions of the newspaper management, but he persuaded the newsagent he wanted it no more.

Returning with clean clothes and a bag of groceries, Grey discovered someone just walking away from his front door. It was a young woman with short dark hair, and as soon as she saw him she smiled expectantly.

"Mr. Grey? I thought you must be out. I was just leaving."

"I've been shopping," he said redundantly. He knew he recognized her, but not from where.

"I tried to telephone you yesterday, but there was no answer." She saw his frown and added, "I don't suppose you remember me . . . I'm Alexandra Gowers. A student of Dr. Hurdis's."

"Miss Gowers! Of course! Would you . . . like to come in?"

"Dr. Hurdis gave me your address. I hope you don't mind."

"Not at all."

He opened the door, went in first, then tried to

stand to one side to let her go in front. She squeezed past
him in the narrow hallway, picking up a slip of paper. "I
had left a note for you," she said, and crumpled it.

He followed her up the stairs at his usual slow pace.

He was trying to remember what she had looked
like before: his memory was of a rather severe face, heavy
and shapeless clothes, spectacles, unstyled and overlong
hair. She had changed since then.

He showed her into his living room.

"I ought to put this stuff away," he said. "Would
you like some coffee?"

"Yes, please."

He moved about in the kitchen, boiling water and
putting away his groceries, trying to think what he knew
of her. He remembered her being there when he was hypnotized the first time. He had heard nothing from Dr.
Hurdis since leaving Middlecombe.

The girl was sitting in one of the chairs when he
took the coffee in.

"I was wondering if I could make an appointment
to interview you sometime?" she said.

"What about?"

"I'm doing postgraduate research at Exeter University. Dr. Hurdis is my supervisor. I'm writing a dissertation on the subjective experience of hypnosis, and I'm trying to interview as many people as possible."

"Well, I don't think I can be much help," Grey said.
He poured the coffees, adding milk and sugar, not looking
at her. "I don't remember very much about it now."

"That's part of the reason I'd like to talk to you.
Could you suggest a suitable time?"

"I don't know. I'm not sure I want to talk about it."

She said nothing, stirring her coffee. Grey was feeling hostile to her, unreasonably. It was as if once you became a case history they would never leave you alone afterward. She was reminding him of what it was like to be
in a wheelchair, constantly in pain and discomfort, help-

less in the hands of those trying to cure you. He had thought that once he left the hospital all that would be behind him.

"So you won't agree to an interview?" she said.

"I'm sure you can find plenty of other people to talk to."

He noticed that the notebook she had been holding had now been returned to her bag.

"The trouble is that I can't," she said. "Dr. Hurdis will only let me approach patients whose sessions I've actually been present at, with their permission. The other people I can interview are mostly experimental subjects—volunteers, other students. Clinical cases are different, and yours is particularly interesting."

"Why?"

"Because you're articulate, because of what happened under hypnosis, because the circumstances—"

"What did happen under hypnosis?"

She shrugged, picked up her coffee to sip at it. "Well, that's what I wanted to discuss with you. I shouldn't have troubled you."

"No, it's all right." His curiosity aroused, Grey was already regretting his feelings of hostility. "We can talk about it if you wish. But look, you've turned up out of the blue. I was going to have lunch in a few minutes. Let's have something to eat, and give me a few minutes to get used to the idea."

Ashamed of the food he bought for himself—when he was alone he survived on sandwiches, fried eggs and fruit—he suggested going to the local pub for a drink and a bar meal. As they walked slowly down the road, Grey suddenly identified the teasing memory he had of her. He remembered the moment under hypnosis when Hurdis had told him to look at this girl, and he had known she was there but had been unable to *see* her. It was an uncanny echo, pre-existing, of everything Sue had said.

They found the pub only half full, and had one of

the tables to themselves. With the food and drink in front of them, Alexandra told him about herself. After graduating she had been unable to find a job, and so had stayed on at Exeter to do research, postponing the problem of work and aiming for higher qualifications. She was surviving on a shoestring because her grant covered only the tuition. She lived with her brother in London, and when in Exeter stayed in a house shared by a number of other students. She thought the research would probably last a few more months, but after that she would have to find a job.

Talking about this led to the subject of her dissertation. She said that the phenomenon that interested her was spontaneous amnesia—the hypnotic subject who, without suggestion from the hypnotist, could not afterward recall what had happened during the session.

"What interests me about your case is that you were being treated for traumatic amnesia, that you seemed to recover some of your memory under hypnosis, but afterward could not remember remembering."

"That about sums it up," Grey said. "That's why I can't help you."

"But Dr. Hurdis says that you have now recovered your memory."

"Only partially."

She reached into her bag and produced her notebook. "Do you mind? I seem to have started interviewing you." Grey shook his head, smiling, as she put on her spectacles and turned the pages quickly. She said, "You were in France . . . before the accident?"

"No, I *remember* being in France. I don't think I was ever actually there."

"Dr. Hurdis said you were pretty sure. You were speaking French, for instance."

"That happened in later sessions, too. I think what happened was that I put together a sort of memory— something that never really occurred, but I felt that it had. At the time it was important to remember something."

"Paramnesia," Alexandra said.

"I know. Hurdis told me."

"Do you remember this?" She produced a piece of paper, curled at the edges and obviously folded and unfolded many times. "Dr. Hurdis asked me to return it to you."

Grey recognized it at once: it was the passage he had written during the first hypnotic session. Gatwick Airport, the departure lounge, the crowds of passengers. It was banal and familiar to him, and after glancing over it he refolded it and slipped it into his jacket pocket.

"You don't seem interested," Alexandra said.

"Not now."

He left her briefly to buy more drinks at the bar. Another memory from their first meeting was tugging at him: as they parted, her ingenuous remark about stage hypnotists and the trick of making their subjects fail to see people's clothes. Sue had been dominating his thoughts at the time, but for a few moments Alexandra had innocently teased him. It was refreshing now to be with a girl who was not Sue, because with Sue there was always the undercurrent of what was allowed to be said, what was admitted, what was in the background. Alexandra had the attractive quality of being uncomplicated, because he hardly knew her. He liked her seriousness and her single-mindedness, the way she intimidated him without meaning to. She was more mature now, less self-conscious. While the barman poured the drinks, Grey glanced back at her. She was looking through her notebook, her short dark hair swept behind an ear—obviously a habit from the time when it fell in her eyes.

Back at the table Grey said, "What else happened that day?"

"You told Dr. Hurdis you couldn't remember the trance."

"Not all of it. I know he told me to go into a deeper trance, but the next thing I knew he was waking me up."

"All right, this is what interests me. Something rather unusual occurred, which Dr. Hurdis did not tell you. It *can* be explained, but neither of us had ever encountered it before, and on that day Dr. Hurdis said it would only complicate matters to talk about it."

"What was it?" Grey said.

"It was when you were speaking French. You were mumbling, and it was difficult to hear, so we were both standing very close to you, looking directly at you. Then something happened. It's hard to describe it exactly, but what it *felt* like was that it suddenly seemed to me we had finished, that the consultation was over and you had left the room. I distinctly remember Dr. Hurdis saying, 'I'm going into Exeter after lunch, so would you like a lift?' I put my notebook away and picked up my coat. Dr. Hurdis said he wanted to speak to one of the other doctors, but would meet me for lunch in a few minutes. We left the office together, and I followed him out of the door. As I did so I remember looking back at the chair you had been in, and you *weren't there.* I'm absolutely certain of that. We walked along the corridor to the stairs, but then Dr. Hurdis suddenly stopped dead, looked at me and said, 'What on earth are we doing?' I didn't know what he meant at first, but then he clicked his fingers very sharply, and this startled me. It was like being awakened out of a dream. 'Miss Gowers, we haven't finished the consultation!' We hurried back to the office, and you were there, sitting back in the armchair, still in the trance and mumbling to yourself."

She paused to take a drink. Grey was staring at the table between them, thinking about that day.

"Do you have any memory of this at all?" Alexandra said.

"No. Go on."

"Well, Dr. Hurdis was very shaken by this. He can be difficult when he's angry, and he started bossing me around. I took out my notebook again and tried to listen to what you were saying, but after a few seconds he pushed me out of the way. He spoke to you in the trance, telling you to describe what you were doing. It was then that you asked for something to write with, and Dr. Hurdis snatched my notebook and pen from me and gave them to you. You wrote that." She indicated the pocket containing the slip of paper. "While you were writing, Dr. Hurdis looked at me and said, 'When the patient comes out of the trance we must say nothing of this.' I asked him what had happened, and he said we could discuss it later. He repeated that we must not under any circumstances talk about it in front of you. You were still writing, so Dr. Hurdis took the pen away from you and gave me back my notebook. You called out that you wanted to go on writing, and sounded distressed. Dr. Hurdis said he was going to bring you out of the trance, and again warned me not to say anything. He calmed you down, then started waking you up. You can probably remember the rest."

"So you made me vanish," Grey said.

"Not exactly."

"You said there was an explanation. What is it?"

"Negative hallucination. It sometimes happens that the process of hypnosis, the repetition of words, the soothing advice, the quiet room, all these can lull the hypnotist himself into a light trance, and he becomes as suggestible as his subject. It's a fairly common occurrence, although there are precautions the hypnotist usually takes. Dr. Hurdis and I are both good hypnotic subjects, and what we think must have happened was that we both became hypnotized. If so, then it's possible that we both had the same negative hallucination, in which we were unable to see you. It's extremely rare, but it is the only possible explanation."

Grey was thinking of something Sue had said, that invisibility depended as much on the unconscious attitude of the observer as the ability of the person making himself invisible. Some can *see*, some cannot. Was it all a negative hallucination?

Aware of his silence, Alexandra said, "I know it doesn't sound very likely, but it *is* possible."

"Has it ever happened before?"

"I've researched it as far as I can. There have been similar cases when a hypnotist was working alone, but I believe there is no precedent for both the hypnotist and an observer to share an experience."

What would Sue say to that? Was her belief in her own invisibility accountable for in terms that Dr. Hurdis and Alexandra could rationally confirm? He remembered the day they had been out photographing the shoppers, and the people Sue claimed were natural invisibles. He thought of the photographs he had seen of Sue and Niall. The camera could not induce negative hallucinations.

"So do you think that's what really happened?"

"Unless you actually made yourself invisible," Alexandra said, smiling. "There's no other explanation."

"What about invisibility?" Grey said on an impulse. "Isn't that possible? I mean—"

"Actual, corporeal invisibility?" She was still smiling. "Not unless you believe in magic. You yourself had a negative hallucination induced by Dr. Hurdis, and you weren't able to see me. But I wasn't *really* invisible, except to you."

"But what's the difference?" Grey said. "I couldn't see you, so you were to all intents invisible. You say that I became invisible to you and Hurdis. Was I still really there?"

"Of course you were. We simply stopped noticing you."

"But that's the same thing. You made me invisible."

"Only subjectively. We made you seem invisible by failing to see you."

Alexandra began to tell him of another case history, a woman who spontaneously hallucinated negatively, and who was treated with hypnosis, and Grey listened to her. But he was also thinking in parallel, trying to reinterpret everything Sue had told him in these terms.

If what she said was true, and she apparently believed it was, then perhaps it was possible that some people had the unconscious ability to hypnotize people around them so they could not be seen. The failure to notice: was it a natural condition? Or something that could be induced by certain people?

It felt as if it might be right. As Alexandra had said, however unlikely it might be it was the only possible rational explanation, even though the *extent* of Sue's claims increased the unlikelihood.

It was difficult to think about this and listen to Alexandra at the same time, and as the conversation became more general he let it go. She asked him about his recovery, how he was adapting once more to normal life, what remaining problems there were. He told her about his recent filming work, and said he had briefly visited Manchester. Somehow, he never mentioned Sue.

When the pub closing time came, they walked together back to his flat. Outside the door Alexandra said, "I must be getting home. Thanks for talking to me about this."

"I think I've learned more than you."

"I just wanted to confirm what I thought might have happened."

They shook hands formally, as they had done on their first meeting.

Grey said, "I was wondering . . . shall we meet again for another drink? Perhaps one evening?"

"Yes, I'd like that," she said, looking at him with a smile. "But no more interviews."

They made a date for the following week.

V

Grey visited Sue in the evening, and as soon as he arrived he knew something was wrong. It was not long before he found out what it was: Sue's mother had telephoned her and told her of his visit.

At first, he tried to lie.

"We had to go to Manchester for some filming," he said. "I decided on an impulse to look them up."

"You said you were working in Toxteth. What the hell does that have to do with Manchester?"

"All right, I went specially. I wanted to meet them."

"But why? They don't know anything about me! What did they tell you?"

"I know you think I was spying on you, but it really wasn't like that. Sue, I had to know."

"Know what? What could they possibly tell you about me?"

"They *are* your parents," Grey said.

"But they've hardly seen me since I was twelve years old!"

"That's why I went. Something happened while I was filming in Liverpool." He told her about the club, and the memory it had prompted of the pub in Belfast. "It made me see everything you had said in a different light—whether, in fact, there might be some truth in it after all."

"I knew you weren't believing me."

"It's not that. I do believe you . . . but I have to know for myself. I'm sorry if you think I've been snooping around, but the idea came to me on the spur of the moment and I didn't really think. I just wanted to talk to someone else who knew you."

"I've been invisible to Mum and Dad since I was a kid. The only times they've seen me have been when I've forced myself to be seen."

"That's not the impression I got from them," Grey said. "You're right that they don't know you very well, but that's because you've grown up and left home. It happens to many people with their parents."

Sue was shaking her head. "That's just the way they account for it. It's how people deal with someone who's invisible around them. They automatically come up with some rational version to explain to themselves what's happened. It's a way of coping."

Grey thought of Alexandra, her rationalization.

"Your mother said she had met Niall."

"That's impossible!" But she looked surprised.

"It's not how it felt to me. You told me yourself that he went home with you once."

"Niall was invisible the whole time. Richard, they *think* they saw him. They know about Niall, I told them about him years ago. The only time he's been home with me was that one weekend. But they couldn't have seen him because it's simply not possible."

"Then why does your mother think she knows him? She's even got a photograph of him—with you, in the back garden."

"I know. They took several. Niall would be in them all. Don't you see, that's how she explains it to herself! When he was there with me they must have been aware of what was going on. Niall registered with them . . . even someone as profoundly invisible as Niall is always *there*. After we had left they would unconsciously have tried to account for all the tension. When they had the pictures developed, the explanation would have presented itself. Thinking back, they would seem to remember having met him."

"Yes, but it's just as likely that they did see him. It doesn't prove anything one way or the other."

"Why do you need proof of all this?"

"Because it's what is coming between us. First it's Niall, now it's this. I want to believe you, and I *do* believe you, but everything you tell me can be explained two ways."

Throughout all this they had been in her room, Sue squatting cross-legged on her bed, Grey sitting in the chair by her desk. Now she left the bed and paced about the room.

"All right," Sue said. "While you were away I gave this a lot of thought. If you're right, and this is what's standing between us, I want to put it right. We're drifting apart, Richard, and I don't like that. If you want proof, I think I can provide it."

"How?"

"There are two ways. The first is simple—it's Niall. He is the proof. He's influenced us from the moment we met, and he's actually been with us, physically been present, yet you've been totally unaware of him."

"You see, that's not proof to me," Grey said. "It works either way. He's here and with us, as you say, lurking around invisibly . . . or he's never been near me and I haven't met him. Just because I haven't seen him doesn't mean he's invisible."

"I thought you'd say that." She was combing through her hair with her fingers as she paced about the room. She looked agitated, but determined too.

"I believe Niall really exists," Grey said. "But try to see it from my point of view. You've only *told* me about Niall, and since I left the hospital you've only told me about him in the past tense. Even you haven't seen him for a long time."

"That's true."

"What's the other proof?"

She halted her prowling. "That's more complicated. I'm hungry now. I've bought some food to cook. I can't afford to keep eating out."

Grey said, "Let's go to a restaurant. I'll pay."

"No, the food will waste." She had already produced a grocery bag and taken down a couple of sauce-pans.

"Tell me while you're cooking," he said.

"It's something I have to show you. Sit there, and keep out of the way."

Grey did as he was told, swiveling to and fro in her office chair. She had only cooked for him once or twice, but he liked how she went about it. She had a casual way of tossing rice and meat and vegetables into pans and coming up with something delicious. It was pleasant to watch her doing something ordinary; they spent so much of their time obsessed with themselves.

But while she was cooking Grey said, "As a matter of interest, where *is* Niall these days?"

"I was wondering when you would ask me that." She had not turned to look at him. "It doesn't matter any more, does it?"

"I suppose not. But from everything you said, he was never going to leave you alone."

"Nor will he." She was chopping vegetables, scooping them a few at a time into the steaming saucepan. "He could be here in the room with us now, for all I know. Because he can make himself completely invisible, there's nothing much I can do about it. But what I can do, and have done, is change myself. I finally worked out what I was doing wrong. I was letting Niall make it matter to me. Now . . . I don't care. Niall is everywhere. He can go anywhere it's possible to be, and almost nothing can stop him. He can do anything he likes. But the point is, if that's so then it doesn't *matter* whether he's actually there or not —the knowledge that he has that ability is the same as him actually using it. These days I assume he's everywhere I go; I take it for granted he's watching me, listening to me.

It makes no difference to me whether he's really there or that I'm imagining it: the effect is that he leaves me alone and that's what I wanted all along." She turned down the cooking rings to their lowest setting and put the lids on the pans. "Right—the food will be ready in ten minutes, and after that we're going out for a walk."

VI

It had been raining earlier, but now the night was clear. Traffic went by, the engines loud against the shiny wetness of the streets. They passed several pubs, a late-opening newsagent, an Indian restaurant with a blue neon sign. Soon they were walking down a wide residential road that ran along the side of Crouch Hill; the lights of north London glittered before them. Overhead, an airliner with brilliant strobe lights crossed the sky, heading down toward Heathrow, miles to the west.

"Are we going anywhere particular?" Grey said.

"No, you can choose."

"What about: around the block, then back to your place?"

Sue came to a halt beneath one of the streetlights. "You want proof, and I'm going to give it to you. After that, will you accept it for what it is?"

"If it's proof."

"It will be, I promise you. Look at me, Richard . . . do I seem any different?"

He looked at her in the orange glow from the sodium lamp. "The light doesn't do anything for you."

"I've been invisible ever since we left home."

"Sue, I can still see you."

"No one else can. What I'm going to do is make you invisible too, and then we're going to go into one of these houses."

"Are you serious?"

"Absolutely."

"All right, but the problem is me."

"No, it isn't." She stretched out a hand and took his. "You're invisible now. Anything I choose to touch becomes invisible."

He could not help but glance down at himself: chest and legs, solidly there. A car went past, its flasher indicating a left turn. Spray flew briefly around them.

Sue said: "No one can see us. The only thing you must do is hold my hand, and whatever happens don't let go." She tightened her grip. "Now, pick a house."

Her voice had taken on an earnest note, a charge of excitement, and Grey felt a tingle of the same.

"What about this one here?"

They both looked at it. Most of the windows were dark, but a pale red glow came through curtains on the top floor.

"It looks as if it's been converted into flats," Sue said. "Let's find another."

They walked along, holding hands, staring at the houses. They went to a few front doors, but where there were several bell pushes and a list of names Sue suggested finding somewhere else. Too many locked doors inside. At the end of the row the house had a darkened porch, and a single bell. Behind the curtains of the front room they could see the glow of a television screen.

"This will do," Sue said. "Now let's hope there's a door open."

"I thought you would break a window."

"We can do anything we like, but I'd rather not cause damage."

They went through the garden and along a narrow passage, pressing past rain-damp trees and bushes. The room at the back was brightly lit with a fluorescent tube, and when Sue tried the door it opened easily.

"We won't stay long," she said. "Don't let go of my hand."

She pushed open the door and they went inside. Grey closed the door behind them. They were in a kitchen. Two women stood with their backs against a work surface, one of them holding a sleeping baby. On the table in front of them were two cheap tumblers containing beer, and an ashtray with a cigarette smoldering. An older child, wearing a soiled romper suit, was playing on the vinyl-tiled floor with a plastic car and some wooden blocks. The woman with the baby was saying, ". . . but when you get in there they treat you like rubbish, so I said to him don't you go talking to me like that, and he just looked at me like I was dirt, and you know what, I'd paid thirty pounds to get in and they look at you like you was rubbish. . . ." Grey felt huge and self-conscious in the cramped room and wanted to edge past the two women, but Sue led him to the sink where she turned on the cold tap. The water splashed down noisily onto the unwashed crockery stacked below, several large droplets spraying up and falling on the floor. Listening to her friend, the woman walked around the table and turned it off. On her way back she picked up the cigarette and put it in her mouth.

Sue said, "Let's see what they're watching on television."

Grey winced because her voice was so loud, but neither of the women appeared to notice. Still clutching Sue's hand, he followed her out of the room and into the short corridor leading to the front of the house. Here a couple of old bicycles leaned against the staircase banisters, and three large cardboard boxes containing bottles were stacked one on top of another. Sue opened the second door and they went inside.

A soccer match was playing on television, the volume turned up loud. The room was full of men, young and middle-aged, sitting forward with their arms resting on their knees, holding beer cans or smoking cigarettes. The air was thick with smoke, and the men were responding to the commentary and the match; England was playing Yugoslavia, and losing. Derision and ridicule poured out whenever the England side lost control of the ball.

Sue said, "Let's have a look at them."

She turned on the overhead light and led Grey across the room. There were three adults and four teenagers.

"Knock that bleeding light off, John," one of the older men said, not looking away from the screen. One of the teenagers got up and switched off the light. Returning to his seat he had to push past Grey, who instinctively eased himself to the side to make way. Sue gripped his hand again.

"Shall we sit down?" she said.

Before he could answer she led him toward the sofa, where two men were sitting. Neither of them looked up, but one shuffled forward so that he sat on the floor and the other moved up to make room for them. Sue and Grey sat down, Grey feeling certain that their presence must register at any moment. The match went on, and England missed another chance. Contemptuous noises roared out in the room, and beer cans hissed wetly open.

"How do you feel?" Sue said, raising her voice over the noise.

"They're going to see us in a moment."

"No they're not. You wanted proof, and this is it." He noticed how her voice had changed; it had a thick, sensuous quality, reminding him of her lovemaking. The palm of her hand was sweating. "Want to see more?" she said.

She got up from the sofa, dragging Grey behind her. To his surprise she went directly to the television set, stood in front of the screen, blocking the men's view, and switched channels. After a couple of tries she found a studio discussion, apparently about banking economics. She stood back, and she and Grey watched the men's reaction.

They were behaving as if the match had suddenly ended. The mood changed and relaxed, the men sat back, lit more cigarettes. They were complaining about the match, the strategy, the management of the side, the selection of the team.

Grey said, "They knew you had turned on the light. Won't they realize you switched channels?"

"Not while we're standing here by the set. For the moment they're all assuming that one of the others did it. They'll go back to it when we leave."

"But surely they know *now?*"

"They know we're here, but they can't see us. Have any of them looked at us?"

"Not directly, no."

"They can't." Sue was looking flushed, her lips were moist. "Watch this."

With her free hand Sue quickly unbuttoned the top of her blouse. Pulling Grey behind her she went toward one of the men, and with a deft movement reached inside and scooped out one of her breasts. She leaned toward him, holding the nipple just a few inches from his face. He carried on talking match strategy to his friend, utterly ignoring her.

Grey tugged Sue back by her hand. "Don't do that!"

"They can't see me!"

"All right, but I don't like you doing it."

She faced him, her blouse open and her breast exposed. "Doesn't this turn you on?"

"Not like that." But he could feel himself arousing.

"I always feel randy doing this." She pressed his hand to her breast, where the nipple was a firm bead of excitement. "Do you want to make love?"

"You're kidding!"

"No, come on—let's do it. We can do anything we like."

"Sue, it's impossible." He was too nervous, too aware of the roomful of men.

"Let's fuck now. On the floor—in front of them."

There had always been an incongruous coarseness in Sue when she made love, but it had never been as blatant as this before. Her free hand was at the front of his trousers, pulling at his zipper.

"Not here," he said. "Outside."

They went quickly into the hall, and then Sue saw the stairs and rushed up them, still holding his hand. They found a room with a bed and threw themselves on it. They loosened their clothes, and coupled almost at once. Sue, when she came, let out a shriek of pleasure, taking his hair in handfuls and snatching it painfully. He had never known her as abandoned as this.

They were lying on the bed, still joined, when the door opened and one of the women they had seen in the kitchen came in. Grey tensed and turned his face away in a desperate attempt to hide. Sue said in a normal voice, "Keep still. She doesn't know we're here."

Grey looked back and watched as the woman opened a wardrobe door. She stood looking at herself in the full-length mirror, then began to undress. When she was naked she stood in front of the mirror again, turning from side to side. Her buttocks were heavy and dimpled, her belly sagged, and her breasts fell flat, pointing outward. The woman leaned forward, looking at her eyes in the reflection, pulling down the lower lids. She farted noisily. When she stood back again she tried to shape her hair with her hands, still turning to and fro, looking critically at herself. Grey could see himself and Sue reflected in the mirror behind her. He felt a deep sense of revulsion, knowing they were violating an intimacy. As his sexual desire faded he began to recoil away from Sue, letting himself slip out of her.

She wrapped her arms around his shoulders, holding him down against her. "Don't move, Richard! Stay until she's gone."

"But she's going to get into bed!"

"Not yet. She can't while we're here."

After another few seconds the woman sighed and closed the wardrobe door, shutting away the mirror. She took a dressing gown from the door and put it on. Before leaving the room she lit a cigarette, tossing the matchbox onto the bedside table. Her cloud of smoke swirled by the door when she had gone.

"Let's get out, Sue. You've proved your point."

He moved away from her and stood by the bed, pulling up his underpants and trousers, tucking his shirt away. He knew that now Sue was no longer touching him he was visible again, but all he wanted was to get out of this house and leave these people alone. Revulsion still filled him.

Sue finished buttoning up her clothes as quickly as he did, and took his hand again.

"Nothing can happen," she said.

"Yes, but we shouldn't be here."

He peered around the open door onto the landing. The woman was standing in the bathroom with the door open, wiping cream on her face. She then closed and locked the door.

"This is what you used to do with Niall, isn't it?"

"I used to *live* like this. I slept in other people's houses for three years. We ate their food, used their lavatories, read their books, used their baths."

"Didn't you ever think about the people you were trespassing on?"

"For God's sake!" She snatched her hand away from his. "Why do you think I tried to get out of this? I was just a kid. Don't you understand that ever since I met you I've been trying to put all this behind me? This is how

Niall lives now, and how he'll live for the rest of his life. We're here because you wanted your damned proof!"

"All right." He kept his voice low, knowing he could be heard. Thinking of her sexual excitement, he said, "But the truth is, you still get a kick from it."

"Of course I do! I always did. That's the curse of invisibility. It's like a drug."

"I think we should get out. Let's talk about it back at your place." He held out his hand for her to take.

She shook her head and sat down on the bed. "Not now."

"We've been here long enough."

"Richard, I'm not invisible anymore. It started to go, after we made love."

"Then get back into it," Grey said.

"I can't . . . I'm drained. I don't know how."

"What are you talking about?"

"I can't just make it happen anymore. Tonight was the first time in many weeks."

"Can't you do it long enough to get us out of here?"

"No. It's gone."

"Then what in hell are we going to do?"

"We're going to have to run for it."

"The house is full of people."

"I know," she said. "But the front door's at the bottom of the stairs. It might be all right."

"Come on, then. That woman will be back at any moment."

But Sue did not move. She said quietly, "I always used to be scared this would happen. In the old days, with Niall. That we'd be in someone's house, like this, and the glamour would suddenly leave us. That was always the kick, the danger of it."

"We can't just wait for something to happen. This is crazy!"

"You could try, Richard. You know how."

"What?"

"Make yourself invisible—you've done it before."

"I can't remember that!"

"We were on a beach . . . there were some girls sunbathing. You pretended to film them. What about the pub in Belfast? Imagine you're here filming. We're in a corner, but you've got the camera and you go on using it."

"I'm too scared of being found here! I can't concentrate on that!"

"But that's when you did your best filming, when you were stuck, when people were throwing petrol bombs."

Grey narrowed his right eye, half closing the lids to approximate the narrow field of a viewfinder. He suddenly imagined the familiar touch of the sponge-rubber eyepiece, the faint vibration of the motor transmitted to his brow. He hunched a shoulder, taking the weight, and cocked his head slightly to the right. There was a power pack on his hip, a cable looping down and behind him, knocking against his shoulder blade. He imagined the soundman beside him, the gray-wrapped mike prodding up and above him from behind. He thought of the Belfast streets, a mass picket outside factory gates, a CND demonstration in Hyde Park, a food riot in Eritrea—all still vivid in his mind, moments of surging and unpredictable danger glimpsed through the lens.

Sue stood up and put a hand on his shoulder. "We can go now."

They both heard the sound of the toilet flushing, a door opening, and then footsteps on the landing outside. A moment later the woman they had seen undressing walked into the room, the half-burned cigarette dangling from her mouth. Grey swung the camera to follow her, tightening the focus. She stepped around them, and went again to the wardrobe.

Grey led the way to the top of the stairs, then walked slowly down, one step at a time. They could hear the sounds of the televised soccer match coming through the open door of the front room. Grey panned to the room, glimpsing the backs of the men's heads. Sue reached past him and unlatched the front door. When they were outside, she pulled it to behind them.

Grey filmed until they were on the street, then he slumped, feeling tired. Sue took his arm and brought up her mouth to kiss the side of his face, but he turned away from her, angry, worn out and repelled.

VII

There was always a next day, a waking to the realities of the present. Richard Grey rarely remembered his dreams when he awoke, although he was always aware of having dreamed. He understood them instinctively as a reorganization of actual daytime memories into a kind of symbolic code that was stored away in the unconscious. When he was at home by himself, each morning was therefore a fresh memorative start. As he muddled sleepily through the first two or three hours, glancing at his mail, reading the headlines of the newspaper, sipping hot coffee, he was aware of a kind of oneiric stew in his mind, an amalgam of mostly forgotten dreams and snatches of the day before. Conscious memories rarely came to him until he forced himself to think properly. Only after he had drunk the second cup of coffee, and had dressed and shaved and was beginning to wonder how to spend the rest of the day would he start seeing the new day in the context of the old. Continuity would return.

In the morning after the visit to the house, Grey found it more difficult than usual to wake up. He had not been especially late to bed, but there had been a long and grumpy conversation at Sue's before he left. Somewhere in it was a conflict over sex: Sue had wanted to make love again, and he had not.

He felt disagreeable on waking. There was nothing in the mail, and the newspaper depressed him. He fried an egg and made a greasy sandwich of it, then drank coffee and stared through his window at the street below.

When he dressed he put on clean clothes and transferred the contents of his pockets. Amid the litter of coins, keys and bank notes he found the slip of paper Alexandra had given him, stuffed negligently in his jacket pocket.

He opened it carefully, flattening it with his hand on the table, and read it through. It began with the words:

> The departures board showed that my flight was delayed, but I had already gone through passport control and there was no escape from the passenger lounge.

The passage continued with a description of the lounge, and concluded in the following way:

> There was nowhere to sit down, nothing much to do except stand or walk about and look at the other passengers. I diverted myself with a ga—

It was at this point that Hurdis had stopped him. The last word, which Grey knew was "game," was only half written and there was a line scored lightly beyond it. He knew all of the rest; the story was familiar to him. Staring idly through the window Grey remembered the long journey through France, the meeting with Sue, their falling in love, their separation over Niall, then their reunion and return to England. The memories ended with his accidental involvement in the terrorist bombing.

It was all very real to him still, the only knowledge

of the period he had subsequently lost. Whenever he dwelled on it, images came starkly and convincingly from it: the first time he and Sue had made love, how it had *felt* to be in love with her, how it felt to miss her, that long and fruitless wait in Saint-Tropez and the consolation of the girl from Hertz, the enervating Mediterranean heat, the taste of the food, Picasso at work in Collioure. These memories had an inner conviction, a sense of story and of events unfolding. Earlier he had thought of it all as a piece of film already edited, but thinking again it occurred to him that a closer analogy was that of seeing a movie. A cinema audience accepted on trust that the whole thing was a fiction, that it was written and directed and acted, that a large crew was somewhere out of sight behind the camera, that the film had been edited and synchronized, and music and sound effects had been added . . . but they nevertheless suspended their disbelief and went along with the illusion.

Grey felt as if his real life had been going on outside the cinema while he was inside watching the film . . . but that the memory of the film was an acceptable substitute.

This fragment of his confabulated past had another importance to him. It had sprung unbidden from his subconscious, a production of an inner need, a desperation to *know*. As a result it was now a part of him, even though it was not what had really happened. It dealt explicitly with his lost period, with the events leading up to the explosion. It gave him continuity.

And it excluded Sue, except as a secondary figure. It did not admit of her invisibility. The real Sue demanded a primary position, and insisted that he accept her claim to be invisible.

Thinking of Sue, Grey was reminded of the events of the night before. Since waking he had not thought about the visit to the house, although in a vague manner it had always been at the back of his mind.

Had he been suppressing it?

He had found it a profoundly disturbing experience, burdened with feelings of intrusion, violation, voyeurism, trespass. The sex with Sue, snatched from her frantic physical need, had provided only neurotic relief, lacking pleasure. He recalled the urgent undoing of clothes, of thrusting himself into her while they both still wore shoes, while their jeans tangled around their knees, while Sue's blouse lay flatly over her half-bared breasts. Afterward the innocent woman, overweight and narcissistic, standing in her own room while strangers appraised her, and then their fear of being caught, trapped like thieves in someone else's home.

This morning, while he stumbled around the flat in his early stupor, it had had all the quality of a half-remembered dream, as if the reality of it had been re-sorted symbolically during the night, encoded and dispatched to his unconscious. Grey thought of something that had happened a few years before: he had dreamed a friend of his had died, and for most of the following day he had felt a vague sense of sadness and loss until, midafternoon, he had realized that it was indeed only a dream, that his friend was alive and well. The feeling about their invisible visit was similar, although its cause was opposite: until reminded of it, Grey had remembered it in a dreamlike manner, his mood subtly affected by it, until the conscious realization that it had really happened.

It was curious that failure of memory surrounded invisibility.

Sue's account of his lost period spoke of his own natural ability, his recognition of hers, the development of his skill at making himself invisible. But because of the bomb he had forgotten all this. Invisibility was a past, unremembered condition: Sue said that he no longer knew how, that her own talent had receded. Even Niall, supremely and terminally invisible, was not around any more.

And last night, intended to be Sue's conclusive proof, had gone half forgotten until now.

Was amnesia inherently related to invisibility? Alexandra told him he had become invisible to her and Dr. Hurdis . . . but this was during the period of hypnosis he could not remember. Then there were the lost weeks of his life, invisible to him now, which he had replaced with spurious, confabulated memories. Was this not exactly the way in which ordinary people accounted to themselves for the presence of invisible people? Sue's parents, bringing up a child they hardly saw, accounted for the mystery as a difficult daughter growing up and moving away. The unseen Niall, selfishly disrupting Sue's visit home, was afterward given the benefit of the doubt and thought to be a nice young man. The soccer fans, deprived for a few minutes of their televised match, agreed among themselves that the game must have ended. The woman in the house acted as if the kitchen tap had somehow turned itself on, and later failed to see two strangers fornicating on her bed.

Sue had said that invisible people were *made* invisible by the people around them, their failure to notice: spontaneous amnesia, followed by confabulation to explain the inexplicable.

There was one experience of invisibility, though, that he could remember clearly, and this was the way it had sometimes helped his filming. But even this was in doubt.

Film crews feel vulnerable in dangerous circumstances. They are weighted down with bulky and valuable equipment, and they generally draw attention to themselves. People are always aware of the presence of cameras. Grey remembered that for a time there had been a problem with the security forces in Northern Ireland, who tried to discourage crews from visiting trouble spots because, it was claimed, the arrival of cameras often created or worsened an incident. Filming at night sometimes meant that lights had to be used, although high-speed stock had to a large extent averted that problem. Cameramen are usually in the thick of whatever is going on, because otherwise there is no point their being there, and if the story involves illegality or political dispute, the crews frequently become the targets of abuse or violence.

When Grey thought back to the reality of news filming as he had known it for several years, the idea of a cameraman working unnoticed was incredible. Yet the fact remained that there had been times when he had obtained footage in extreme situations. Sue's interpretation had an odd plausibility, one that touched an inner instinct in him.

He simply did not know what to think.

After lunch Grey went for a walk by himself. Exercise for his hip was still essential, so he drove his car up to the West Heath near Hampstead and walked for a couple of hours through the oak forest. It was a small but attractive area, often neglected by visitors in favor of the more open main part of the Heath.

While he was there he came across a film crew from the BBC who were shooting some exterior action for a play. He recognized the cameraman, so he walked over and talked briefly between takes; Grey was now actively seeking work, and was not afraid to let it be known. The two men agreed to meet for a drink in a few days' time.

He watched the unit at work for a while, wishing he were a part of it. The story was an episode from a thriller series, and the scene they were shooting involved two men chasing a blond actress through the trees. She was wearing a flimsy yellow dress, and between takes she stood with her boyfriend, shivering inside her coat and chain-smoking. She looked, off camera, utterly different from the frightened and vulnerable character she was playing.

Walking on, Grey thought about the one incident from the night before that had fundamentally affected his outlook. This was his discovery that Sue, when she thought herself invisible, became sexually highly charged. Because he had been there, had seen the change coming over her, had felt it too, he responded. He could still recall the urgent need. But it was an insight he had not expected; what he found attractive about Sue was what he had always thought of as her shyness, her modest dislike of being stared at, her physical neutrality. Sometimes in the past her lovemaking had been uninhibitedly coarse, and he had always believed that this was something he had brought out in her. Sexual knowledge is frequently revealing. But she had never been assertive in that way before. He was not repelled sexually, but it made him feel that until then he had perceived her wrongly.

That actress back there was in real life unlike the part she was playing. Sue, thinking herself unseen, switched from the role she habitually played to another character. She was two people: the woman he usually saw, and the one he had never seen until last night. In her invisibility, her concealment from the world, she had revealed herself. To Grey, it felt as if his other doubts coalesced around this. If the revelation had come earlier it might have made no difference, but at this late stage he felt unable to cope with yet another reversal.

By the time he returned to his car Grey had resolved not to see Sue again. They had an arrangement to meet in the evening, but he decided to call her as soon as he was home and cancel it. He drove back to his flat, thinking of what he would say to her. She was waiting for him, though, sitting on the steps of the small porch outside his front door.

VIII

In spite of his decision there was a part of him that remained pleased to see her. She kissed him warmly before
they went inside, but Grey felt cool and resistant to her.
Reluctantly he took her up to his flat, wondering how to
broach the subject. He felt like a drink, so he took a can of
lager from the refrigerator, but made some tea for Sue. He
could hear her moving about restlessly in the front room
as he drank some of the beer and waited for the kettle to
boil.

When he took her the tea she was standing by the
window, looking down into the street.

"You don't want me here, do you?" she said.

"I was just about to give you a ring. I've been thinking—"

"I've come about something very important, Richard."

"I'd rather not talk about it."

"It's about Niall."

He put down her cup by the spare chair, noticing
that she had brought with her a large manila envelope
stuffed with papers. It was lying on the cushion of the
chair. Outside in the street someone was trying to get a
car going, the starter motor making a repeated nagging,
whining sound. The noise always made Grey think of a
sick animal, flogged endlessly by its unforgiving driver.

"There's nothing else I want to know about Niall,"
Grey said. He felt remote from her, the distance between
them lengthening.

"I've come to tell you that Niall's left me for good."

"That's not what you said yesterday. Anyway, I don't care. Niall's not the problem any more."

"Then what is?"

"Everything that happened last night, everything you've ever said. I've had enough."

"Richard, what I've come to say is there's nothing left to come between us. It's all over. Niall's gone, I've lost the glamour. What more do you want?"

She stared at him across the room, looking helpless. Grey remembered suddenly how it had felt to love her, and he wished it were possible again. Outside, the irritating sound of the fruitless attempts to start the car came to an end. For the last minute or so the car battery had been running flat, the starter motor grinding with a pathetic, hopeless sound. Grey walked across to where Sue was standing and looked down into the street. He was always distracted by the sound of a car being started, because it crossed his mind that somebody might be interfering with his. He could see no one around, and his car was standing where he had parked it.

Sue took his hand. "What are you looking for?"

"That car being started . . . where is it?"

"Haven't you been listening to me?"

"Yes, of course I have."

She released his hand and went to sit down, moving the envelope to her lap. After looking up and down the street once more, Grey went to his chair.

Sue said, "Last night was a mistake, we both know that. It'll never happen again. It *can't* happen again. I've got to explain. . . . While I believed Niall was somewhere around I could still feel able to make myself invisible. But last night was wrong, something failed. I thought I was trying to prove invisibility to you, but really I was trying to prove to myself that Niall's influence had left me. Now I'm sure of it."

She held up the envelope for him to see.

"What's that?" Grey said.

"It's something Niall gave me, the last time I saw him." She drew a breath, watching him. "He came to see me, gave me a newspaper which listed the names of the people injured by the car bomb. This was a few days afterward, long before you were transferred to Devon. At the same time he gave me this envelope. I didn't know what it was, and I didn't care. I never even opened it. I knew it was something of Niall's, but by that time I was sick to death of him. But this morning I was thinking about last night, why it went wrong, and I knew Niall was somehow responsible. It felt, well, it was as if that part of my life no longer made sense without him. I remembered him giving me this, and I searched through my stuff until I found it. You ought to know what it is."

"Sue, I'm just not interested in Niall."

"Please at least look at it. It's important."

He took the envelope from her and pulled out what was inside. It was a sheaf of papers, handwritten, torn from the sort of writing pad found in any stationery shop; the left-hand side of each sheet was slightly corrugated where it had been ripped off. The top page was a brief note, written in the same hand as the rest. It said: *Susan— Read this and try to understand. Goodbye—N.*

The handwriting was legible, but it was distracting to look at because of the use of extravagant loops and curls. Periods and the dot above the letter "i" were drawn as minute circles. On most of the pages the color of the ink changed intermittently as different pens were used, but the most favored colors were green and radiant blue. Grey had no knowledge of graphology, but everything about the handwriting bespoke self-consciousness and a wish to seem prestigious.

"What is this? Did Niall write it all?"

"Yes . . . you ought to read it."

"Now? While you're sitting there?"

"At least look through it long enough to realize what it is."

Grey set the note aside and read the first few lines at the top of the next page. They said:

> The house had been built so that it over-
> looked the sea. Since its conversion to a con-
> valescent hospital, two large wings had been
> added in the original style, and the gardens
> had been relandscaped so that patients wish-
> ing to move around were never faced with
> steep inclines.

"I don't understand," Grey said. "What's this all about?"

"Look at it further on," Sue said.

Grey put several of the pages on one side and read at random:

> She tossed her hair back with a light shak-
> ing motion of her head and looked straight at
> him. He regarded her, trying to remember
> or see her as he might have done before. She
> held his gaze for a few moments, then cast
> her eyes downward once more.
> "Don't stare at me," she said.

Grey said, beginning to feel confused, "This is a description of you, I think."

"Yes, there's some of that. Read more of it."

He started turning the pages, picking out odd sentences to be read, constantly dazzled by the extraordinary handwriting and its elaborate curlicues. It was easier to skim than to read, but at another random he found:

> Grey felt comfortable and relaxed and
> drowsy, but was still aware of all that was
> around him. He had his eyes closed and was
> listening to Dr. Hurdis, but he could also

sense further. Outside in the hall two people walked past, talking to each other, and somewhere in the room Alexandra Gowers had made a clicking noise with a ballpoint pen, and rustled some paper.

Saying nothing to Sue, Grey turned the rest of the pages quickly. He knew what the writing said; the sense came through to him without having to read, because it was all familiar to him. There was not much farther to go. The text ended with the words:

> Late, far later than he had expected, she called him from a pay phone. She had arrived at Totnes station, and was about to hire a taxi. She was with him half an hour later.

When she saw he had finished, Sue said, "Do you understand what it means, Richard?"

"What *is* this?"

"It's Niall's way of dealing with the inevitable. It's a story, something he made up about us."

"But why should he give it to you?"

"He wanted me to know. He wrote it to say that he finally accepted that I had finished with him, and wanted you."

"This is what happened, though! How the hell could he have *written* it?"

"It's just a story," Sue said.

Holding the sheaf of papers in his hand, Grey slowly rolled them, making them into a short truncheon.

"But how did he *know?*" he said. "When did Niall give you this? You said it was just after the car bomb—but this is what really happened later!"

"I don't understand it either," Sue said.

"Niall didn't make this up! He couldn't have! He must have been there—all the time I was in hospital Niall was there too! That's what this means. Don't you see that?"

"Richard, that story's been in my room for months."

Suddenly Grey moved in his seat, looking wildly from side to side.

"Is Niall following us now? Is he *here?*"

"I told you, Niall is always here. Don't let it matter."

"He's here now, Sue! He's in this room!" Grey stood up, lurching on his weak hip, and took a clumsy step to the side. He flailed at the air with the papers in his hand. The beer can at his feet fell on its side, the frothy lager pouring in gulps onto the carpet. Grey swung about, groping with one hand at the air around him, prodding and punching with the rolled-up pages in his other fist. He moved awkwardly to the door, snatched it open to peer outside, then slammed it closed. He reached blindly for me as the air swirled about us both.

I stood back, keeping my distance, not wishing to be struck with a truncheon of my own making.

"Hold it!" I shouted, but of course you did not hear.

I heard Susan say, "Richard, you're making a fool of yourself!" but neither of us paid her any attention. You were directly in front of me, balancing your weight on your good leg, your fist raised against me, your eyes in their desperation seeming to stare straight at me. I turned away from your disconcerting gaze, even though you would never be able to see me.

It has gone far enough. Here it ends.

Hold that position, Grey; nothing more is going to happen. Susan too; stay still!

I pause.

My hands are trembling. You scare me, Grey. We both threaten each other, you with your blundering ability to cause pain, I with my freedom to manipulate you.

But now I am in control, and you can stay there as you are.

All right, Grey, let me tell you what you least wish to hear:

I am your invisible adversary and I am somewhere around you. You can never see me. I have been everywhere with you: I watched you at the hospital, I was there when Susan came to see you, I overheard what you said. I was in the South of France, I followed you about Wales, I have been with you in London. You have never been free of me. I have looked at you and listened to you; I know what you have done and everything you have thought. Nothing is private to you because I know you as well as you know yourself. I said I would fix you, Grey, and that is what I did.

I am everything you have ever feared. I am indeed invisible to you, but not in the sense you mean.

IX

Consider the room in which the three of us now find ourselves. We are in confrontation once more, facing up to each other ineffectually, and as ever failing to see. Yet there is a difference: you and Susan are both here, but I am not. I am no more *here* than I can be *everywhere*, because each is an absurdity.

Consider this room, the living room of your apartment.

I feel I know it intimately, although in reality I have never visited it. No matter; I can *see* it. I can move around it, walking or even drifting, look at it in its generality or inspect it in the closest detail. Here the white-painted walls that Susan so dislikes, covered with the cheap emulsion paint used by the builders who converted the house into flats; here the slightly worn carpet and furniture once owned by your parents. A television set in one corner, a layer of pale dust over the screen, a video recorder beneath it, the digital clock blinking on and off because you have never bothered to set it properly. I see a couple of bookshelves attached to one wall, and they are sagging in the middle because you or whoever put them up did not properly measure the distance between the brackets. I can scan along the shelves to look at your choice of books—some technical manuals, books of photography, a stack of glamour magazines, a random selection of paperback novels with broken spines—and I know you are not a serious reader except when you travel. On the sill against the window are the marks on the white paint where your houseplants stood; the sunlight has yellowed the paint except for five circular patches, themselves slightly marked by grains of dried potting compost. There is a faint smell of dust, also of damp. Your room speaks of transience, impermanence. I judge you are often away, that you do not feel settled or comfortable here even though you have owned the place for some time.

I know this room. I have inhabited it mentally from the day I first knew of you. It is real to me because this is how I have always visualized it, how I have imagined it when I have known you are here. I know the rest of the apartment in the same way, my interest in you extending to everything about you.

Your real life does not concern me, nor does the reality of where you might actually live. This is what I have created for you.

So here you are in this room, and Susan is with you. Both of you are motionless, because for the time being I have stilled you. Susan is sitting wide-eyed in the chair by the window, watching what you are trying to do. She has placed her canvas bag on the floor beside the chair and its strap snakes lightly over one of her feet. On the carpet in front of her is the opened envelope in which I had given her my story. A dark pool of moisture lies in the weave of the carpet beside the overturned beer can. You are a few feet away from Susan, frozen in your aggressive search, just as you were when I decided to call a halt.

And I am here too, of course, although neither of you can see me.

What do you hope to achieve as you search for me? If you found me what would you do? Do you seek some kind of conclusion to all our wretched dealings? Surely I cannot matter to you anymore, as for weeks I have left you alone, or at least have left you alone as far as you were aware? You have stirred me from my quiescence by this sudden eruption of interest in me. Left to yourself, you had decided to break off your relationship with Susan. That suited me; only Susan concerns me, and as soon as you have finished with her I will be finished with you. So why should I matter to you anymore?

Yes, but Susan has shown you what I have written about you!

You clasp it in your hand, knowing that it describes you. It invalidates you, Grey. What you remember of the hospital now becomes false because I created it for you, and by extension it invalidates your memories of France, and by extension from that it invalidates everything else. You thought you could trust those memories because they have conviction, but I can tell you they have not.

Do you believe me? How good is your memory? Can you believe anything you remember or do you trust only what you are told?

We are all fictions—you, Susan, to a lesser extent myself. You are a fiction in the special sense of having been a different voice, which I used to speak for me. I have made you, Grey. You disbelieve in me, but not as much as I disbelieve in you. You are real enough in your own life, but when you impinged on mine I took you and used you.

You are "real" only so far as it pleases me to make you seem "real," and from the day you met Susan you gave me no pleasure.

Why should you resist this? We all make fictions. Not one of us is what we seem. We rearrange our memories to suit our present understanding of ourselves, not to account accurately for the past. When we meet other people we try to project an image of ourselves that will please or influence them in some way. When we fall in love we blind ourselves to what we do not wish to see.

The urge to rewrite ourselves as real-seeming fictions is present in us all: in the glamour of our wishes we hope that our real selves will not become visible.

This is all I have done. You are not you, but how I have made you seem to be. Susan is not Sue. I am not Niall, but Niall is a version of myself; once again I have no name. I am only I.

So you are denied the conclusion you thought you wanted. None of this tells you what you think you want to know, but I owe you no explanations. Susan has already told you the truth and you can and should believe her, even though I have taken her words and written them down myself. The facts in this are hers, but the fictions are mine.

What remains for you of Susan? Because I have frozen you in mid-action, and you cannot even turn your head, you will not see her as we leave. You will feel no bitterness at losing her—you have already reached your own decision about her. But I will ensure that you never see her again, because that much is in my power.

I could leave you here, stuck forever in this moment, a fiction abandoned without an ending . . . but that would not be right. Your own real life continues, and it is time I released you to that. Your life will now be tidy, your body will heal, matters will improve. I doubt you

will every know why. You will forget, induce your own
negative hallucination. You are no stranger to this, because for you forgetting is a way of failing to see.

X

The summer was hot that year, and with the breaking of
the warm weather came the prospect of a full-time job for
Richard Grey. His friend at the BBC put him in touch
with the head of films at Ealing, the place where his film
career had begun, and after an interview he was told that a
staff job would be his from the first week in September.

Given the long summer to fill, Grey was stricken
with his customary restlessness. He did a free-lance camera job in Malta, but the trip was a short one and afterward he was more at a loose end than before. Cash compensation at last came through: it was less than he had
expected, but more than enough to cover his immediate
needs. Although he was no longer in pain and could use
his hip normally, Grey bought a new car, one with automatic transmission. The old one had begun giving him
trouble, starting with the annoyance of a flat battery.
When Alexandra returned from Exeter to complete her
dissertation, he waited around for a week or two, then
suggested a holiday.

They took the new car across to France, driving
slowly from place to place, following whim and a certain
curiosity of memory. They visited Paris, Lyons, Grenoble,
then drove south to the Riviera. It was still early in the
summer, and the later crowds had not yet arrived. Grey
found Alexandra's company delightful, even though she
was several years younger than he was. They never spoke

of the past, or how they had met, or of anything that was not their immediate world of the holiday and each other. They spent a long time in the south, sunbathing, swimming, visiting museums and landmarks, touring around to see the sights. They visited Saint-Tropez only briefly, but here Grey came across a little shop that sold reproduction postcards. There was one he particularly liked: a photograph of the harbor while it was still used for fishing. He bought a copy of it for Sue. "Wish you were here," he wrote, in a studiedly elaborate handwriting, and he signed it with an X.